AFRICA JUNCTION

Ginny Baily was born in Halifax in Yorkshire, grew up in Cardiff and now lives in Devon. She has taught English as a Foreign Language, Italian and French, has lived and worked in both France and Italy and has long worked on the *Africa Research Bulletin* – a monthly journal of African affairs. She is also the co-founder and co-editor of *Riptide*, a journal that champions the short story. She has won various prizes for her poetry and short stories. *Africa Junction* is her first novel. She has two sons and lives in Exeter.

'A finely written and incisive story of global connections'
Philip Hensher, *Spectator*, Books of the Year

'Forceful debut . . . The astonishing landscapes of
Mali, Liberia and Senegal over the last 30 years are
compellingly crossed'
Guardian

'A novel of grave emotional weight and colour. Whether
she describes terrible or magical events, to read Ginny
Baily is to pick up riches in every paragraph . . . It's a
rare achievement'
Sam North, author of *The Old Country*

'Highly ambitious . . . the constant flickering between the
familiarities of the UK and dry deserts and sweltering cities
of West Africa accentuates the descriptions of each and
gives powerful resonance to the nuances of difference that
dictate our lives'
New Welsh Review

'Fascinating and unusual . . . beautiful writing . . . Baily
is clearly an intelligent writer . . . Deftly brings the reader
inside the story . . . and the tragic individual fallout of
war and political unrest are truly brought home to us'
Planet

'Ginny Baily writes with perception and insight, telling
the stories of her many characters with great skill and
eventually weaving them together into a satisfying whole
. . . A compelling read'
Claire Morrall

GINNY BAILY

Africa Junction

VINTAGE BOOKS
London

For Ben and Harry

Published by Vintage 2012

2 4 6 8 10 9 7 5 3 1

Copyright © Ginny Baily 2011

Ginny Baily has asserted her right under the Copyright,
Designs and Patents Act 1988 to be identified as the author
of this work.

First published in Great Britain in 2011 by
Harvill Secker

Vintage
Random House, 20 Vauxhall Bridge Road,
London SW1V 2SA

www.vintage-books.co.uk

Addresses for companies within The Random House Group Limited
can be found at: www.randomhouse.co.uk/offices.htm

The Random House Group Limited Reg. No. 954009

A CIP catalogue record for this book
is available from the British Library

ISBN 9780099552727

'Songs of Sorrow' © 1967 George Awoonor-Williams (Kofi Awoonor) can
be found in West African Verse: An Anthology, chosen and annotated by
Donatus Ibe Nwoga (Longman, 1967). Every effort has been made to
trace and contact the copyright holder and the publishers would be
pleased to correct any omissions in any future editions

The Random House Group Limited supports The Forest Stewardship
Council (FSC®), the leading international forest certification organisation.
Our books carrying the FSC label are printed on FSC® certified paper.
FSC is the only forest certification scheme endorsed by the leading
environmental organisations, including Greenpeace. Our
paper procurement policy can be found at
www.randomhouse.co.uk/environment

Typeset in Bembo by Palimpsest Book Production Limited,
Falkirk, Stirlingshire
Printed and bound in Great Britain by Clays Ltd, St Ives PLC

Ask them why they idle there
While we suffer, and eat sand,
And the crow and the vulture
Hover always above our broken fences
And strangers walk over our portion.

Kofi Awoonor, 'Songs of Sorrow'

The Sand Eaters

Nimba County, Liberia, 1990

The old woman was folded into the base of the tree, her back propped against the trunk. Her patterned blue wrap was rucked up around bony knees and her flint-thin shins stretched out into the sunlight. Her bare black feet, baking in the sulphurous sun, flopped outwards at a careless angle. A pair of green flip-flops was placed neatly beside her. From the knees up she was obscured by the shadow of the tree's branches, as if she'd been planted and had taken on the characteristics of an extra knobbly root, quiet and deep in the narrow shade of the high afternoon sun. She sat unmoving, seeming to gaze through a gap between the huts that encircled this central space. She stared past her own hut and her neighbour's, Old Man Sebo, to the empty track beyond.

At her back, behind and around the houses of the little village scratched out of the bush, stood the great, dank expanse of rainforest. It covered the uplands and stretched out over the borders into the countries beyond.

In front, eddies of a wind that had travelled from the Sahara, thickened with flakes of charred thatch, played with the sandy soil, lifting it into ridges and flattening them again. Gusts billowed Old Man Sebo's jacket, which hung from a nail on the back of his flung-open door. They puffed up the sleeves, animating them into weakly flailing arms. The jacket was now so threadbare and filthy that its original colour had dulled to the sludge brown of dead leaves after the rain, but Old Man Sebo had cut a dash when he wore it. He had completed his daily outfit with a yellow cane and a pink brimless hat worn low on his brow. At night he had always hung the jacket on the door hook, smoothing its creases with a respectful motion of his hand. He had never let it be cleaned because it was only the weave of age-old dirt that held it together. The hot wind that wore it now didn't show the same restraint.

The rice kitchen was still smouldering after three days. The torched huts had gone up like kindling, but the tightly packed sacks of grain held the fire in a slow pungent burn. The smell came through the village like a profligate feast. Both the rain-fed upland rice and the swamp rice the villagers cultivated, that they had sown, picked, dried and stored to last the whole season, all blown in one blaze. The old lady, who was known for her jollof rice, which she served with hot pepper sauce, fried plantains, green bananas and collard greens or sweet-potato leaves, didn't stir from her place beneath the tree.

The people who'd swarmed through the village hadn't wanted the rice. They'd taken only what was easy and wouldn't slow them, what could be carried without breaking their stride: the dried meat, eddoes, cassava and palm nuts. They'd taken the cane juice to drink later around their campfire but left the sacks of rice, as if their futures were so assured they had no need of long-term supplies. Their life was only then, in that dazzling blade of a moment.

Brightly coloured items of clothing were scattered about the dusty pathways of the village like fallen bunting, caught on fences or half trampled into the earth: women's wraps in bold patterns of yellow and emerald green; a red T-shirt and a torn blue one; a child's plastic sandal, its strap broken; two bobble hats with dirty yellow rims; a strip of cloth in bright turquoise that might have served as a scarf, belt or bandanna. Another wad of cloth, a faded pink coil used for balancing a load upon the head, was wedged between an overturned red-and-yellow-striped bowl and a kettle. In front of the largest house, the only one to have a tin roof and a veranda, lay a battered brown suitcase. Its contents spilled on to the earth between two spiky clumps of elephant grass. Strewn like diamonds among the enamel cups and plates, a crimson blanket and a tub of palm butter were broken pieces of mirror. They caught the sunlight and shimmered it up into the air or held it in sparkling little pools of concentrated light.

The mirror used to hang on the wall opposite the doorway, showing the comings and goings of the family and their visitors. Often it held the daughter's face, her lips, the curve of her cheek and the braids in her hair. When the shout came to run for your life, the soldiers were coming, people scooped up their children and fled. Some snatched up food, blankets, clothes and cups. There was no time to pack.

The brown suitcase must have been for a different, scheduled journey. The girl, spinning round in the house to find her most precious possession, saw the mirror, pulled it from the wall and ran, clutching it to her chest. Sometimes the mirror had held a child spinning his hoop through the door and grinning at his sister's sly looking-glass expression. Today, it held only sky.

The emptied village was filling with grit and sand like a bottle cast up by the tide. The wind seemed to draw a whistle from its lips, the high, keening sound of the emptiness.

Not all the villagers had run. The old, the slow and the sleepy were left behind. The sun had shifted and now the old lady was almost entirely exposed to its blistering heat, as she had been the day before and the day before that. She sat unmoving, not even brushing sand from her eyes. She was used to extremes. It would have been cooler in the dark corners of her little house on the other side of the clearing. The bamboo window was propped open. Through it came a slanting shaft of golden light flecked with sparks of dust and sooty embers. A yellow gourd filled with palm wine gleamed on the sunlit table. Flies landed on the white tin plate and scaled the remains of a mound of rice, treading it down, palpating and reshaping its contours with their spindly black legs. Ants and beetles and other winged insects came creeping and scuttling and whirring across the dusty floor or through the hazy air. The old lady's broom and a shovel lay beside her as though she'd thought to sweep away the debris and the unseemly mess but had sat down to take stock before beginning. Inside her house, the insects' scratchings and swishings and buzzings ventilated the silence as they found their way into unswept corners and under the bed where the old lady had dutifully lain, three days earlier.

'Get under there,' her husband had told her, 'I'll be back in a minute.' He believed in respect for the elders and the power of parley. He had stood at their threshold and waited. From her squeezed and breathless hiding place she had seen only his trousered legs and sandalled feet, planted firmly in their open doorway. There had been the clamour of a wild party outside. Music with a beat as fast as her heart had blasted from somewhere nearby and voices had joined in, not singing but chanting. Men had shouted, ordering the remaining people out of their houses, demanding to know what tribe they were. The doorway had lightened momentarily as the old woman's husband had moved back inside. He had resumed his position, but now the knife for cutting into the rubber trees swung from his right hand. The shouting and yelling had continued and someone had burst into laughter, a wheezing cackle, that had stopped suddenly.

Then there had been screams and the crackling of flames. The sweet smell of thatch like burning stubble, the poisonous fumes of plastic, the sickening stench of singed animal hair and seared flesh, like bush meat. Booted feet had crowded her husband and he had disappeared. There had been gunshots just outside the window and a grunt that had sounded like a pig, but wasn't.

The soldiers had dragged Old Man Sebo out into the yard. They had rolled him inside his own mattress, tied him up with string like fufu wrapped in plantain leaves and put a match to the parcel they'd made. Smoke had risen in a bluish plume.

Later, when most of the fires had died down and the old lady had taken up her place beneath the tree, the vultures came. After them came the monkeys. It started with one monkey, scattering husks from the branches above, and then dropping down to the ground in a rustle of leaves. It landed near the old woman's feet, batted at her flip-flops, and as if disturbed by her indifference, danced backwards with its tail raised. It paused at the open doorway of Old Man Sebo's house and yowled, a piercing shriek which summoned a horde of other monkeys down from the trees. Suddenly, there were monkeys everywhere, darting in and out of the burnt-out huts, squawking from the ruined roofs. For a brief time, the village belonged to them. Then came a boom, a distant sound that might have been the thunder announcing rain at last, or might have been gunfire. The monkeys ran back into the forest and left the village empty again.

Now there were only the swooping cries of birds, the buzz and hum of insects, the creak of branches.

The sun had sunk low. It balanced on the treeline, casting its last light before it dipped away. The village seemed less a man-made thing than an organism thrown up by the ground itself. In the light that filtered through the treetops, the earth, with its matted roots and trampled fence posts, its buried and unburied bones, glowed red.

The Iron Fist

Exeter, Devon, 2003

On a cold December evening, Adele looked in a mirror and saw a visiting angel. Her coming was like the man in the moon winking or the sun shining at midnight. It undercut everything that had come before. Adele looked at the walls as if they might, all at once, melt into a fog.

The night before Adele had hugged her knees in a corner of the sofa, locked in her silence, watching the segments of a multicoloured pie chart rise and fall on the television screen. Africa's slice was bright blue and disproportionately large, a greedy boy's fat helping. Senegal, where she and her family had lived for a few years when she was a child, was picked out as a success story. Only about 2 per cent of the population was thought to be infected. Adele worked it out. That was about 200,000 people; more than the whole population of Exeter. She switched off the TV and went to bed.

The iron fist came most often at night, uncoiling its metal fingers and clutching her from sleep. Pedro, her erstwhile lover, had brought it into her life. The fist was increasingly easy to provoke. It didn't need another split condom. An overheard word, graffiti in the school toilet, a defenceless look in her child's eye, sufficed these days. That night it woke her in the early hours, squeezing her chest as if she were strapped into a metal bodice, a medieval instrument of torture. She lay for what felt like hours, pinned between cold sheets, eyes staring, the compressed beat of her heart like the flap of leathery wings.

It was her son, Joe, who released her, shouting out in his sleep from the bedroom next door. 'He's trying to take it, he's trying to take it,' he wailed.

She didn't know who 'he' was or what he was trying to take but the voice she found to call back with was soothing and motherly. 'It's all right, Joe. Mummy's here. I won't let him take it.' When Joe quietened, Adele felt herself quieten too, as if his nightmare had been the cause of her panic. She tumbled into sleep.

'Did you have a bad dream?' she asked Joe over breakfast, rootling in the cupboards for something to put in his lunch box. It would have to be Marmite sandwiches again.

'No!' He slapped the cornflakes box down on the table indignantly. He was a composed child by day but a wild, passionate one by night. Sometimes he stumbled into Adele's room and climbed into her bed where he slept with his foot in her hand, consoling her with his need. He would look at her accusingly in the morning on these occasions, as if she'd kidnapped him.

'You were shouting in your sleep.'

'No. You were,' he said, examining the instructions on how to make an Advent calendar on the back of the box. Adele felt the iron fist start to flex its fingers and she put her hand to her chest.

Joe let out an eerie wail. 'Woo-woo,' he cried, tilting his head up to an imaginary moon.

'What's the matter?' Adele said sharply. 'Why are you making that horrible noise?'

'That's what you were shouting in the night,' he said.

'Go and clean your teeth,' she said.

'Like a wolf,' he said. He slid down off his chair and left the kitchen, woo-wooing all the way up the stairs.

Halfway to school, in the middle of traffic, the car engine died. Adele pumped the accelerator up and down and twiddled the key. The engine turned over but didn't start again. The sound of the vehicles behind tooting their horns reverberated through the car and set her teeth jangling. She gripped the wheel, staring ahead as the lights turned from red to green and back again.

Joe sat implacably calm, strapped into his booster seat. 'Do we need petrol?' he said.

Adele tried to remember when she'd last filled the car up. The petrol gauge had been broken for months. She couldn't think with all those furious people beeping at her. One swerved past, gesturing angrily. Others followed and the cars in the next lane seemed to squeeze up accommodatingly so that traffic flowed again around them, leaving her and Joe stuck in the middle, like a snagged branch in the stream.

A man tapped at her window. 'Need a hand?' he said. He and his mate left their van with the hazard warning lights on and pushed them to a side street, then ran off, waving.

Joe waved back. 'Those were nice men,' he said.

They abandoned the car and walked the rest of the way. Adele knew they should be hurrying but she seemed to have developed a limp, one leg suddenly shorter than the other. On the way, Joe described what the ancient Romans had for breakfast and how they used honey instead of sugar, and she wondered, distractedly, if the limp was the first sign of something ominous, if her bones were infected and crumbling. She left Joe in the playground with his friends, resisting the urge to lift him up and carry him with her, a stalwart ally through the day. She blew him a kiss instead, which he dodged because kisses were for girls, and then she ran lopsidedly up the hill to the secondary school where she taught French, arriving just as the bell rang. She wasn't even late. It was amazing. A little triumph. But she didn't have time for her pre-school cigarette in the pine trees behind the car park.

As soon as she entered the classroom, she knew that something was wrong, that she'd forgotten something important. She must have left it in the car. It was a sixth-form class, mostly girls, quite bright and motivated. They were all staring at her. She couldn't remember if they always stared like that or if this was unusual. She felt naked in front of them, and glancing down to check her trousers were fastened, her shirt tucked in, she saw that she was wearing odd shoes, a blue one on the left, black on the right. It explained the limp. She shuffled behind the desk to hide her feet and glanced at her notes. The subjunctive seemed an elusive thing to explain to seventeen-year-olds. A grammatical mode to express hopes, wishes and regrets, she had written. If she just stood there, exposed to their teenage gaze, perhaps they would absorb the concept. She kept her eyes down and fiddled with the papers on her desk. She swallowed. Her mouth was dry. They were starting to fidget. Kelly Simons, she noticed out of the corner of her eye, had her hand up.

She turned to the board and began to write sentences exemplifying the subjunctive mode. 'If I were braver, I would do things differently,' she wrote. 'Whatever he says, I don't believe him.' 'If he had told the truth, we mightn't be in this mess.' The sentences flowed from her pen until the board was covered with a variety of expressions of how things could have been, should have been, might have been, but weren't. She turned to the class, ignoring their mutterings, and fixed her gaze through the window on the spot in the car park near the pine trees where she usually left her car.

'With a partner,' she said, 'analyse what is going on in these sentences. See if you can detect a pattern.'

'Miss,' Kelly said, 'I don't understand.' The rest of the class tittered.

Adele swivelled to face the board again and saw she had written in the wrong language. The phrases were in Spanish instead of French. Keeping her back turned, she sidled towards the desk and reached for the board rubber. Her fingers flicked painfully against the edge of the desk and sent the rubber clattering to the floor. She didn't pick it up. Instead, she turned and walked quickly out of the room and down the corridor. She shut herself in a cubicle in the loo and sat there for a while. After a few minutes she went back.

She dragged herself through the rest of the school day and that first lesson, where on her return the board had been wiped clean and the students were hushed and compliant, was not the worst. She found it increasingly difficult to answer questions. The inside of her head was like the hold of a stricken ship, the cargo bobbing about on scummy water, and she felt a pressure at her temples, as if she had been underwater too long. She plucked bits of language from the flotsam and jetsam and offered them cautiously, not knowing whether they were the appropriate responses or not. She couldn't imagine how she'd ever managed to do this job. Nor how she was going to do it all again tomorrow.

She wandered round the car park in the four o'clock dark looking for her car. She knew she hadn't parked it in the usual place. It was nowhere to be found. It must have been stolen. She heard the head's voice somewhere behind her, talking in the patronising tone he reserved for the kids, and she slipped into the pine grove. She steadied herself against a tree and lit a cigarette. The nicotine went straight to her head and she started to shake. She slid down the trunk and sat, leaning against it, on the damp resinous earth. She would make a list, prioritise. First, she would phone Joe's friend's mother and tell her she would be late picking him up. Then she would phone the police and report the car stolen. Two simple phone calls. She could surely manage that. It was easy.

With that thought, a wave carrying other debris came crashing into her head and frothed there; the damp patch in Joe's bedroom, the intermittently functioning boiler, the rubble on the landing where Pedro had abandoned the upstairs bathroom he'd embarked on to replace the mildewed downstairs lean-to, the blocked guttering, the dying fish in the pond in her back garden, their bellies swollen, tangled in poisonous weed. She had meant to do something about the fish before Joe noticed. The poor, innocent fish. Two simple phone calls, she reminded herself. She crumpled her cigarette end into the pine needles, picked herself up and went back into the building.

The caretaker was standing between her and the phone at reception. 'There you are,' he said. He was holding out a green plastic petrol can. 'It should be enough to get you home,' he said. She blinked at him. Then she remembered the car stalling on the hill and telling him about it at lunchtime. 'Looks like it's been one of those days,' he said.

That was the night of the visitation. Adele was standing blearily in the bathroom, cleaning her teeth, when she noticed a shadow, a kind of smudge in the steamed-up mirror. She rubbed the glass and the figure of an African woman came slowly into focus, like a photograph emerging from developing fluid.

The other woman was also cleaning her teeth, but she was using a twig. She was more or less Adele's size because she replaced Adele's face in the mirror exactly. Yellow and red beads were woven into the tiny little plaits on her head and her skin glowed like chestnuts. Adele's eyes met the steady gaze of the other woman and recognition flashed – Ellena, her childhood friend from Senegal. As Adele let out a cry and raised her hand to her mouth, the other woman did the same. Then she vanished.

Adele was looking at herself again, her own incredulous face, scrubbed of colour, like a peeled and greying potato. She touched her cheek and her skin had a rubbery, unconvincing quality. She laid her hand flat against the sweaty glass and leaned her forehead next to it. Her heart thumped. The electric toothbrush was still whirring in her other hand. She switched it off and placed it on the shelf above the sink and then ran her fingers along the edge. She hung on to the shelf and pressed her hand more firmly against the mirror, testing its permeability, as if she could make it melt and step into another world, away from the dirty mess. 'Come back,' she said to the hard glass.

And Africa was in her head. There was Ellena as a child cross-legged on her sack in the silver and black of the garage. There was the unreal glittering blue of the swimming pool at the clubhouse, where Adele and her brother Louis floated face down pretending to be dead or did handstands under the water, where she'd had her tenth birthday party, her last in Senegal. There was the red dirt road outside the gates of their house where the watchmen congregated, the bougainvillea dripping pink and purple over the walls, the wooden kiosk at the junction three gates along where she went to buy baguettes in the morning and the man with the blue cap and an orange rope for a belt who sold the bread. The tree at the end of the garden and her climbing it, the notch to press the toes of the left foot against, the skinny branch to stretch the right hand around, the way to shift your weight and pull. Adele saw again the golden open ground behind the house threaded with meandering paths, the giant baobab tree in the distance. She was running and jumping, swinging and climbing, bold and free and defiant.

Adele opened her eyes and looked into the merged, cyclops darkness of their reflection, wondering where in the maze of paths the running child got lost.

She tuned into the boom of her heartbeat in her ears. She was a veteran of palpitations and erratic rumblings. On one of her whispered night-time conversations with the helpline, she had described the iron fist. The man on the line, a brusque Scot, diagnosed panic, but the feeling now, a powerful thump of excitement, was different. It awoke in her an urgent need to talk to her big brother, to hear him say 'Still in your mad Spanish phase?' or something else that cast a little shaft of light down the dark well she'd fallen into. She pushed the unwilling cat out through its flap and stacked dishes next to the sink, thinking of Louis in the hot, dry savannah of the Malian outback where he worked. She had him riding to meet her on a cart pulled by a donkey, because he'd mentioned such a journey in one of his rare emails.

As she put the empty milk bottle outside the front door, the image of Ellena glowed in her mind. There was something self-contained in Ellena's bearing that Adele yearned for. She should have done more to help Ellena all those years before. Yet the Ellena she'd seen in the glass had gained in substance while Adele had diminished. She pulled her dressing gown tight against the December-night chill.

She curled on to the sofa phone in hand. She was trying to work out what time it was in Mali and to convince herself it didn't matter, she was allowed to call her own brother day or night, when it rang. She held it to her ear, smiling, ready to laugh with Louis at their hitherto undiscovered psychic connection.

It was Pedro and he was shouting. Usually their conversations started with his litany of woes, all the terrible things that had happened to him, the injustices and the wicked fools who were blighting his life. The conversation would only move on to the bellowing rage after a few minutes, by means of some twist that Adele was unable to avoid. The twist, and Adele could never see it coming, was that it was all her fault. Because she used to love him.

Love had become the dirty word they used to berate each other.

She'd have let the answer machine respond if she'd thought. Only Pedro phoned past midnight. She steered clear of him these days, drove past him in the street, walked past her own house and hid round the corner if she saw his van outside, didn't answer the phone. She didn't know when he'd reduced her to this quivering, skulking creature. He was still there, inside her all the time, whispering or shouting. It was the opposite of sweet nothings.

She thought of Ellena in the mirror and hung up, yanking the phone out of the wall as she left the room.

In the morning, after a night of deep and dream-filled sleep, she came to with a feeling of determination and clarity, as if her daring childhood self had been reawoken. She phoned in sick. Within two hours, she was sitting in a clinic in a town forty miles away from Exeter, a town where she didn't know anyone and no one knew her. The test was anonymous and confidential, they said, but, just in case, she lied about her date of birth, making herself a year and three months younger, and gave them a false name, Ellen George.

In front of her there was a white rack full of leaflets with titles like 'Safe Sex and You'. She turned her head away, looking at the potted plant near the door she'd come in through, an avocado plant. She and Joe had grown an avocado plant from a stone. He took it into school to show. She'd told him about the avocado trees in the yard of her school in Senegal, how the avocados would drop, overripe, to the ground and they would have avocado fights, flinging the squishy fruit at each other, hiding behind the trees. Like a warm, green snowball fight.

Adele's heels clicked across the floor when the nurse called her in. She had dressed carefully in smart shoes, a suit, lipstick, to give herself courage. The room smelt of witch hazel and Dettol. 'Before we start, you're sure you don't want to see a counsellor? They can answer any questions you have and make sure that having the test is the right choice for you,' the nurse said in a fake, bright voice, as if she were discussing a better kind of washing powder.

Adele shook her head. She'd been to see a counsellor before. He'd asked, 'What do you get from this relationship?' and there'd been a silence. 'Take your time,' he'd said. 'Grief, confusion, guilt on a scale that is almost unimaginable,' she'd wanted to reply. How could she articulate the intensity of the feeling, the horrible, inescapable sensation of a shared doom? 'He'd walk through fire for me,' she'd said eventually.

The counsellor had scrutinised her. 'But is there much call for that?' he'd asked. Adele hadn't gone back.

While the nurse was lining up bottles and fixing labels on them, she told Adele about the procedure, that she could telephone for the results if she preferred. It was advisable, she said, to have a friend with you when you phoned, not to be on your own when you got the news. 'Do you have someone?' she asked, her eyes and hands still busy with her task. An old schoolmate, Jill, the most dogged and loyal of her friends ever, appeared, fat plaits intact, in Adele's mind. She'd lost touch with Jill years before for reasons she couldn't now remember. Her mind flew all over the place like a frightened bird, thinking of her mother, father, Louis, her friends and colleagues, all the people she hadn't told, until it found Ellena and settled there. She nodded.

The nurse looked up, a needle in her hand. 'Are you sure?' she said, and Adele couldn't think what it was she was supposed to be sure about. She shook her head.

She swallowed and took a breath and then, taking both her and the nurse by surprise, as the consensus in the room seemed by then to be that she was mute, she spoke. 'My boyfriend's HIV-positive,' she said in an unnaturally loud voice. She had never spoken the words aloud before, only whispered them into the ears of the people who manned night-time helplines. 'Ex-boyfriend.' She nodded again, as if the nurse had been about to contradict her.

'Right,' the nurse said in a matter-of-fact way. 'He's been tested, has he?'

'Yes. A long time ago. In Spain.'

Adele looked down at her knees, tugging her skirt over them. She could feel a rattling inside her skull, flecks of something that had broken loose. It was tempting now to keep going, to tell this stranger about how Pedro had said he'd kill himself if she became infected. She could relate how he let out a cry like a wounded animal when the first condom had split and had disappeared for three days afterwards so that she'd thought he was dead. 'Can we just get on with this now?' she said, rolling up her sleeve.

The nurse's eyes widened as if she'd been slapped. 'Right,' she said. 'Let's.' While she was filling the various containers with Adele's rich, red blood and listing all the sexually trans-mitted diseases it would be tested for, Adele wondered if there'd been a point when she could have done things differ-ently to set another, more wholesome, chain of events in motion. She thought again of the night Pedro had turned up with a bottle of vodka in his pocket and an anarchic bunch of friends and whispered in her ear as he led her in a drunken dance around her living room. What if she'd taken a step back, sent him packing and insisted she needed her sleep because she had to be up early for school in the morning? But she had no sensation of choice when she revisited that moment. No, it was another night, the one when they'd first slept together. They'd been out somewhere with the same wild group and she had invited him in, but he'd said no, he was going home. And then, five minutes later, he'd turned up again at the door and said, 'You want me to come in?' and later, 'You want me to stay?' and so on. Now, she realised he'd been giving himself an alibi. He was only ever doing what she wanted. There had been a conversation about condoms. It was coming back now. How come she hadn't remembered this before?

The nurse stuck a plaster into the crook of Adele's arm and told her to apply pressure. Neither of them had had any condoms and she'd said that it didn't matter because she was on the pill, but – she had to allow this thought in now – even then she'd had the sense that procreation wasn't the issue. She shook her head, pressing against the soft hollow of her arm, conscious of the blood pulsing in her ears. She'd wanted him and she hadn't cared what price there was to pay. I jumped, she thought. No one pushed me. That was the contract she'd made with Pedro. She'd offered him her life. No wonder he was angry that she was trying to reclaim it.

'Miss George, are you feeling faint?' the nurse was saying.

Adele became aware that, still shaking her head from side to side, she'd allowed it to loll forward on to her chest. 'No, no. I'm fine,' she said.

'Shall I fetch you a nice cup of tea?' the nurse said.

Adele sat up straighter. 'Please,' she said, thinking of the dark green frothing tea in Senegal. Thrice brewed, each glass less bitter than the one before.

Toubab

Sine-Saloum, Senegal, 1977

It went quiet in the Land Rover after Louis' stepfather slammed his foot on the accelerator. They had to beat the tide or they wouldn't make it to the beach house that day. The car bounced along the hard wet sand near the ocean's edge trying to keep up with the one in front. When they veered round the black rocks in the shallows, seawater smacked against the side and sprayed through the window. Mrs Travis, Marge, in the passenger seat had stopped twisting round to chat and was gripping the strap above the door. She'd turned the colour of a pale frog. Or a toad.

There were four people and the cool box wedged on to the back seat, including Danny Travis, Marge's husband, who was whale-sized. Louis didn't understand why he wasn't in the front. Then they'd have had enough room. As the bumpy drive jolted and shook them all about, the big man seemed to sink further at the same time as expanding widthways, his massive thighs spreading out like softening butter. Louis calcu-lated he had about two square inches on which to perch his bum. His knees were jammed into the back of the driver's seat and his face was practically touching the red nape of his stepfather's neck where two trickles of sweat rolled out of his hair down into his collar. His stepfather seemed not to see the boulders until he was nearly upon them. He would wrench the wheel at the last minute as though a waiting beast had suddenly reared. Every time he did it something twitched under the skin of his neck like a lizard's tail.

Louis' mum, Claire, who was squeezed between his little sister and blubber-man, had her eyes closed and her lips pressed together. With one hand she held on to the back of the seat and with the other she clutched Adele's bare foot. Adele, squashed against the opposite side from Louis, had pulled herself up to kneeling. Holding the strap with both hands like reins, she was riding the bucking, rolling vehicle, whooping whenever spray shot through. She was only seven. She didn't know any better.

They pummelled along the narrowing strip of beach towards a place that looked impassable, where the mangrove forest spilled down to meet the ocean. Then, suddenly, with a slap of waves and the skewing sigh of mangrove roots beneath the tyres, they were through and out the other side. A massive empty expanse of yellow beach stretched away from them. The cars slowed down to a steadier pace. Dr Mercure, the driver of the car in front, stuck his hand out of the window and gave the thumbs-up sign. Louis' stepfather did the same. His mum leaned forward to pat his stepfather's arm. 'Brilliant driving, darling,' she said. Marge, still with a greenish tinge, swivelled in her seat. Louis accidentally intercepted the look of raised-eyebrow disbelief that passed between her and Danny Travis. He turned to look out of the window. There was a hand-painted wooden sign with a finger pointing in the direction they were heading: 'La Falaise 5km'.

'Only five kilometres to the beach house,' he said.

'Praise the Lord,' Danny Travis sang in a booming voice as if he was in church. 'Praise the Lord.' Louis glanced sideways at him out of the corner of his eye and the fat man winked.

La Falaise was made up of three bungalows tucked behind a fringe of palm trees under a craggy outcrop of rock that bordered the beach. It belonged to his stepfather's work and people could borrow it for trips. A boy at Louis' school whose dad worked at the centre too had told him about a rope swing in the thicket up and over the cliff behind. He unpacked boxes of food, sleeping bags and towels with the adults and put up a camp bed for himself. Adele went off with Dr Mercure's girls to put her things in the kids' room in Dr Mercure's bungalow. Louis wasn't sure when he'd stopped qualifying as a kid, although it had first become apparent last Christmas. The bulging sock full of sweets and little presents was missing from the end of his bed. 'Dominic thinks,' his mother had said, glancing at his stepfather who looked stiff and solemn, 'we both think, darling,' she corrected herself, 'that eleven is a bit too old for Christmas stockings.' His stepfather nodded slightly. Later, Louis had thought of a string of replies to demonstrate how he hadn't for a moment expected a stocking and had long outgrown them. But, at the time, horribly conscious that he'd let Adele run protesting that Father Christmas had forgotten him, he'd been dumb. Anyhow, it was fine. He didn't want all those silly toys. He really was too old for stockings. And now it meant he got a room to himself. Those Mercure girls screeched when you didn't look at them and gaped silently when you did.

Everyone put on their bathers and trooped down to the sea for a dip, except for Marge who went for a lie-down. Louis held back from running ahead with the girls. Instead, he trailed behind the adults. He'd have liked a friend to come along, but there wasn't room in the car because of Danny Travis and Marge.

White foam frothed the sand sloping down to the water, but the sea itself was calm. The three men all went straight in without discussion and swam out in a businesslike way. For all his bulk, Danny Travis was a strong swimmer, tunnelling powerfully through the immense quantity of water he displaced. Louis' stepfather thrashed in his wake, like a tug chasing a liner. Dr Mercure made slower progress and was the first to turn back. The two women waded out to thigh height with the girls jumping and splashing and shrieking around them. Adele started showing the bigger girls how to do handstands under the water.

Louis turned away and looked back up the beach. The escarpment behind the beach huts was bright orange in the sunlight. It looked soft and crumbly, as if you could break off a piece and eat it and it would taste like sticky marmalade cake.

He kicked off his sandals and trotted into the sea to ask his mum what was for dinner, but she was nowhere to be seen.

The water was chillier than he'd expected. Madame Mercure was still standing in the shallows, comforting a snotty, wailing child. A cloud of mosquitoes swarmed around his head and he dived under, feeling the water ripple deliciously fresh over his sweaty face and down his chest. This was his new thing, underwater swimming, but it was the first time he'd done it in the sea. He could go a whole width in the swimming pool without coming up for air. Now he counted ten strokes before he emerged, took in a great lungful and slid back under. Ten more long pulls away from the shore before he broke the surface, gasping. He was out of his depth and for a moment, spinning, unable to see land, he felt like he'd come up in a different world, a bowl of deep salt water where blue sea met bluer sky in a vast dizzying circle and he alone at its centre. Then he saw someone swimming towards him. When she lifted her face to draw breath he recognised his mother in the flick of her ponytail. He trod water, waiting. She swam behind him and laid her arms over his shoulders, draping herself over him as if he were a resting place. He took her weight, bobbing lower. Her arms were smooth and silky with water.

'Are you having a nice time, beautiful boy?' she said.

He wondered when she'd last called him beautiful boy. He nodded.

'I'm going back to start the dinner,' she said.

'I'll come and help,' he said. Before she could pull away, he twisted inside her arms to face her. 'Do you want a tow?' he asked. She used to let him tow her up and down the pool at the clubhouse sometimes.

Her hair was flattened against her head and the sea had washed her face clean of all make-up. She craned her head over her shoulder as if someone might be following her. 'Best not,' she said.

She kicked off and away from him, her toenails scraping for an instant against his stomach. Twisting over on to her front, she resumed her easy crawl.

He watched her go but then, all of a sudden, he flung himself after her with great, thrashing urgent strokes, feeling the strength in his legs as he powered through the water, straining every muscle to catch up. Then he was churning alongside her and they were neck and neck. Her mouth formed a surprised 'oh' as she realised he was there. He felt the sinews in his neck stretching. With a final heave, he left her behind and pulled ahead. His knees grazed the sandy bottom of the shallows and he staggered to his feet.

The Mercure family were sitting in a row at the water's edge, draped in towels. Madame Mercure gazed at him with an uncertain smile. Adele, crouching further up the beach, was banging sand into a bucket with the back of a spade and didn't look up. His mum appeared beside him. She was panting. She bent forward, hands on knees, catching her breath. The bones of her spine pushed white against the skin of her back. He could easily have pushed her under.

Louis was bending to do up his shoe strap a minute later when a shove from behind sent him sprawling face down in the sand. He looked up and there was his mother skipping backwards away from him, laughing. He hauled himself up and she turned away, running up the beach towards La Falaise.

Laughing too, his feet sinking into the sand, he ran after her, heavy-legged. He ran skew-whiff and lopsided, snorting with laughter, drunk on hilarity, but still he caught up and got to the beach house first. He did a slow handclap for her arrival.

'I can't run properly in a bikini,' she said.

'Excuses, excuses,' Louis said.

He went into his room, peeled off his wet trunks and pulled on long trousers and a shirt. He brought his transistor radio out and perched it on the veranda. It was playing West African jazz. His mother had wrapped a blue cloth around her waist and knotted it like the Senegalese women did. She shuffled sideways to the music, swinging her hips. Louis laughed loudly. It wasn't that funny but he felt like laughing for some reason. 'Hey, lady. You dance like African woman. You no dance like *toubab*,' he said, imitating the speech pattern of Ernest, their garden boy. Once, when Louis was practising his football skills, Ernest had told him he didn't play like a *toubab*, a white person, but like an African. It was a great compliment.

Louis and his mum found a trestle table in a storeroom next to the toilet behind the main bungalow and put it up in the space in front of the veranda. While she started preparing the food, he loaded all the lanterns with candles and went round hanging them from the hooks so that they'd be ready to light when night fell. His mum, still swaying to the music, was cutting the white fish they'd bought in Dakar that morning into cubes and dropping them into a mixture she'd made. She smiled at him from under a strand of hair that had fallen in front of her eyes and held out her slimy fishy hands helplessly. He pushed the hair off her face. She smelt of garlic and ginger and the sea.

'What you making?' said a voice from behind Louis. It was Marge, emerging after her nap. 'Can I help?' she asked.

Louis didn't get why they had to have all these people along on their weekend away. He retreated to the hammock on the veranda while the two women cracked open a beer each, although Marge said that she shouldn't really.

'Don't then,' he muttered, turning the radio up louder.

'Do you actually like this music?' Marge asked after a while.

His mum wrinkled her nose. 'Not really,' she said.

He snapped the radio off and stowed it in his room. 'I'm off for a wander,' he said.

'Don't be too long. Remember how quickly it gets dark,' she called after him.

He walked away without answering. He kept inside the palm trees so that he wouldn't bump into the others coming up from the sea. He could hear their voices. His mum always said that. As if he would forget that he lived in Africa now, close to the equator, where night came down fast like a big black bird spreading its wings. Those long English evenings when the whiteness of the sky held out for hours against the creeping dark and where kids romped through the back lanes past bedtime was a life that belonged to someone else, to the little kid he used to be.

His shoes were filling with sand. He bent down to take them off, hooked them by the straps from his forefinger and walked on. The sand oozed between his toes and his thoughts shot to another beach, back before he'd come to Africa, an English beach. He was playing French cricket with his dad. It was the longest day, his dad said, but it couldn't go on long enough for Louis. Even when he couldn't see the ball and was swinging the bat through the air blind, he hadn't wanted to stop, because then it would be over and he and his father would be living on different continents. Just throw one more ball, he kept saying.

'Louis.' His sister's voice, calling from behind, startled him. He spun round. She was trotting after him. 'Wait for me,' she said.

'You can't come,' he said.

'Mum said I could if you look after me,' she said.

'Well, you can't because I don't want to look after you.'

'That's OK,' she said, taking hold of his hand, ''cos I don't need looking after.'

'You're still in your beach stuff,' he said. She had a pair of shorts over her bathing costume.

'I'll get changed when we come back.' He shook his head. 'OK, I'll run back and get a T-shirt. Will you wait for me?'

'No. I'm going now.'

She pulled on his arm. 'Come on then,' she said. 'It doesn't matter about the T-shirt.'

He stood his ground. 'I'm not going to carry you if you get tired,' he warned. She gave him a fierce look. He didn't need to say 'school trip' or 'Niokolo-Koba National Park'. 'I was only little then,' she said.

'It was two months ago.'

'Yes. When I was little,' she said, swinging his arm.

He smiled. She always made him smile eventually. 'Come on then,' he said, tugging on her hand. 'What you waiting for, slowcoach?'

They ran along the rocky base of the escarpment pulling each other and shouting come on, come on, come on. Soon the trees came to an end and the crag petered out, giving way to dunes. When they came to the first of many upturned fishing boats, painted bright yellow with blue patterns on the side, Louis knew they were at the place where they had to turn. They swerved to the left away from the sea and started to climb the dune. Tufts of grass like spiky fringes of green hair stuck out between the ridges. They scrabbled up, on hands and toes, sand shifting and dimpling beneath their feet.

The top of the dune wasn't the summit; it folded into the base of another, more solid hill beyond, where the scrub was denser and the roots bound the sand together, converting it into something more like soil. Louis sat on a rock to pull his shoes on and saw that Adele was wearing flip-flops.

'You haven't even got proper shoes on,' he said.

'I'll be careful,' she said.

There was a sort of path curving up just as his friend had described. It took them back on themselves, so that as they climbed higher, they were moving parallel to the beach below. When the land levelled off, they were hot and breathless. They were on the bluff almost directly above the beach house.

'Look, there's Mummy,' Adele said. Their mum had come out from the shower block, wrapped in a towel. Dominic was right behind her. He wrapped his arms around her waist and pulled her against him.

Louis turned away and tugged at Adele's arm. 'Don't look,' he said. 'It's private.'

They scrambled up the last stretch away from the cliff edge, pushing through dense undergrowth that closed overhead like a tunnel. Louis led the way. The path became so steep they had to use scrubby bushes as handholds. The rust-coloured earth let out a musty ancient smell. Insects buzzed all around them, winged ants batting at their noses. Louis put his face through a spider's web and saw, cross-eyed, the spider scuttle up a thread to the refuge of a leaf. He righted a giant armoured beetle that lay on the path wriggling its legs uselessly in the air and then he crunched it underfoot with his next step. It made a popping sound. They pushed on up until they emerged again in the light where dazzling yellow flowers caught the sun and sent out a sharply sweet smell.

They were on the edge of a fold in the land before the final ridge which formed the horizon above them. Louis didn't know what lay beyond; he pictured fields and massive mountains, villages, forests and mysterious pathways through giant, strangely shaped trees, and part of him, having come so far, wanted to keep going, to clamber up and over into that unknown world. But the land dipped away at their feet and there below them, over a hollow bursting with plants, hung the swing. A blue rope like the ones the fishermen used was knotted around an overhanging branch of a tree that rose up out of the leafy crater. It was looped over a lower branch to hold it in place.

'Hooray,' Adele shouted, slithering past him down the slope.

Her voice echoed. 'Shh,' he said. Seabirds cawed in the sky above the ridge but down there in the crease it was hot and still.

Louis saw that if let dangle, the rope would hang in the centre of the dip and be impossible to reach from the edge, unless by some extraordinary flying leap. Adele was unhooking it. 'Wait,' he said, calculating. 'Let me go first. To see if it's safe.' She squatted on the side of the hill to watch and stuck her thumb in her mouth. As soon as he had the weight of the rope in his hands, it pulled at him, dragging him towards the ditch. He had to dig his feet in firmly not to slide. The rope was too thick to get his hands around comfortably but he spotted a stripped piece of wood propped against the tree trunk. He picked it up and slid it through the loop. Now he had a crossbar to hold. Whoever made this swing, some boy's dad probably, had thought of everything. He tugged on the rope and it held firm. They'd made a good job of it, he thought, squinting up. Those were proper fishermen's knots.

He wiped one sweaty hand in turn on each trouser leg, gripped both ends of the stick and backed up the slope as far as he could, resisting the downward drag. With a scuttling, skidding kind of run, he launched himself, the ground falling away beneath him. He felt the shock in his armpits and down his sides when his body yanked out to full length. The soles of his shoes skimmed the bushes as he flew over the pit, twisting and drawing his knees up at the top of the rope's arc so he didn't crash into the hillside. The rush of air that he fell through cooled his hot face, lifted and dropped his hair as he careered back and forth. Adele, squatting on the bank with her face upturned, grinned at him and he grinned back.

It was only when he started to think about landing that he realised the design fault. He would have to let go of the rope so as not to be dragged into the ditch but, if he let go, the rope would be out of reach. He glanced down at the mesh of interwoven branches, wondering how deep it was and whether there were snakes. Then he saw that in between the grey-green leaves, thin white thorns like sharpened knitting needles stuck out at angles. There was a piece of flatter ground by the place where the tree pushed up from the hollow. Without giving himself time to think, as he touched his feet to the ground, in the split second before gravity pulled him backwards, he flung out his left arm and grabbed a handful of the sinewy fronds of a side branch. For a sickening moment he was stretched between the two, his arms being yanked from their sockets, and then, twisting sideways, he flipped the rope end over the branch and caught it on the other side. The crossbar slid to the ground, the branch took the strain and he was able to straighten up, the blood pulsing behind his eyeballs and his heart hammering.

He became aware of Adele clapping. 'That was fun,' she said. She sidled towards him round the edge of the hollow. 'My turn.'

'Do you want the good news or the bad news?' he said in as jokey a voice as he could manage, holding the rope away from her. He had a sick taste in his mouth. She stared at him warily. 'The good news,' he said, 'is that it is brilliant fun. The bad news . . .' She put her finger to his mouth to stop him speaking. He shook her off. '. . . the bad news is that it's too dangerous for you.' She bit her top lip with her bottom teeth and shook her head. She looked like their mother when she did that. Mostly she favoured her father but just sometimes she had a look of their mum and so, Louis thought, she probably looked like him too. It was funny because people always commented on how unalike they were, he so blond, she so dark. 'Look,' he said, 'when you swing, you have to get back to this little ledge. It's the only place you can land. And you can't let go of the rope swing. You have to be like a trapeze artist.'

'I can do that,' she said. 'I can do trapeze. I go upside down on the swing at school and standing up, one leg and everything.'

He shook his head.

'That's not fair,' she said in a little voice.

'Look at those thorns, Del,' he said. 'What if you fell?'

'I won't fall.'

'*I* nearly slipped. You won't be able to land.'

'You can catch me,' she said.

He hadn't thought of that. 'But, you won't be able to grip. Your hands are too small.'

'I'll sit, like on a proper swing,' she said.

Louis couldn't come up with any more objections. He didn't know why he bothered. Feet wedged behind a protruding root, he held the rope while Adele straddled the crossbar and folded her arms around the rope. When he let go and she soared out over the dip screeching, he squatted down on the slope, hugging his knees. He watched her and at the same time he took note of handholds on the tree trunk, calculated distances, worked out where he would stand to haul her in. He was just waiting for that moment, rehearsing it in his head. But by bending and straightening her legs she was able to maintain the momentum and prolong her go. He started to count the seconds each swing took. 'One elephant, two elephants,' he muttered under his breath. He would give her another minute.

'Watch this, Louis,' she called. She let go of the rope and her body toppled backwards. He was on his feet with a yell in his throat. She was hanging by her knees, laughing. She flung her arms wide. 'I'm a bird,' she shouted.

'Don't be so stupid,' he said. 'Sit back up and hold on properly.' She flapped her arms and made clucking noises. 'Sit up,' he said. 'Or I'll never bring you out again.' He meant it as well. The stupid little girl.

The quality of light had changed. He twisted round and looked up towards the ridge. The sun had shifted so that the top was a fiery line. He had the feeling something had moved and he'd just missed it. 'We've got to go,' he said.

Adele was flailing, reaching up and dropping back, her body flipping about like the time she was stung by a jellyfish. The span of her swing had shrunk.

'Come on, Del,' he said. 'Stop mucking about.'

'I can't sit up,' she said, 'my tummy won't pull me.'

Louis felt a prickle in the back of his neck and swung round again. There, up on the ridge, something had definitely moved.

Several somethings. He turned back and shuffled quickly down the slope to the edge of the hollow, positioning himself on the ledge. 'Next time,' he said, 'grab hold.' When she swung towards him they caught each other's sweaty hands. Adele screamed and he let go. It was simple. If he pulled her in, he'd pull her off. Into the thorns. She had slipped so that she was hanging by her calves now. 'Can you make it swing higher?' he said. If he could catch her further up, she could tumble on to the side of the slope. They'd lose the rope swing, but he didn't care about that any more.

'I can't,' she said, her voice shuddering. He balanced on the rim, bouncing on the balls of his feet, his teeth clamped together. He still had his arms stretched out towards her, even though she was now out of reach. He flapped his hands, making a panicky moaning noise. Why'd she have to hang upside down in the first place?

'Get me down, Louis,' Adele wailed.

He eyed the other side of the crater for inspiration. The ground there was too sheer, only a rim of flat land to stand on. He cast his eyes down again. He wondered if he could lower himself into the ditch, in between the thorns, wade into the middle beneath her and then do something, he didn't know what it would be, but something. He teetered on the edge like an idiot.

'My legs,' Adele's voice came out jerkily, 'my legs hurt.'

He didn't have time to run for help. It would be dark by the time he brought anyone back. A picture of himself leading Dominic up the cliffside by torchlight flashed into his mind. He thought again of the mysterious land beyond the ridge and saw himself running along the tree-lined path, simple and free and alone. He shook his head, pulling his thoughts back. What could he do? For a wild moment, he had a notion of flinging himself on to the thorns to be her landing place. He would rather die than have his sister die. He looked again at the cruelly sharp tips and saw Adele's flip-flops wedged among them. He stared, enraged at this new evidence of her idiocy. He shuffled pointlessly, still crouching, along the edge of the gully, his scuffling feet dislodging little stones. Adele was making a ghastly whining noise. He didn't look at her in case she had slipped even further.

'Shut up,' he shouted. 'Let me think.' She fell silent and instantly an idea came into his head. Up, not down, he thought. He'd climb the tree and shin down the rope on to the crossbar. He wasn't sure what would follow because his imagination wouldn't stretch any further. He glanced at Adele. She was staring transfixed at something behind him. He realised that she hadn't shut up just because he'd told her to. It was something else. The prickling in the back of his neck shivered down his back and into his shoes. Slowly, he turned.

There were three African boys squatting a yard or two further up the slope, watching. Louis had the sensation they'd been there for a while. They'd seen him flapping about. They'd heard him shout. They watched him with their black eyes and Louis felt his own eyes water, his skin stretch taut on his cheekbones, in an effort not to blink. A memory of a previous situation like this one nudged at him and a strand of his awareness chased it, trying to nail it down, but it slid away. He stood there clenching and unclenching his fists, trying not to buckle under the thick layer of impotence and fear that swaddled him. He was weak with it and his mind was blank.

Suddenly, the biggest boy stood up and the other two followed. He had a coil of rope slantways across his bare chest. He lifted it over his head and handed one end to another boy who wore cuffs of red rags around his wrists. This other one, a compact and muscly sort of boy, built like a little man rather than a child, moved swiftly away, carrying his end of the rope. The third, the littlest, sank back to the ground. The big one stepped down towards Louis, speaking to him in fast Wolof in a scratchy, intermittent voice like a radio with a bad signal. He jerked his head back and made a tutting noise, motioning Louis away from the edge of the ditch. He clicked his teeth and indicated the thorns, shaking his head as if Louis might not have noticed them, and Louis, grasping that, whatever else was going on, the boy didn't intend to tie him up and throw him on the spikes, moved to the side and made room on the ledge.

Then, so fast that Louis could hardly understand what was happening, the rope, lobbed by the red-rag boy from the narrow rim on the other side of the ditch, came hurtling through the air like a flying blue snake. The big boy reached out and grabbed it and Louis saw that they'd lassoed the rope swing. The next moment a rope end was thrust into his hand and he found himself, alongside the other boy, reeling Adele in, and all the time, as she dangled there like a stranded bat, she remained utterly silent, as did the African boys. He should have been glad that she wasn't whining any more but it was unnerving, no one speaking. As they backed up the slope, the tall boy and Louis, shoulder to shoulder, hoisting Adele ever further away from danger, he glanced sideways. The boy's head was shaved so close that his hair was just stubble and the dome of his skull was apparent. He had an outside sort of smell, like the garden in the rain, like hot mud.

Adele's hair brushed the hillside. She slid off on to the ground and lay there on her back. Louis knelt beside her, conscious of the big boy behind him doing things with the ropes. 'Are you all right?' he asked. She was gazing at the sky with a faraway look in her eyes. She looked demented and he thought she might be putting it on. His fingers itched at his side with the desire to give her a sharp slap. The smallest boy came and stood right next to him, peering down into Adele's face. With a faint frown, like a girl being woken from a trance, her eyes came into focus. She nodded at Louis. The boy laughed, a gurgle, like water going down the plughole. Adele pushed herself up on to her elbows and looked at him. He laughed again. His two front teeth were missing. Louis helped Adele to her feet and let go of her hand. She clung on to his sleeve, leaning into his side.

The little boy slid down to the ledge to join the other two. The biggest one was leaning against the tree trunk. He'd looped the spare rope back around his chest and the rope swing around its hook. The red rags that had encircled the other boy's wrists hung loosely from his hand. All three stood looking blankly up at Louis and Adele. Louis' sense of their camaraderie faltered. He searched in his mind for the right thing to say. The only words he remembered in Wolof were traditional greetings. He could ask them how their families were and whether they'd slept well the previous night, but those weren't the sort of words that he needed, the sort that would bridge the gap. Perhaps they would invite him to come back and play on the swing with them tomorrow. The right words were on the tip of his tongue.

'*Jerejef*,' Adele said in a sudden, loud voice. That was 'thank you' in Wolof. Louis remembered now. He should have been the one to say it. The boys all laughed. The big one replied to her in his harsh voice, but she hung her head and pressed herself into Louis' side. When Louis tried to detach himself she clung on to his shirt, hiding her face in it. Short of actually shoving her off, he couldn't get free. He raised his eyebrows at the biggest of the boys but the other wasn't even looking. He had turned away and was concentrating on bandaging the middle boy's hands with the red rags, as if his business with Louis and Adele was over and done with.

'Um,' Louis said. The boy stopped what he was doing and looked up. He made a noise in his throat, a kind of growl. Perhaps he spoke in that husky way because he had a sore throat. Louis found himself giving an awkward little bow. He spoke in French. 'Thank you for your help,' he said.

The boy stared at him. He must at least understand French. Everyone in Senegal spoke French. It was the official language. It was what they used in schools. He tried again. 'You saved my sister,' he said, 'with your rope.' He flapped his hand towards the rope to make himself clear and inclined his head again. Louis wanted this boy to know that he was his friend, was in his debt. The boy continued to look at him with an unreadable expression on his face. Perhaps this boy didn't actually go to school. Louis put his hand to his chest in a gesture he'd never used before but which he hoped conveyed sincerity.

The boy spoke then, but not to him. He muttered something to his companions and they replied in low voices, without taking their eyes off Louis. Louis had the feeling that he'd seriously missed the mark. The half-remembered thing from when he'd first turned and seen the boys behind him on the hillside flew into Louis' head. It was a scene from an old Western. Some cowboys ride into an apparently deserted Cherokee village down in a valley. They kick over the ashes of a cooking fire, upsetting the pot. They are standing laughing as if they own the place, the liquid from the cooking pot draining into the dirt, when they become aware that they are being watched. Cherokee warriors, bows and arrows at the ready, have surrounded them on the hillside above. 'Sorry,' Louis blurted out. 'I thought it was a swing anyone could use. I didn't know it was yours.'

The boy eyed Louis up and down.

'I'm sorry,' Louis said again.

'It's OK,' the boy said, eventually.

Adele was tugging at his sleeve, whispering that they should go. When she set off round the slope, Louis saw that the backs of her legs were scraped red raw. He was going to be in such trouble.

'What if I come tomorrow?' Louis said.

The boy furrowed his brow and flicked his head backwards as if to say 'Can't you see I'm a busy man?' He made the clicking noise with his teeth again. 'Come if you want, *toubab*,' he said.

When, at the entrance to the tunnel of leaves, they looked back down, the boys were flying through the air. The red-rag one was standing on the crossbar, keeping the swing moving, his back arching at the forward high point, knees bending as they swept back, propelling them to and fro at speed. The other two were taking it in turns to leap and take hold, swing, turn and fly back off to the ledge. They were like a circus act, performing only for themselves. The word 'aerodynamic' sprang into Louis' head. Of course this swing hadn't been put up by somebody's stupid dad for stupid white children.

They turned away without speaking and Louis followed Adele into the tunnel. She stumbled ahead of him down the slope, her bare feet sliding on the loose earth. When they reached the flat part above the beach hut, he saw she was drooping with tiredness. If her brothers were those African boys, they'd probably make her a carrying thing out of rope and branches. They wouldn't have let her get hurt in the first place. Louis was suddenly tired too, like someone who'd been on a long journey and still had a way to go before home, but he squatted down and offered Adele his back. She clambered on, letting out a little whimper when her sore legs rubbed on his sleeves.

He set off down the dunes. The fat sun hung low in the wide orange sky ahead so that he had the sensation of walking into the light. An evening breeze blew up off the sea, charging the salty air with freshness and carrying the shouts and cries of voices. The beach below them was so transformed from earlier that he almost forgot his disquiet.

Black silhouettes furrowed weightless boats across the liquid copper sand. Louis could hear the slap of the waves again and the clamour of the fishermen as they called to each other. From the water's edge came the deep mellow voice of a man singing as he boarded his craft and pushed off. Others joined in.

By the time they were down on the flat, the boats were all in the sea. Gulls and other seabirds, terns and skuas, wheeled around the shoreline. He put Adele down and held her hand, half towing her back along the beach to La Falaise. When they were close, she let go and ran ahead into the circle of lanterns. The little pods of light illuminated bits of faces, edges of things, but left the blackness of the surrounding night untouched. A smoky fish smell wafted through the air. Louis hung back in the dark as Adele squeezed in between their mum and Dominic at the far end of the trestle table and Dominic clapped his arms around her, scooping her on to his lap. A glowing cigarette butt chucked by someone at the near end, Marge probably, landed at his feet. He bent to retrieve it and took a puff. It tasted disgusting and made his head swirl. He took another puff. Then he stepped forward and slipped quietly into the empty seat. Danny Travis passed him a beer.

'You're old enough to drink beer, aren't you, kid?' he said.

He took a cautious swig. He placed the can on the table halfway between his place and Danny Travis's so he could deny ownership if spotted, but no one paid him any mind. A paper plate of rice and fish was passed down to him and he caught a brief smile from his mum. He looked down the table at the pink balloon faces jiggling in the lamplight, wondering where the rope-swing boys were right then and what they might be eating for dinner. He thought of the spikes beneath the swing, imagining their ghastly whiteness by moonlight, feeling that this impunity wouldn't last and that, sooner or later, he'd have to pay, but not right then, not that night, under the swaying palms.

Boubacar's Journey

Dakar, Senegal, and Nouadhibou, Mauritania, 2002–3

On what turned out to be his last day at school, Boubacar Dieng learned about Senegal's first president, Leopold Sedar Senghor, and his philosophy of *la négritude*. He studied the meaning of the red, yellow and green colours in the Senegalese flag and, along with the other fifty-seven children in his class, he sang the national anthem, which Senghor had written. '*Senegal, give to us the honour of our ancestors, splendid as ebony, strong as muscle.*' The words made him feel powerful and full of hope. His friend Abdou gave him a lift most of the way home on the back of his bicycle. They flew along Rue Parchappe.

In his house he found his mother wailing and his sisters covering their faces. His father had been killed in a road accident that day when the bus he drove collided with a lorry beside the docks and crumpled like a paper bag. They'd had to use cutting machines to get the bodies out. They brought him home and laid him out on the table. The marabout came and his father was buried the next day before sunset.

Every night for three nights his mother came home from her work cleaning the *toubab* house and she cried. The first night she cried for her lost husband who had never taken another wife and rarely raised his hand to her; the second night she cried for her poor fatherless children; and the third night she cried because she had no reason to stop. Boubacar told her not to worry. He was the man of the house now and he would provide. His sisters could stay at school because he would pay for their books. Fatima, who was eleven, wanted to be a nurse. It was important, he said, for her education at least to continue. His mother stopped crying, and in the sudden hush, they could hear his grandmother, the one they called Other-gran, mumbling her prayers behind the curtain. Fatima looked up from her book. His mother unwrapped the baby from her back and handed her to his second sister, Husna. He waited for his mother to tell him not to be silly. 'You're a good son,' she said at last.

His grandmother, the one who couldn't see, was sitting on a stool in the last bit of sun just beyond the doorway. She held out her hand to him but he brushed past. He stood in the enclosed space between the wall and the neighbours' washing. A lizard with a stripe on its back ran up the yellow bricks. Fatima came and stood next to him. She slid her hand inside his.

'Me and Binata,' she said, naming one of her friends, 'we've got a competition going on.' The lizard disappeared into a crack. Boubacar didn't know why his sister was speaking in that sing-song voice. 'And I think I've won,' she said.

She tried to swing his arm. He held it stiff.

The neighbour, Madame Talla, came out and began un-pegging the clothes. 'Salaam aleikum,' she said when she saw them there. She called down blessings on them and on the spirit of their father. The ancestors would give them strength, she said.

'Salaam aleikum,' they replied.

'Ah, ah, ah. The widows and the children. The children and the widows,' she said and went back inside with her clean, dry clothes.

'It's a competition to see who's got the best brother,' Fatima said.

Boubacar studied the mortar in between the bricks. Everything further away was blurry, as if a mist had descended.

Instead of going to school with his friends in the mornings, Boubacar looked for work. He went with his mother and asked at all the *toubab* houses in the area. He liked it there because it was where he used to play as a child. He offered to labour in the garden or the house, to clean their cars or fix their broken things, but they said they didn't need him. He tried to get a job on the buses like his father. The only work for unqualified people was as an apprentice and there was a waiting list of boys wanting to be taken on. The list was closed. The man in the office said because of his father he would add Boubacar's name, but it might be a long time. He went round the shops and banks in the city centre. He discovered he needed more education, some kind of qualification or experience to work in these places.

He thought he might become a tailor and spent some days studying the men with their sewing machines. He watched the way they fed the material in and manoeuvred it round, how they licked the thread before pushing it through the needle, popped the bobbin out and slotted a new one in, all very quick-fingered with a light but sure touch. It was something he could learn because he was fast and nimble, but he didn't have time. He needed the work now.

Sometimes he got a day's shift at a garage on Rue Gazoduc, clearing the forecourt and putting their supplies in order. He handed all the money to his mother when he got home and she sent Husna out to buy something for their dinner.

A man who came into the garage said that there were jobs in the southern region of Casamance, in the tourist places. The man mentioned the ferry that left Dakar for the southern capital, Ziguinchor, twice a week. Boubacar tried to think about getting on that boat and travelling down the coast, but his mind wouldn't go there. He kept seeing the sea rising up and sucking him down into a dark, slippery tunnel. The sea was like a monster to him.

One Wednesday, he waited at the side of the road for Fatima to come home from school. He'd spent that day looking for work in the artisan market. He'd sat at the edge of the carvers' workshop and his hands smelt of wood shavings. He saw Fatima before she saw him. She was barefoot.

He stepped out in front of her. 'Where are your shoes?' he asked.

'In my bag,' she said.

'Then why don't you put them on?' he said sharply.

She made a face at him. 'Because they don't fit any more,' she said. 'I'll put them on nearer the house.'

She walked on. He watched the up and down of the pink soles of her feet, the movement of her thin legs. Her school uniform was too tight across her back and around her arms. She turned and saw him still standing there. 'OK,' she called back, 'I'll put them on now.' She sat down on the ground and fetched her shoes out of her bag. He caught up with her as she stood up. She hobbled along next to him.

'I'm going to the Casamance to work,' he said. She stopped and put a hand on his arm.

'Don't be silly,' she said, 'there's still fighting going on there.'

'The separatists signed a peace agreement last year,' he said. He was glad to know more than she did for once. The garage man had explained to him that the latest deal between the government and the rebels who wanted independence for the Casamance region seemed to be holding. 'The tourists are coming back and there'll be tourist money sloshing around.'

'Sloshing?' Fatima said, laughing.

'Yes, rivers and lakes of cash. I'll be swimming in francs and dollars.'

'Wow.'

'I'll send money back and you can get new shoes,' he said. 'Two pairs probably.'

'What about Husna?' she said.

'Yes, Husna too. And a wrap for Mam. A carved walking stick for Gran.'

'And some chickens for Other-gran. She's always saying she doesn't get enough meat. She'll get out of bed again if she has chickens.'

'And some new teeth for her. Some big white dentures so she can crunch the chicken bones.'

The whole way home, they conjured up all the clothes and food and comfort his earnings would buy. Boubacar talked in a loud extravagant voice to keep his mind from sliding down into the tunnel.

Before he left, Other-gran called him to her. She was sitting on the edge of the bed the two grans shared. She wore her best dress with a yellow-and-scarlet headscarf tied around her little hairless head as if this were a special occasion. He sat down opposite on a low stool. 'They tell me that the fighting has stopped in the Casamance,' she said.

'Yes, Grandma. They've done a deal with the government,' he said. 'Now the tourist places are going to reopen and there'll be plenty of work, painting and decorating, getting them ready.' She didn't say anything. Although this was his grandma who could see, her eyes were whitish like a cloudy sky and you couldn't tell whether she was looking at you or had floated away. He continued. 'There's a big hotel right on the tip, Club Med they call it, and now the French tourists will be flying direct from Paris and I'm probably going to get work there.'

She held up her hand to stop him. 'Even though the fighting is over, men have killed each other. Remember that it's a scarred place.'

'I will, Grandma.'

'When elephants fight, it's the grass that suffers most,' she said.

He thought of trampled grass and crushed things and then the idea of the dark lonely tunnel surged in his head.

'Be careful,' she said, 'but be fearless. Because you are young, strong and brave. You are a lion,' she said.

He was going by road with a travelling salesman the man from the garage knew. He didn't need to keep thinking about the sea. He was a lion. He moved his jaw in a silent roar.

His grandma pressed two round metal pieces into his hand. One was a silver coin. The other was a medal with an engraving of a white man with shaggy hair carrying a child on his shoulders across a river. 'When you can't find your way, St Christopher will help,' she said.

'Grandma, I'm a Muslim,' he said.

'Put it in your pocket,' she said. 'Saints are saints.'

'Next time I see you,' he said, 'it'll be me putting coins in your pocket.'

★

He walked between the tight-packed houses, his bare feet slapping the dry mud. The light spilling out from open doorways and the cracks around shut ones lit his way. Voices speaking in Wolof came from the houses on either side. He quickened his pace. He was nearly home.

When he'd passed the barbershop on the corner and was close to the house, he stopped. He stepped into a dark side alley and pulled his grubby T-shirt over his head. He put on a clean white shirt, tugging the material down to stretch out the creases. The shirt was for a much bigger man. It hung like a cut-off boubou over his trousers, as if he'd started to dress in traditional clothes but changed his mind halfway. When he'd snatched it from a washing line, his thought hadn't been for the size but the wealth of clothing hanging there. He took out his shoes, polished each of them with his old T-shirt and then put it in his bag. He looped an elastic band around the right shoe to hold the flapping sole in place.

There were people sitting in the yard of his and the neighbour's house watching television. From the other side of the wall he examined their faces in the flickering bluish light from the screen. Five children of different sizes were sitting on little stools or upturned crates. Three young men sat in a row on plastic bags. There was a girl about Husna's size sitting on the ground with her legs stretched straight out in front. Behind her an older woman sat slumped in a plastic chair.

He took a step back and looked up and down the dark street. He could make out the sign above the barbershop, and although there wasn't enough light to read the writing, the sign was the right shape and he knew it said 'Ali Coiffeur'. He smoothed the big shirt down, adjusted the bag across his shoulder and went quietly into the yard. The girl who looked a bit like Husna tugged on the woman's dress and the woman sat up. 'What is it?' she said. She peered at Boubacar. 'Who is it?' she said.

Boubacar saw it was Madame Talla, his neighbour. 'It's me,' he said. 'The son of your neighbour.' He nodded at the shut door of his house, but he didn't move towards it. The children in front of the TV glanced up at him and then back at the TV, except for the littlest boy who swivelled round on his stool and sat wide-eyed, thumb in mouth, staring at Boubacar.

'Oh,' the woman said, standing up. 'Welcome, young man. I didn't recognise you at first. You are welcome.' On the TV screen two men were fighting on a high roof. 'Just wait a minute. I'll fetch the bag,' Madame Talla said. She disappeared into her house.

The door of Boubacar's house opened and a woman appeared. She wore a pale headscarf and something glinted silver at her neck. 'Time to come in now,' she said in a low voice. The little boy picked up his stool and went inside. One of the men on the TV had a ponytail. He kung-fu-kicked the other in the head and leapt across from the roof to another lower one.

The neighbour came out with a zipped plastic holdall. 'Say hello to your mother for me,' she said. 'Tell her to come and visit.'

'I will,' he said. 'Thank you.'

She put her hand on his arm and pulled him close, patting his back. 'I'm sorry for your loss,' she said.

He took the bag and went out of the yard. He walked quickly to the junction where there was a tree with hanging branches. He ducked under the leaves, up close, and laid his forehead against the trunk. He thought about his father who was dead and who he'd never see again. That wasn't the loss she was talking about. He thought about the places he'd been turned away from in the Casamance and of his journey back, passing like a ghost through the leafy villages as if he'd lost himself.

As if he were no longer a solid person but something the light and the shadows could pass through. It wasn't that loss she meant either. She might mean the loss of his home where it seemed unknown people now lived, but he didn't think so. He prostrated himself on the ground.

After a while, he got up and went back to the yard. Everyone had gone, the TV had been put away and the yard was empty, but there was a light from inside Madame Talla's house. 'I don't know where I'm going,' he said when she came to the door.

She looked smaller without her headdress. Her short hair was grey and tufty. 'Oh my poor child,' she said, 'I thought you'd just come to collect the last things. I thought you knew.'

He sat on her plastic chair drinking a cup of water while she told him. His mother had lost her job at the *toubab* house and they couldn't manage the rent any more so they'd had to move. 'Your sister wrote to you,' she said.

'I kept moving around,' he said. 'I didn't get a letter.'

She didn't ask him why he hadn't written. It wasn't her business. He knew she was thinking it. How to say that a letter would be one long scream and it was better to stay silent?

She gave him the new address and explained how to get there. 'Your mother will be glad to have you home. It will be a comfort for her in her loss.'

There it was again. He couldn't bring himself to ask. He got up to go. At the door he faced out into the night. He made his lion face in the dark. He turned back to her. 'Someone else has died?'

'Your grandmother,' she said. 'I'm sorry to be the one to tell you. She passed away four, five months ago.'

Just after he'd left, she must have died. He put a hand in his trouser pocket and felt for St Christopher. He couldn't wish either of his grandmothers dead.

'Not the blind one. The other one,' the neighbour said. She looked at him crumpled there against her doorpost. 'Come back inside and stay here tonight. Time enough for all that tomorrow.'

She made a bed for him on the floor and he lay wrapped in a blanket, not sure if he was asleep or awake.

Early in the morning she sent a child to the baker on the next street. She made Boubacar coffee and gave him fresh bread. He ate sitting in the yard. The woman from his old house came out with her children, but he turned his face away.

He set off to the new house following Madame Talla's directions. At first he walked quickly as if he were in a hurry to get there, pushing through the stream of women with baskets on their heads on their way to market. But then he slowed his steps and let them overtake him, chattering and laughing as if all things were right in the world. He caught sight of himself in a shop window, shaking his head like an old man with a palsy. He steadied himself. Then he walked on. The streets near the market at Khar Yalla were teeming with people and smelt of fish and bread.

The first person he saw when he got to the place was his blind grandmother. She was sitting on her stool with his baby sister playing nearby, on the edge of a gully choked with plastic bags and rotting things. His legs buckled so that he knelt on the ground at his grandmother's feet. She held his head and cradled him, mumbling and crying into his hair.

The house was a one-room shack. He couldn't see how they all fitted in even without him. Clothes hung from hooks around the walls. He left the bag Madame Talla had given him inside.

He found his mother at a crossroads on the edge of the market. She was sitting on a bucket behind a little stall she'd laid out on a cloth on the ground. She had tomatoes, carrots and dried fish to sell. She looked worn. She must have been up before dawn to buy the goods wholesale. 'My son,' she cried, 'my son is here.' And she called to the other women stallholders to witness the wonder of her son returned. He stood straight, trying to make himself taller and more impressive. These women didn't need to know that his pockets were empty and his shirt stolen.

'How was Casamance?' one asked.

He thought of arriving by road in the grief-choked streets of Ziguinchor. The ferry that he hadn't caught had capsized in a storm on its way back to Dakar and hundreds were drowned. He thought of Club Med at Cap Skirring which employed cooks, kitchen porters, cleaners, tennis coaches, maintenance men, waiters, bar staff and receptionists, but had nothing to offer Boubacar. He'd stayed there anyway, camping out in the bush near the beach, climbing into the compound at night to scavenge for thrown-away food, waking to the dazzle of the sun on the ocean. 'Very beautiful,' he said, 'but treacherous.'

'Did you see the rebels?'

'I only just escaped,' he said. He didn't know he was going to say such a thing.

They gasped at him and clustered round exclaiming and asking questions.

'Ladies, I will tell you the story another time. Just now I must speak with my mother.' She'd sat back down on her bucket and was looking at him with a light in her eyes. She'd never been any good at knowing when he was lying.

He squatted beside her and she stroked his hand. 'The important thing is that you're safe,' she said.

He wondered if that were true.

'Your grandmother died,' she said.

'I know,' he said.

'My *toubabs* went back to England and I lost my job.'

'Didn't they give you a reference?'

'They did, son. And they recommended me very highly to the new people who took over the house. French people. Very nice and polite.'

'So how come you're not working for them, Ma?'

'Oh, they wanted to start afresh. Choose for themselves.'

He rocked on his haunches.

'When I've sold these last bits, I'll buy some rice. We'll go home and eat together,' she said.

'Home,' he said. He didn't like the sound of his own voice. A child's treble.

'Now you're back, things will start to get better,' she said.

He cleared his throat, spoke in a lower voice. 'I need to go and see a man about some work and then I'll meet you at the house when the girls return from school.' He got to his feet. She looked up at him as if from a far distant place. 'What is it?' he said.

'No,' she said, shaking her head, 'it's a good thing.'

He looked up at the sky where high clouds swirled. His heart fluttered like the wings of a bird on the verge of flight. 'What is it?' he said again.

'Husna still goes to school,' she said.

He waited. He thought he'd felt dread before, but this was worse.

His mother stood up. She said something to the woman on the next stall. She led him away to a quieter place down a side street. 'Fatima has gone away. She's got a job in another country,' she said. 'It's a very good job where she will be able to continue her education and will be hosted by a respectable family.'

'What country?'

'Ivory Coast,' she said. 'Or it might be Nigeria.'

'What nonsense is this?' He'd never spoken to his mother like that.

'A man came. A businessman. He was recruiting young people to go and work on cocoa plantations and in people's houses. He wore a suit. He paid a fee. It's a guarantee. I've kept it safe. I haven't used any of it.'

Boubacar had heard of this business, these child traffickers, during his travels in the south. 'Where's this man?' he said.

'He went with them. I'm waiting for a letter.'

He took a step back. 'Don't get your hopes up,' he said. 'You've sold her.'

He left his mother crying in the street.

★

His first lift was a good one because the driver was going all the way up to the border. Boubacar's plan was to cross into Mauritania and find a place on a boat going the short distance across the sea to the Canary Islands. That was the best way to get into Europe.

He was the second passenger and so he sat up front where it was comfortable. In the wing mirror he could see the fingertips of the passengers who'd joined later, holding on to the rim of the truck. He rolled the driver's cigarettes for him. The driver was thin but his stomach hung over his trousers. He shifted restlessly on his seat, letting farts escape into the tobacco air. He smelt like he was rotting from the inside.

When they stopped for diesel, he picked out one of the girls with lips purple like bruises. 'Go and ask her how much,' he said to Boubacar.

'How old are you?' the girl said to him.

'I'm sixteen,' Boubacar said, 'but it's not for me, it's for him.'

She went off into the bushes with the stinking man. Afterwards, the driver went to buy a hot drink. Boubacar had nuts and oranges in the pocket of his jacket and all the money from selling Fatima sewn into the hem. He offered the girl an orange. 'I don't do it for oranges,' she said.

'I don't want anything,' he said. She took an orange. 'Why do you do it?' he asked.

'Why do you think?' she said. He turned away from her, thinking of Fatima. He had logged her details with a charity that tried to reunite children with their families. When he returned from Europe with funds, her whereabouts would be known and he would get her back.

Somewhere in the north a woman with a baby got on. Boubacar watched her struggling to lift the baby above her head and the people reaching down to help. 'Is it OK with you if I give her my place?' he asked the driver.

'You're not going to get far in Europe if you let others get in front,' the driver said.

There was no space left in the back of the truck around the side where you could hold on. He sat on the metal in the middle with his feet braced against the floor, his thighs tensed and his hands splayed either side. An old lady was lifted in at one of the stops. He found a better position against the back of the driver's cab and tried to keep her from being thrown about. Her headscarf had yellow lions standing up on their hind legs. She fell asleep on his lap. He was sorry to hand her out, although she didn't say goodbye. She might have thought he was an armchair.

The border was easy. On the other side he got a lift to the outskirts of Nouakchott. There were two other young men waiting by the roadside. They were brothers from Mali but they could speak French like him. They were heading for Europe too. They shared their food of bread and hard-boiled eggs with spicy tomato paste and told stories of people they knew who'd made it, of the jobs they had and the money they sent home to their families. They were full of hope. They would do this or die, they said. No trucks came by. The sun went down and they were still sitting by the roadside.

Boubacar and the Malian boys took it in turns to sleep so they didn't miss a lift. The one called Mohammed squatted next to Boubacar. 'We saw dead men in the desert,' he whispered.

'They were sitting against a rock and their water bottles were empty.'

When it was his turn to lie down, Boubacar wrapped himself in his blanket and lay on the ground on the edge of the Sahara. He could feel the desert behind him, the vast waves of sand like the sea, pulling him down. He remembered the ocean at Cap Skirring and how the tourists threw themselves in as if it held no fear for them and was only a place to laugh and play. When no one was looking he'd waded in and imitated them, spreading his arms through the water, flapping one of his legs. It looked like he was swimming but, for a long time, he kept one foot on the ocean floor. On his last day there, he'd dared to lift his toes off and the water had held him afloat.

The moon over the desert was so strong it was like a powerful spotlight from the sky. It pushed against his eyelids, trying to prise them open.

In the morning they got a lift to Nouadhibou where the men selling passage on the boats to the Canaries came and found them. They handed over their money. When it was dark, the men took them to the boat. It was just a rowing boat with an engine and it was already full.

Salt water churned in Boubacar's stomach as if the sea had got inside him and was bubbling up through the holes it found there. He knew he was a leaky vessel. Even before he clambered aboard, he felt the waves crashing over his head.

The Lodger

Cardiff, South Wales, 1986

The man was in the breakfast room, leaning against the window ledge with his back to the high, narrow window. His hair against the diffuse white light of the setting sun beyond formed a silvery aureole around his head while his face was in shadow. When he greeted her, he inclined his head. The suddenly blinding light spilled over the top and on to Adele's face. She closed her eyes. The outline of his placid smiling face shimmered gold and wavering black against the crimson of her eyelids. 'How do you do?' he said as he enfolded her right hand in both of his, and Adele, eyes shut, face tipped up into the beatific unfolding glow, rocked giddily and felt him tighten his grip, steadying her.

'He's got a what?' her friend Jill said the next day in the bus on the way home from school.

Adele wished she hadn't begun. She didn't so much doubt Jill's willingness to allow this man, the new lodger, a halo if Adele said he had one. Jill made bigger leaps of faith than that on a regular basis, whenever Adele required her to. It was more that she herself was explaining the magic away.

It was like the time in the scripture lesson when the teacher told them that manna from heaven was really some nutritious fungus that wafted in the desert wind and not a miracle at all. Enraged, she'd come home and asked how come she'd been sent to this heathen school and her mother had laughed. But she had been younger then and her faith total and unassailable. 'I said his hair *looked* like a halo,' she said, 'a bit like a halo. It was a trick of the light, probably.'

'And you must have been quite stoned,' Jill said in her matter-of-fact way.

'Yes, I was,' Adele conceded, 'reeling with stonedness.'

They'd taken to stopping for a smoke in the park between their houses on the way home sometimes. They pooled the money from their Saturday jobs to buy the occasional quarter ounce and liked to think of themselves as connoisseurs. They could roll three-skin joints and five-skin joints and thought it cheating to use a king-size cigarette paper or a rolling machine. Yesterday, for the first time, Jill had given her something called a blowback she'd learned off the Newport Road squat guy. Jill had provided her with a short scientific explanation of how it doubled the effect while Adele leaned against the tree with her head swimming, wondering if she was going to be sick. But afterwards, when the nausea had calmed down, it felt nice. It took the edge off things. Adele liked that. 'You know when distances stretch and time goes all funny?' she said. 'It was like that walking home yesterday. I was so stoned I was tottering along and I thought I was never going to get there. The house seemed to be getting further away the more I walked. Like Alice in the garden of Looking-Glass House.'

'Alice who?'

'The book,' Adele said. 'And,' she went on quickly so she wouldn't have to explain which book or see Jill's incomprehension, 'and another thing is, it was unexpected him being there, a stranger in the house. There's usually no one in when I get back on a Wednesday.' She had expected that emptiness, to be able to revel in the delicious floatiness of her stoned state, to drift around making herself tea and then to listen to David Bowie in her room before having to speak to anyone. Guiltily, she remembered her father, whose doleful, shambling presence in the house was so close to absence as to not quite count. Although physically much bigger than he'd been when younger, he was somehow less substantial and more wispy in terms of impact, inconsequential. He rarely spoke. So much so that on the occasions when he appeared somewhere unexpected or made an utterance, it was as if the wardrobes had suddenly loomed or the wallpaper had unpeeled and whipped out as you passed.

'Oh, you mean *Alice in Wonderland*?' Jill said.

Before she was even through the door, her mum had called out to her in that brittle voice she sometimes used as if someone had a gun to her head but she was determined to be brave. 'Adele,' she'd warbled, 'come into the breakfast room. There's someone here to meet you.' Adele had been shaken by a queasy memory of a previous time when her mother had called out in that querulous way, perhaps using the same words, which was when her father had come creeping home six months earlier.

Jill had been tearing tiny holes out of her folded bus ticket.

She spread it out on her lap. 'Look at my snowflake,' she said.

'Very nice,' Adele said, standing up and catching hold of the overhead strap. It was her stop next.

Jill looked up. The sun through the bus window glanced off her glasses, so that she appeared to have a pair of gleaming white moons instead of eyes, like an owl creature from a different dimension. Adele, swaying above her to the motion of the bus, thought an unsuspected aspect of Jill's nature had been revealed, unknowable and alien. The ray of sunlight shifted away to reveal Jill's glassy green eyes. They held the same gawpingly trusting look that had flipped Adele into the realisation two years before that Jill was her responsibility and that, without really meaning to, she'd taken her on.

The two had met when Jill, a new girl and latecomer to the Davies Academy, the independent girls' school where Adele was by then a veteran of two years, turned up at Catholic prayers. On Fridays, the Catholics held separate prayers in one of the classrooms. They would kneel on the wooden floor in the space in front of the teacher's desk to mumble a Confiteor and a few Hail Marys, then queue up in the corridor to go in to general assembly for the final announcements. Adele's attendance wasn't due to piety. Her faith, swallowed whole at a tender age, had risen up to choke her by thirteen and a half. She had been spitting it out ever since, although the sensation of sin still coated her innards and the impetus of guilt drove her. The reason she went was because it was up to her whether she did or she didn't. There was no obligation. At the Davies Academy where everything

65

was obligatory, from the shade and thickness of the tights you wore (caramel beige, 30 denier), to the number of tests you had to pass before being allowed to play a game of lacrosse (seven, including scooping up a rolling transverse ball while running), that was a sliver of freedom. The prayer meetings provided quarter of an hour of unregimented time, when Adele could walk, with legitimacy, in the opposite direction to the rest of the school. They made her feel as the prisoner in the tower might when she squeezed her fingers through an arrow-slit and wafted them briefly in the air outside.

The girls were in silent contemplation, heads bowed. The door creaked open, and a voice that sounded unnecessarily loud in the reverent post-rosary hush said, 'Is this the Catholics?' Adele looked up at the speaker in the doorway, a girl she'd not seen before, and gave an involuntary little smirk at the girl's appearance. Her uniform, while conforming in a general way to the regulation grey pleats and bottle-green woollens, undermined them in the wrinkled, baggy slouch with which it was worn. The oversized cardigan, each button a mismatch, hung off one shoulder to reveal the strap of her pinafore beneath in schoolgirl imitation of decadent décolleté. The straggling waist-length golden plaits that hung either side of her broad pink face, like badly drawn curtains, were loosely tied with what appeared to be shoelaces. She had only one eyebrow.

The spotty sixth-former who led the prayers with majestic self-importance put a finger to her lips and beckoned. The girl remained where she was, half in and half out, not committing herself. She pushed her glasses up her nose. 'Well, is it though?' she said, her face impassive. 'Or is it the Jews?'

Adele smiled her most brilliant and welcoming smile.

The girl knelt next to her, palms pressed together and eyes squeezed tight shut with every appearance of pious sincerity. She gave off a damp, musty aroma like a wet carpet. There were holes in her cardigan and safety pins held two of the buttons in place. The uniform was second-hand, unwashed and unmended. Perhaps what Adele had taken for perverse chic was nothing of the sort. She felt resentful, as if the girl had deliberately duped her.

When prayers ended the girl said, 'You get the number 28 bus, don't you?'

Adele kept her gaze averted.

'Shh,' said the sixth-former in charge.

The girl lowered her voice to a stage whisper. 'So do I,' she said with the air of someone uncovering hidden treasure, as if she were announcing that they were long-lost sisters. 'But,' she added as they set off to assembly, 'you get on two stops after me.'

In a moist, breathy murmur, undaunted by either the frowns and shushings or Adele's averted gaze, the girl, Jill, imparted more pieces of information. Among other things, Adele learned Jill had a poodle called Pester who only understood Welsh, that her mum had bought the uniform from the lost-property store but had forgotten to get it cleaned, that she'd won a maths scholarship to the school and that she had twin brothers who were altar boys which wasn't fair because girls should be allowed too.

When they were sitting on the benches in the corridor waiting to go in to assembly, Jill subsided into silence. Adele would discover Jill had bouts of talk, when strings of words like tapeworms would emerge, but her natural state was mute. Right then, however, sitting next to Jill's hunched form on the bench, Adele felt responsible. She hated to think how many other little defeats and rejections this odd, malodorous girl must have suffered in her first week. When Adele had come back from Africa and started at the school she hadn't fitted in either. She still didn't, but she disguised it better.

The sixth-former, standing on duty near the glass panel in the assembly door so as not to miss the moment when they would make their discreet entry, swung round and said in an undertone, with a little smile on her face, 'I don't know what you think you're playing at.'

Jill looked blankly up. Her lips hung slackly open. It wasn't clear whether she grasped she was being addressed.

'Talking in the corridor, wearing improper uniform, refusing to be quiet when warned.'

Adele felt a surge of protectiveness. 'She's new,' she said. 'She doesn't know the rules.'

'Are you going to explain them to her?' the sixth-former snapped, emboldened perhaps by the passive slump of Jill's shoulders.

'Yes,' Adele said, 'if you don't report her.'

'Well, I'll be checking on that,' the sixth-former hissed.

Jill had turned her pondweed eyes on Adele, waiting for her next move, waiting, as Adele later understood it, to be given instruction. Just as she was doing now, on the upper deck of the 28 bus.

'We're not going for a smoke today then?' Jill asked.

Adele shook her head. She'd promised to help her mum get the room ready for the new lodger.

When she got home, her mum, Claire, had already started. There were grunts and scraping noises coming from the front room and her father was standing in the hall, rattling a box of matches, an unlit cigarette hanging from his mouth. Her mother was sitting on the floor, her back braced against the bedstead, pushing a wardrobe into the alcove with her feet. 'You should have waited for me,' Adele said from the doorway.

'Your father,' Claire panted, 'was helping me.' Adele waited for her to say something disparaging like she usually did – 'your useless father' – but, instead, she gave another mighty shove and the wardrobe teetered dangerously.

Adele darted into the room and grabbed hold. She glanced back at her father, dithering in the hall. 'It's all right,' she said to him, 'I'll take over now.' He wandered away. A moment later she heard the back door open, the strike of a match and then the aroma of his cigarette wafted down the hall.

Together they humped furniture about and tugged a rug over the stain on the oatmeal carpet. Adele wiped down the skirting boards while her mum sprayed furniture polish and rubbed vigorously at the chest of drawers. 'There,' she said when she'd finished. 'You'd think it was real, wouldn't you?' A rare smile was on her face. It was a beleaguered little smile, but still, not to be wasted.

'No.' Adele shook her head solemnly. 'I still think it's a figment of your imagination.'

'Silly.' Her mum gave a laugh, patting Adele's shoulder. 'You know what I mean.' With the smell of polish, the sheen on the grain, the hardboard back concealed, the chest seemed like old wood. It might be an heirloom instead of a bit of tat from a junk shop that she'd wildly nailed back together in the shed.

'Yes, it looks really nice in here,' Adele said. She straightened the rug with her toe. 'Lucky new lodger.'

'Please God this one works out,' Claire said.

Since Dominic had come out of hospital, they'd had a succession of lodgers. Claire worked 'all the hours God sends' to pay the bills and the mortgage but, still, it was difficult to 'keep the wolves from the door', she said. Sometimes, when she was stoned, Adele could hear those wolves and would howl into her pillow along with them. One of the expenses her mother had to meet was the cost of constantly updating the Davies Academy uniform. Adele offered to go to the comprehensive down the road but that, apparently, was just flinging her mother's sacrifices back in her face. Her father took no part in these debates. He would retire to 'his' room upstairs, the room Louis had vacated when he'd gone off to university, where he sat in a fug of smoke, staring out of the window. Smoking was his new hobby. He'd taken it up when he was in hospital.

None of the lodgers lasted long. There was always something not right. In the case of Peter K, it was his hair. Usually he ate in his room, but on the day he cashed his giro, he'd treat himself to tandoori chicken and chips at the kitchen table, a beer mat from his collection under a can of strong cider, a piece of toilet paper tucked festively into the front of his T-shirt. As he munched, he nodded his head in time to the heavy-metal beat of Megadeth buzzing through his headphones, and the ends of his long hair would dip and trail into the sauce, anointing them with curry. For days afterwards the foremost locks of hair would have their last inch or so encased in an orangey crust. Eventually, Claire claimed to have seen something that confirmed her worst suspicions and she asked him to leave. 'He sucks the crust off,' she told Adele.

Claudia, the Italian student, had to go because she wandered about the house in her underwear, thrusting her breasts at Adele's 'poor bewildered father'. Arthur, the electrician, was the only one to leave of his own accord after Claire caught him heading off out one evening wearing Adele's velvet jacket. The wig, stockings, frock and heels were all his own. 'I suppose you want me to go,' he'd said mournfully and Claire had admitted that she did.

The trouble with all of them, as Claire explained, was that they were there. 'I just don't like them in the house,' she said. 'I wouldn't mind if it weren't for that.'

Now, after a pause, Robert had appeared. According to her mother, Robert even coming to know about the room showed it was meant to be. He'd spotted the ancient yellowing postcard announcing the room's dimensions and reasonable price in the window of the local post office. The card should have been taken down ages before because Claire hadn't paid the 25p a week. It had been stuck there, forgotten both by the postmistress and by Claire, until Robert came along. What made Robert perfect was that he didn't actually intend to live there. His home was in some sleepy village in mid-Wales and all he wanted was a bolt-hole for when he was too tired to drive home or might have a late meeting at the university where he taught. He would come sometimes in the daytime for an hour or so. He would pay in cash weekly. They wouldn't even notice him.

So it proved. He glided in and out, seeming never to stay the night. Once or twice, on a Wednesday when she came straight home from school, Adele would catch him just before he left. A couple of times, he had a woman with him whom he introduced as Daisy. Daisy looked more like a dandelion. She wore her feathery yellow hair in bunches despite being at least thirty-five or forty. Although he never spelled it out, Adele had the impression that Daisy was a lame duck of Robert's. Sometimes whole weeks went by without anyone even seeing him and the only evidence that he had been in the house at all was the envelope containing seven five-pound notes that he left on the side in the breakfast room. Adele, though, could feel it when he was in the house. A kind of benevolence that seeped under the doorways.

'I feel that there's a rebalancing of the arrhythmic pulse of our household going on,' she announced to Jill one after-noon. They were in their den in the park. The heavy scent of hot hash was in the air.

Jill glanced up at her. 'You what?' she said.

'It's the lodger,' Adele said.

'What is?' Jill said.

'He's causing the rebalancing.' Her mother had given up her frenzied insomniac hoovering. Her father had started to leave the house for the first time in months to take short walks in the park.

Jill offered Adele the joint and held out the lighter. Adele relit, took a deep drag and held the smoke down in her lungs. She let it trickle out through her nostrils and took another drag. 'Even Louis,' she said, 'has phoned up to say he's coming home at Easter. He hasn't been home for aeons.'

'What's it got to do with the lodger though?' Jill said.

'I don't know,' said Adele. 'He just has this soothing effect. He emanates calm.'

'We could do with him in my house then,' Jill said. 'Though I don't know where we'd put him.'

Adele didn't like to think of the fragrant Robert migrating to Jill's house, where towers of mouldering magazines blocked the hallway and the sofas were covered in dog hairs. 'Anyway,' she said briskly, 'what's next?'

Outside of school, over the two years that they'd been companions, Adele and Jill had escaped their homes regularly of an evening and climbed the railings to roam the dark park where they had many secret places. More recently, they had ventured out into the city and once to a nightclub, where they had drunk a nasty, but potent and cheap, concoction of barley wine and blackcurrant until they were sick.

Adele would have liked a best friend who understood her, but what she'd got was Jill. There were things you just couldn't do with Jill. You couldn't have a conversation that started 'What would you do if . . .' Adele didn't tell her half of what went through her mind, the pictures of herself crossing the Sahara by camel under a huge jewelled sky; a tiled apartment on the Moroccan coast with the turquoise oceans glittering from the window; the white house on a hill in the scorched south of some unspecified country, Greece or Spain or France, where people would know of her and she would speak their language, but would remain apart. It wasn't that Jill was stupid. She was just a different sort of clever. The mismatch in their consciousness made Adele fidgety, but Jill, she knew, would do anything for her.

One afternoon, when the lodger had been in peaceful part-time residence for a couple of months, Jill found herself sitting on the edge of his bed, gripping a mug of herbal tea. It was the first Monday of March, a half-day holiday to celebrate St David's Day. Adele hadn't been in school that morning so Jill had come round to see if she was all right. She hadn't even been home to change out of her uniform.

The tea tasted of dry wood and had bits of stalk and slimy leaves like seaweed floating in it. When she'd agreed to his offer of a brew, she hadn't imagined he meant here, in his room. She was wondering now if this was a chance for one of Adele's 'threads of silver light', a special moment outside of the ordinary. If so, she must live up to it. She thought it might well be one of those moments because he'd answered the door in a blue silk robe. Adele had been training her to look for the signs. Colour came into it.

'Oh, sorry,' he said. 'I thought you'd be Daisy.'

Jill had blinked at him.

'There's no one in,' he said. 'Only me.'

The robe was like a summer dress. It was tied loosely just below his waist. 'Excuse the kimono,' he said. 'I was meditating.'

74

Jill, aware that she might have what Adele called her gormless face on, closed her mouth and nodded.

'Come in and wait,' he said, stepping back into the hallway. He threw his arm wide to gesture her in. His robe gaped to show his smooth and hairless chest.

He had an electric kettle and two blue-and-white mugs made of thin china with bamboo handles. His room smelt like church on a Sunday afternoon, the incense of benediction. The music playing was like church too, monks singing far away.

He sat near the window at the little table where he made the tea. He leaned back in the chair, hooked his right arm over the back and lifted the edge of the net curtain. His bare legs were stretched out into the room. He had square toenails like miniature television screens. 'What's your favourite subject at school?' he asked, peering out under the curtain.

He thought her just a child. It wouldn't do to tell him about trigonometric functions. Jill took her time, thinking what Adele might say. 'The school has stupid rules,' she said. 'It's our duty, as citizens of the wider world, to disobey.'

He ducked his head back into the room, laughing. 'How do you do that?' he asked.

'All sorts of things. Skiving off lessons; going places that are out of bounds.' The lodger nodded, but he didn't ask another question. She needed something more. 'Taking drugs. Sneaking out and going to clubs to meet boys,' she said.

'And I thought Adele was such a good girl,' he said.

'She is,' Jill said. 'I lead her astray.' That was what Jill's parents said about Adele. She was a bad influence, they said, getting her to wear weird clothes and make-up, staying out late, putting strange ideas into her head.

'Do you?' he asked. He tipped his head on one side and looked at her from that angle with his sludgy blue eyes; eyes the colour of the sky after rain, Adele had said once.

Jill nodded. She couldn't think of anything else to say.

He went on looking at her, his head still cocked at that angle. Jill's face was getting hot. 'Are you feeling a bit subversive right now?' he said eventually.

She nodded again. She wasn't sure what he meant.

He looked at his watch and tapped his fingers on its face. He flipped the net curtain and glanced out again. 'She won't come now,' he said, pulling the chair across the room to sit with his knees almost touching Jill's. His beard would be ginger if he let it grow. He smelt of pine bath oil. He took the mug from her hand and laid it down carefully on the floor. He lifted her school skirt up and they both examined her pink legs with his freckly hand stroking them and then prising them apart. 'This is OK, is it?' he said. He was naked under the robe.

Afterwards, Jill didn't feel special and daring, but stupid and dirty. It was how they'd made her feel at the Davies Academy until Adele had come along and helped her. She avoided going to Adele's house for fear of bumping into him. Every time the memories of his hot fast breath on her back and the creak of the bed springs appeared in her mind, she pushed them back out until they seemed made up, like one of Adele's stories.

One Sunday lunchtime in late May, not long before the

O level exams were due to begin, Jill was sitting at the dinner table with her family. It was the one meal of the week they always ate together, 'like a proper family,' her mum would say, as if they weren't. The table was erected in the dining nook rather than in the kitchen and they had paper napkins. Outside it was a yellow kind of day. Jill was going to meet Adele in the park after lunch. She was dying to get out of the house. She was pushing a piece of fatty lamb around her plate, waiting for her mum to be distracted by her bickering brothers so she could slip it to the dog under the table. Then, quite suddenly, her mum barked, 'What's the matter with you?' and she said it in a way as if she was at the end of her tether and Jill had been doing something very bad for ages, instead of just pushing a slice of meat around for a few minutes.

'I feel sick,' Jill said.

'Again,' her mum said.

Jill didn't say anything. She had a horrible feeling. Her brothers fell silent. The dog under the table made a snorting noise. She pronged the piece of meat and lifted it towards her mouth. She couldn't put it in.

'Get into the kitchen,' her mum said, scraping her chair back.

Jill stood shaking her head in the kitchen while her mother talked about morning sickness and missed periods. 'I can't be,' Jill said.

'Don't pretend you haven't done it,' her mum said, her face flushing red and her voice rising to a thin scream. 'You and the doctor's daughter, out whoring.'

Later, when she was in the den, she spread her jacket on the ground and sat cross-legged on the bank of the stream. The water bubbled over the stones and the leaves above her rustled in the wind as if everything was still normal and everyday. She fetched her tobacco pouch out of her pocket. On the patch of jacket between her legs she laid out the bits she needed to make a joint: papers, little lump of hash, tobacco, cardboard for the roach. She rolled herself a quick single-paper one. Just looking at it made her feel sicker than she did already, but she lit it anyway and smoked it in a few deep drags so that the end glowed in a red-poker point. It was the same way she and Adele sometimes smoked at school, fast and furtive in the secret places they had – the boiler room, the old air-raid shelter behind the kitchens or the bell tower, from where they'd emerge blinking and reeling to the blur of their afternoon classes. A purply-black inkspot behind her eyes seeped and spread wider just as a washing-machine noise filled her ears. The earth behind rose up to hit the back of her head.

'Are you asleep or dead?' Adele's voice echoed around Jill's skull. She opened her eyes woozily. Adele was kneeling over her. The damp earth was soaking through her jacket. She could feel herself motionless and heavy on the ground, but everything about her was in a state of dizzying movement. Adele's face, hanging upside down, framed by the dancing leaves of the tree above, seemed to dissolve and re-form as she looked. She closed her eyes again. She couldn't answer yet. 'Is it just that you're stoned or are you ill?' Adele said.

'Stoned,' Jill managed.

Adele patted her arm. 'Sorry I'm late,' she said. 'There was a furore at home.'

Jill opened her eyes again, pushed herself up on to her elbows and adjusted her glasses. Furore. She examined the word. She hadn't heard that one before. Roaring fury, she thought. A picture of her mother, red-faced and shouting, came into her head.

'You're very pale,' Adele said. 'Are you sure you're not ill?'

Jill sat all the way up. 'Not ill,' she said.

'I'll roll one, shall I?' Adele said. She reached across for the lump of hash and held it in the flame of her lighter.

Jill got groggily to her feet. She was going to pull herself up on to the low branch they called their sofa but she still felt light-headed. She leaned against it instead, dropping her arms behind so that her hands dangled and the branch supported the curve of her back. She watched Adele sticking the papers together. It was her job usually. In a minute she would tell her and Adele would help her talk to Robert.

'It's our lodger,' Adele said.

Jill's branch shuddered. She freed her arms and clutched them around her middle, trying to hold everything in.

'High drama in our house,' Adele said, twisting the end of the joint and giving it a businesslike little shake. 'That Robert isn't like I thought he was at all.'

Jill took her glasses off and put them in her pocket. She let her eyes go out of focus while Adele told her about the lodger. He'd phoned breathless at midnight asking if Daisy was there, that he couldn't find Daisy. Daisy's husband had found out about their liaison and now she'd run away. He'd screamed down the phone that Daisy's husband was violent and then the phone had gone dead. Adele's mother had phoned the police who said it sounded like a prank. But just now, as Adele was about to come and meet Jill, Robert and Daisy had turned up, hand in hand with two spindly children in tow. He'd found Daisy and her children at her sister's house. 'We didn't plan it like this,' he'd said.

'No,' Jill said, stepping away from the tree and shaking her head. She took no notice of Adele standing up and putting a restraining hand on her arm, asking her what was the matter, why was she crying. She kept shaking her head from side to side. She was like a dog, like Pester, shaking the wet out. 'No, no, no,' she said, her hands wrapped around her stomach. Hot little tears spun out and away from the top of her nose.

Adele lay on her bed, hugging her pillow to her chest. Her mother was violently vacuuming the landing just outside her bedroom door, cracking the nozzle repeatedly against the skirting board. Her father had turned up the radio in his room. He was listening to jazz. The cacophony didn't mask the underlying emptiness, the sensation of loss. The month before there'd been a huge explosion at a nuclear power plant thousands of miles away at Chernobyl in Russia. Radioactive dust was falling all over Europe, even reaching here in South Wales where the sheep on the hills were contaminated because they'd grazed on the polluted grass. Adele's dreams had been doom-laden and stayed with her by day; flayed skin and choking dust, poisonous spores spilling from the clouds, soaking into an earth where nothing wholesome could ever grow again. She felt herself to be in the aftermath of the explosion now; holding to the rim of a dust-filled crater, hardly knowing why she suffered when she was only a bystander, and ostensibly unscathed.

Robert had apologised for using the house for their trysts. 'We had nowhere else to go,' he told Claire. Perhaps he was hoping Claire would say they could stay until they'd sorted themselves out, but Adele could see from the thin, deceived line of her mother's mouth that she wanted rid.

When Adele was running down to the park to meet Jill, she was trying to imagine how she would reconfigure the episode in the telling of it, turning it perhaps into a funny story. But there was no laughing to be had, no shrugging off of anything, because Jill was lying white-faced and unconscious on the ground, her glasses askew, her mouth open, and Adele thought for a second that she was dead and that her foreboding had presaged this. Jill turned out to be pregnant, with no intention of telling Adele who the father was, ever. It was then that Adele had the sensation that the blasted ground was crumbling under her feet. 'Don't bother asking,' Jill had said once she'd stopped flailing about like a demented dervish, picked up her jacket and wiped her face on the sleeve.

Adele couldn't believe what she was hearing. She didn't even know Jill had had sex. 'You're only just sixteen,' she'd said. 'You can't have a baby.'

Neither of them mentioned abortion. They were good Catholic girls.

It was the last few weeks at the Davies Academy with attendance only required for the O level exams. Adele saw Jill across the exam hall but she disappeared straight afterwards and was never on the bus. Someone was ferrying her to and fro. She didn't turn up at her Saturday job either. Adele made herself call round at Jill's house. It was always someone else who answered the door – her fraying grandmother, one of her brothers. 'She's not here,' they said. The third time, Jill's mother came to the door. 'Go away,' she said. 'Haven't you done enough damage already?' She shut the door before Adele could protest that whatever this rabid little woman thought, she'd been a good influence on Jill. Not benign, but enriching.

After that, reluctantly but with a sense of relief, Adele gave up. She'd tried. For a while, she speculated that Louis might be the father of Jill's baby and that was what it was all about. She tried to persuade herself that she'd nearly caught a knowing look between them when her brother had been down at Easter.

Adele spent the summer at her aunt's house in Aix-en-Provence. When she returned, she was finally allowed to move to the local comprehensive for her A levels. Sixth-formers there didn't have to wear school uniform. There was a whole new set of people, including boys. She worked backstage on the school's Christmas show. A boy called Lance was her assistant. He was desperately in love with her, but she kept him dangling.

It was her mum who told her that Jill had had a baby girl at the end of November, that she was called Leanne, had red hair and freckles and that still no one knew who the father was. Claire had heard all this from someone at church.

'I haven't said this before,' Claire said, 'but I was surprised at you, the way you just dropped that girl.'

Adele was shocked. 'Me? Drop her?' she said.

'When she was in trouble,' Claire said, 'and most needed a friend.'

The Road to Timbuktu

Cardiff, South Wales, and Mopti, Mali, 2004

I'd never even have come to Africa if my nan hadn't kicked up a fuss. I wanted to go to Tenerife but Jack had this idea of travelling around, playing his guitar in the desert. He'd seen a TV programme. Where we're all from originally, he said. He is quite dark, actually, Jack. His grandfather was from Jamaica.

'Touch of the tarbrush,' my nan said, even though I'd told her off a hundred times for talking like that, told her it wasn't PC. 'PC?' she went. 'It's not against the law.' 'That darkie boyfriend of hers is putting ideas in her head,' she told my mum.

I despair absolutely of raising my nan's consciousness. I haven't entirely given up on Mum yet. She was younger than I am when she had me and she's had Nan telling her what since time began so she never had much of a chance. Now she's doing the teacher training thing, though, she's much more open to new ideas.

Jack said we'd ride on camels over the dunes and that the blue men of the desert would sing in praise of my pale beauty, like a desert rose.

My nan said, 'Why don't you go to Tenerife? You could stay in Uncle Ned's apartment. It's nice, lovely beaches and great nightlife. And you,' she nudged me, to say she knows me better than I know myself, 'you like your creature comforts, Leanne.' She thought she'd got me there. 'How'd you straighten your hair if you were in Africa?'

Nan had a point, I'll give her that, but it really pissed me off, as if I'm so shallow I can't live without my hair straighteners for a few weeks.

Mum was looking at me in the solemn way she does sometimes.

Then Jack piped up. 'It's not all begging bowls and famine, you know.'

'You don't need to tell me what it's like,' Mum said, looking daggers.

'Don't worry, Jill,' Jack said, totally not realising that he'd already rubbed her up the wrong way, 'I'll look after her.'

My mum turned her attention to him. She's never said it outright but I don't think she trusts Jack. 'Leanne is only seventeen,' she began.

I made my mind up right then. I was fed up of people trying to make decisions for me as if I was a baby. It wasn't just about being with Jack. 'I'm going, Mum,' I said.

'Don't you let her,' my nan said.

Then this funny look came over Mum's face. 'Yes,' she said. 'You go for it.'

'You what?' I said. I was only winding her up. Africa didn't sound like my cup of tea really.

'Go for it. This is your time,' she said cryptically.

So, it's like she made me come.

Jack booked everything. Said he was going to surprise me. He did it all online at work. He worked shifts as a porter at the Imperial Hotel in town. He wore a very cute uniform – smart, high-waisted black trousers and a bolero jacket, with a frilly white shirt underneath. He looked fit as a flamenco dancer. I didn't say that to him though, because he thought he looked like a ladyboy. He did a bit, but he always does. He's got thick black eyelashes that make him look like he's put kohl round his eyes. He told me they were always picking on him at school. I didn't realise. I'd fancied him since I was thirteen but I was two years below so we occupied different dimensions; I could gawp at his but not enter it and mine was invisible to him.

It was only at my leaving prom, last summer when I was sixteen, that we first spoke. He'd left school for a couple of years by then but he gatecrashed the party, which was in the function room at the Imperial. I was doing formation dancing with my mates, we thought we were so cool, and he skidded on to the dance floor, wearing his cute uniform, and came to a stop in front of me. I didn't know whether he was aiming for me or for Frannie who was next in line but I'm where he landed. He was well oiled, else he wouldn't have had the face to do it. I'd had a few glasses in the limo on the way there too, or I might not have just gone for it like I did. There he was, gift-wrapped.

Most of the time the Imperial is dead quiet at nights though, because it's a chandeliers and polished banisters kind of place and the guests are mostly old folk, and so, when

Jack was on the night shift, he got to use the computer behind reception.

We were sitting on the grass in the park sharing a mango-and-strawberry smoothie in my break one Saturday morning when he told me where we were going. I'd been working in Woolworths cafe every Saturday since I started college but in the holidays I was there full-time, which was less than no fun. I had to wear a manky nylon uniform the colour of bacon with my hair tucked up in a red cap – because of health and safety supposedly, but really to make you look and feel crap so you didn't question any of the stupid rules. I'm nothing much to look at without my hair. I shook it out before I went to meet Jack of course, but I still stank of fat. The people who worked there permanently were always telling me I'd got a lot to learn, as if there was some special expertise required for wiping grease and cake crumbs off tables and dishing up reheated shepherd's pie. There was this old guy, Jim, who was the worst. I'd go 'Shall I take these trays out the back, Jim?' and he'd go 'College girl doesn't know where to put the trays' to no one in particular. Pathetic. The customers were either half starved and spindly or so lardy they could hardly squeeze themselves into the chairs, which were bolted down as if a gang of plastic-seating thieves might run off with them. I couldn't wait to get out of there.

'We're going to Timbuktu,' Jack said.

I thought he was joking. I laughed.

'What's so funny?' he said frowning.

'That's not a real place,' I said, not quite so sure of myself. 'It's just an expression. From here to Timbuktu.'

'It's in Mali,' he said, 'in West Africa.'

I didn't know he'd actually gone ahead and booked it or I'd have kept quiet. 'I've been looking at West Africa on the Internet at college,' I said. 'Gambia looks pretty cool. They do an all-in trip, hotel on the beach with optional excursions and one of them is a drumming workshop on an island in the Gambia River.'

I thought he'd love that. He was so into his sounds, especially West African music. He slurped the smoothie through the straw and stared at me. He had his brooding Heathcliff kind of look on. I should have shut up.

'If I got good on the bongo or whatever, I could do the percussion when you play guitar,' I said. 'That'd be so cool, wouldn't it?'

Jack sucked up the rest of the drink we were supposed to be sharing with a gurgling noise and scrunched the plastic cup in his hand, still staring.

'What?' I said, standing up. I had about three minutes to get back to work. Jack fetched his tobacco out of his pocket and started to roll himself a cigarette. 'I've got to go,' I said.

He lit his cigarette and stuck it between his lips, lay back on the grass, hands behind his head, eyes screwed up against the smoke. 'Go on then,' he said nastily.

I watched him a minute. He looked so cool; his dreads splayed out on the grass and the way he held the cigarette in the corner of his mouth. I didn't know what I'd done. 'I really have to go,' I said.

He waved his hand in the air, dismissing me. 'I thought you were up for an adventure,' he said, 'didn't realise you just wanted a package holiday.' He said 'package holiday' as if it meant dog muck.

'Plenty of people go on package holidays,' I said. I left him there. I had to. I stuffed my greasy hair back into my greasy cap as I ran back to work. We were really busy that afternoon and I hardly got a chance to think. When it was home time, I stayed behind giving the counter an extra swipe or two, thinking about how I'd stolen Jack's thunder. I'd make it up to him straight away. 'En't you got a home to go to?' Jim asked.

Jack wasn't waiting for me at the usual place outside Boots. I must have really offended him. I called in at the Crypt for an iced vodka. It was happy hour and trebles were the price of doubles. They never ID you at the Crypt. I sent Jack a text saying sorry and asking him to call. I didn't have enough credit to phone. Halfway home the effect of the triple vodka made my head bang so all I wanted to do was get back, wash my hair, have something to eat and watch the TV with my mum.

Jack phoned when I was on the doorstep. He wanted to meet me by the clock tower next to Woolworths. I didn't even have a shower, but I ran a wet comb through my hair, splashed some water about, washed two paracetamol down with a jug of water, put on some eyeliner and my red heels.

'It's *Moulin Rouge* on Channel 4 in a minute,' Mum called, but I was out the door and running.

'I'm sorry,' I said as soon as I saw him. 'Tell me about Timbuktu. I was being a wimp. I know you've got it all sorted.'

'I have,' he said in his masterful voice. 'Trust me, moll. We're going to have a ball.'

When we got out of the plane in Mopti, it was like stepping neck-deep into hot gravy. This wasn't air as I'd ever known it. My whole body heated up as if I was a piece of meat on a barbecue, being chargrilled. The smell was like a barbecue too, smoky and fume-laden, and I felt a bit panicky. Then, all of a sudden, sweat burst out from everywhere and I was dripping. It was the weirdest sensation but I felt better in a flash. 'Wow!' I said. 'We're in Africa.' I turned to Jack but he was looking past me, down the steps to the guys with a trolley who were unloading the bags.

'They'd better have looked after my guitar,' he said. We went into the terminal building.

Jack had been fretting about his guitar the whole journey. They wouldn't let him take it on the plane as hand luggage because it was too bulky. He should have brought it in a hard case, not a gig bag, they said. 'It'll be all right,' I kept saying. He loved his guitar. He'd customised it with stickers of his guitar heroes. Ali Farka Toure was one of them and the main reason he'd picked Timbuktu. We were going to pay our respects.

'Perhaps we have to collect your guitar from a different place?' I said, once all the cases had been unloaded and it wasn't among them. Jack gave me a dirty look as if it was my fault. 'Why don't you go and ask at that information desk? I'll guard the bags.' He looked towards the desk at the far end of the concourse, biting his lip. Then he took a breath as if about to dive in the deep end and set off.

I sat on my pack and watched everyone who'd been on the plane from Paris with us collect their bags and leave. The Europeans' queue was shorter and more serious. They were all oldish and all wore the same kind of clothes, khaki-coloured trousers and white T-shirts, as if they were off to do something strenuous like climbing a mountain. They had smart, new-looking rucksacks with lots of zips and pockets. The women's heads with their flat brown hair looked really small compared to the Africans who had fantastic headdresses like sculptures, as if bright-feathered birds were perching on their heads. Or they had amazing hairdos, plaits wound round their skulls and coiled into complicated designs. I patted my own hair. I could feel it was already frizzing up in the humidity. If big colourful headgear was the thing in Mali, then I was going to do fine.

When there was no one left but me, I put my pack on my back and dragged Jack's along the concrete floor to the far end of the hall where he was standing at a cubicle. His shoulders were hunched and he was drumming his fingers on the counter. There was no one there.

'Any luck?' I said, which was obviously a stupid thing to say.

Jack didn't turn to face me. 'The man just disappeared,' he said. 'He took the baggage receipt thing and he just disappeared.'

'What did he say?'

'I don't know, do I?' Jack spat.

'Didn't he speak English?' I said.

Jack made a puffing noise and shook his head.

A man suddenly appeared in the kiosk as if he'd come through a secret door. He was wearing a grey-blue uniform and a gun hung from his belt. No sign of Jack's guitar. He didn't look at us, just started to fill out a form. Jack was staring at the man and his lips were pressed tightly together. I hoped he wasn't going to kick off.

The man looked up and smiled at us. He had a fantastic smile; he could have been in a toothpaste advert except he had a gap between the two front teeth. He handed the paper across to Jack who took it, shaking his head, looking crushed.

'Come back tomorrow,' the man said. He had a strange accent but he was definitely speaking English. 'Or the next day.' He closed the kiosk and disappeared again while we just stood there like lemons.

All the time leading up to the trip Jack'd been lecturing me on how I was going to suffer from culture shock when I got there, not having been to a developing country before, and how I had to adjust my expectations. Not that he'd been to a developing country either, unless you count Brixton, but his Jamaican ancestry gave him an edge. So when these two guys came and pressed up against us just outside the airport building, shouting stuff about taxis and guides and hotels and I don't know what in our faces, one trying to pull us one way and one the other, I tried not to panic. Jack said something about the bus, where do we catch the bus, and one of them said, 'No bus, no, monsieur.' Though there were only two of them they managed to crowd around and jostle us along to the most decrepit car ever, rusted-out with ill-fitting doors in different colours and one side totally dented. I thought any minute Jack was going to take control, but he started to swing his backpack off as if he was going to get in. It was a post-joyride sort of car. The kind that you see lying at the bottom of steep valleys round where we live. 'We can't go in that,' I said to him. 'It's a death trap.' Jack stood there, with his pack half on and half off. I put my hand on his arm and he was shaking. 'Let's go and ask about the bus in the airport,' I said. Jack pulled his pack back on. I took hold of his arm. 'We catch bus,' I said to the taxi driver. The man didn't leave us alone all the way back to the airport building. He was going, 'No bus. Taxi.' The whites of his eyes were yellow and I didn't like to look at him. The other one had sloped off.

The lights had been dimmed inside the airport. They made a kind of buzzing noise. Jack sat down on his pack and rolled a cigarette while I walked all round the foyer saying excuse me into dark corners, looking for someone to ask or an information sign or something. There were people-sounds from the other side of the passport control but this part was deserted. It was quite spooky. 'There must be someone to ask,' I said. Jack ignored me, puffing on his cigarette as if he wasn't bothered. 'What now?' I said.

He looked up at me through the smoke. 'You tell me,' he said.

'You what?' I said.

'You're the one wouldn't get in the taxi,' he said.

'You said there was a bus.'

He shook his head at me as if I'd let him down.

'There must be a bus or something. You can't have an airport where there's no public transport,' I said.

'It's not Heathrow,' he said.

I don't know if he was expecting an apology or something but he didn't get one. 'Better go and get in that stinking death trap then, hadn't we?' I said and swung out the door.

Outside, even though we'd only been in the building five minutes, it had gone dark and a torrent of rain collapsed out of the sky. The rain beat down and bounced back off the ground, bubbling and frothing like boiling water in a pan.

By the time we got out at the other end, the rain had stopped. There was a strange smell in the air, a smell called up from the ground by the rain. It was earthy and unearthly at the same time. It made my skin tingle.

Oh my God, that hotel room. 'Squalid' would be too good a word. It had a saggy bed with a pink nylon sheet and a mosquito net full of holes big enough for a major swarm to enter and leave by without going single file. There was a bare bulb hanging from a dodgy-looking wire above the bed which gave off less light than a candle and a ceiling fan that moved so slowly. You couldn't have both of these on at once. The window didn't have any glass. It was basically a window-shaped hole in the wall with a dirty mesh in it and a ledge where an army of insects had been defeated and lay in little heaps like dirty desiccated coconut. It was like being underground.

Five days in a row, we went back to the airport to ask about the guitar. Every time we went out, we were pestered. According to Jack, it was because of my whiter-than-the-drizzled-snow skin, my freckles and my red hair that they targeted us. I might as well have been carrying a placard saying: 'Rip me off. I'm a rich white foreigner.' If he'd been on his own, they'd have acted differently because of the common ancestry thing. That was a load of tosh though, because, whether he liked it or not, Jack stood out too. That African blood must have got diluted over the generations. There were a few people around in Mopti who, like him, weren't that dark-skinned. Some of them were Mauritanians, who looked more like Arabs, and some were the Tuaregs, who strode about as if they owned the place, tall and elegant. Most of them were black though, not black like coal but black like dark chocolate and Jack was more cappuccino. But it wasn't that. It was other things that set him apart more. Like his clothes for instance. Not all the people there were in traditional dress. Some of the men at least wore Western-style clothes, like jeans or baggy shorts and T-shirts, but although their clothes were much tattier than Jack's, they wore them as if they weren't. As if they were dressed for a night out at the Imperial, though they'd never even have got through the door. And then they'd all do a little something, a battered hat pushed back or a purple cloth tied around their trousers, that marked them out, made them special. And then with Jack, I think it was something about the way he walked maybe, a bit awkward and hunched, as if he didn't want to be seen, and that actually had the opposite effect.

The touts would go 'You going to Dogon? I am from Dogon, I can show you the best sights. Maybe later, maybe you want to book a guide for later? What? You're going to Timbuktu? Aha, do you want a guide to Timbuktu? I am from there, I have many friends there, I can show you the best sights. First time in Africa? First time in Mali? What's your name? You visit Dogon? You visit Timbuktu? You want a *pinasse* trip? Ah, I see you are walking. Yes, you can walk this way, this way there is a market, what do you want, food, water, maybe tickets? I can get you anything. Yes, we meet before, you remember me, I show you bus stop.' On and on.

We'd queue up for hours at the airport in the heat only to be told to come back again tomorrow. No one had any answers about when or whether the guitar might arrive and that, more than anything, drove Jack mad. He got me to do the talking because of my French being better. He'd skulk behind me and come up with a load of questions I should have asked them after I'd finished at the counter. I always had to ask what time we should come back and they'd look at me like they didn't know what I was on about and then they'd say some random time, two o'clock in the afternoon or ten in the morning, as if we were in a game of What's the Time, Mr Wolf? It would have been funny if Jack hadn't been so stressed.

In between our airport trips, we hung around at the hotel. Jack lay about on the bed smoking, flicking through his Josh White blues riffs book or staring at the ceiling. Or he slept, wrapped in the pink sheet like someone in a coma. There was a table and a chair against the wall where I spent hours sitting reading the guidebook. Or I'd go for a shower. The shower we shared with everyone else on the ground floor was always cold but worked best in the daytime when the other guests weren't around. I kept trying to cool down. I wasn't the right skin type to cope with the climate and my face was red the whole time. The people staying in the hotel were mostly backpackers like us but they came and went. It was more an overnight stop place than somewhere you'd stay for your holidays. We didn't go out. Jack said it wasn't worth it because we'd have to set off for the airport any minute. Every time I suggested a walk or something, he'd say, 'Nah, I'm a bit tired just now.' Or, 'Stop nagging.' Or, 'You need to chill, moll. You're getting a heat rash.' I couldn't go out on my own. It was too scary.

We missed the boat we were supposed to catch to Timbuktu. We went down to the river to watch it leave, which made a change from sitting in the hotel room or doing the airport trek. The port was a noisy muddle of people and crates of fish and trucks and piles of rope and rickety wooden buildings. There were women washing clothes, men unloading fish, children kicking about and climbing over things, and rubbish everywhere. Dead fish were rotting in the sun and the waterline was a swirling mass of plastic bags. It looked like everything had been thrown up into the air and had landed all higgledy-piggledy and broken and what got me was that everyone just carried on as if it wasn't a shambles.

Beyond all the mess and hubbub flowed the river, big and full and definite. There was nothing makeshift about the river. Long, low, curved boats were loading up. Some of them were painted with geometric designs in rusty red, indigo blue and bluish-white. Close to the shore a fishing boat was stuck in the mud. The driver was manoeuvring a long heavy pole into the water, trying to push off. He shifted the pole effortfully to the other side, bent and pushed again. Up and down, in and out, over and over again. It was hard work and he didn't look up to it. He was small and thin with an angular little beard and a pirate scarf tucked behind sticky-outy ears. He looked done in. Then something loosened and shifted and the mud let him go. He found the current or the current found him and it lifted him and drew him away. He took up his position at the far end, steering the boat with the pole, dipping and lifting it, bending and straightening his body in a fluid movement. He was beautiful. I turned my eyes back to the bustle of the shore. The ramshackle shelters and stalls held together with salvaged bits of string and corrugated iron and tacked-on cloth and the people working, shouting, laughing there, the hardness of their lives and their cheerfulness made my heart ache. They were heroes. I looked back at the river. The boat had glided away to join others in the silver distance.

Jack nudged me. He pointed at a big boat with a sacking roof stretched over curved sticks. It was the *pinasse* we should have been boarding. Women with bowls of bananas and peanuts and other food on their heads had waded into the water to sell their provisions to the passengers on the upper deck. There were so many people crowded below that the lower deck sprouted arms and legs like oars. I really wanted to be getting on board that boat. 'This place is beautiful, isn't it?' I said.

'That boat's much too low in the water,' Jack said.

'We could get a place in one of the four-wheel drives

going up to Timbuktu when the guitar arrives,' I said. Neither of us ever said 'if the guitar arrives'. It didn't bear thinking that it mightn't come.

'You know we can't afford that,' he said.

'Can't we?' I said. It was the first I'd heard of it. We'd been saving for this trip for months.

He just shook his head.

'How come?'

He sighed. 'The air tickets were really, really expensive,' he said. He looked straight at me for a minute with a hard, black look in his eyes that made me feel like he hated me. 'It's not a package tour, is it?'

I couldn't get why Jack didn't seem that bothered about Timbuktu though. It was supposed to be the whole point of being there.

The idea floated into my head that we weren't actually going anywhere at all and were going to spend the month cooped up in one dingy room. Still, it wasn't all bad. In the afternoon of the day we went to the river I discovered the mesh thing would open if you used a bit of force. It gave on to an inner courtyard where women did the cooking. I sat and watched them while Jack snored. There was one woman who prepared the food and another, younger one who did the running around, fetching charcoal and tidying up. The cook usually had a baby tied to her back and it'd stare at me, hidden in the dark of our room, with huge wide eyes as if it could see a ghost. The woman would gut and clean the fish the girl carried in from somewhere, flicking her knife up and down the scales like she was playing a tune and slicing them open, throwing the guts into a stinky pile that the girl cleared away. The fish were mostly tiddlers but sometimes there'd be a great fat brown one, the size of your arm, with ugly spikes sticking out of both sides, and they seemed really chuffed when that one turned up.

A little barefoot boy wearing a very short yellow nightie and nothing else played about in the dirt. When the cook sat on an upturned crate and fed the baby I realised she was very young. A picture of my own mum came into my mind – not as she is now but as she must have been aged sixteen with me as a baby on her lap. I had a tight feeling in my chest. If I'd had my phone with me I'd have called her up right then. As it was I put in a reverse-charges request through the hotel reception. It was rejected. Nan, I suppose.

It was because of the little boy that the kitchen women noticed me. He was bouncing the baby on his knee and the baby was, as usual, staring wide-eyed and unblinking at me – I swear that baby could have won a competition for not blinking – and the boy followed the baby's gaze, spotted me and jumped up with a shout, pointing. I was embarrassed to be caught spying but they didn't seem to mind. They were dead friendly. They told me the names of things, the fish and the vegetables. Knobbly yellowish sticks called *igname* had to be boiled, then peeled and bashed up into a mush. *Goyo* was their name for aubergine and *banane* wasn't like our bananas but a kind of starchy vegetable. It was hard work cooking in Mopti. You couldn't just shove a ready meal in the microwave. You had to wash and gut and chop and pummel and grind. You had to send a child to fetch the charcoal and pile it up in the burners.

I ate that ugly brown fish in the bar later with hot chilli sauce, fried *banane* and rice. It tasted delicious. I never much liked fish before. Jack said it looked disgusting and told me to go and clean my teeth afterwards. He stuck to the chicken, said it was safer. Of course, he hadn't seen the chicken running round the yard earlier pecking at the fish innards before the woman with the baby, Assetou, had chopped off its head without even pausing in her conversation.

I'm not sure when Jack stopped mentioning the motherland and his cultural heritage. I tried to make allowances for him being upset about his guitar but it was like he had it in for me and for Africa. He hated the way the airport officials just smiled and said, '*L'Afrique c'est comme ça*,' instead of giving an explanation. Everything had gone wrong, he said. 'They haven't even got any fucking pavements. Where you supposed to walk?' he'd say. And when you thought about all the other things the people in Mopti didn't have, like running water and electricity and shoes some of them, it seemed funny to pick on pavements. We were walking along one day and I came over a bit faint, so we stopped for a minute and from the shack behind us, which was a barbershop because it had a painting outside of the different haircuts you could choose, two boys carried out a wooden bench for us to sit on. They wouldn't do that for you back home even if we do have pavements.

I don't know who was happier to see his precious guitar when it finally turned up on the sixth day, him or me. And there wasn't a scratch on it apart from the ones it had had to begin with, which weren't scratches, Jack said, but graffiti. With his guitar on his back he seemed to grow, walked with more of a swagger, nodded at the people hissing at us from doorways when he'd always ignored them before. He even gave me a hug. He hadn't touched me since we got to Africa. Said he was tired and that the yucky fish I kept eating put him off.

'Shall we go out tonight?' I said when we were back in our room and he was strumming the guitar on the bed.

'I told the guys I'd play for them in the bar,' he said. The bar was part of the hotel and was where we went every evening. It was pretty dire. Dark and dingy with a bitter swampy smell and suspicious-looking men whispering in dark corners and drinking clear liquid out of polythene bags. There weren't many places to get a drink in Mopti, so all the locals who fancied one, which wasn't many because they were Muslim, congregated in our hotel bar. The guys were three Japanese boys who we'd acquired at the airport the day before and whose taxi we shared back. They were on a mega world tour. They'd done Asia but Mopti was their first experience of Africa.

You could tell they thought Jack was pretty cool. They listened awestruck to everything he said, nodding and saying 'aah' all the time as he pointed out the sites we'd never even visited from the taxi. They all gasped when we went past the mosque, which was glowing orange in the evening sun, its towers pointing skywards like ancient rockets about to blast off. 'This is the largest mosque in the country,' Jack explained casually.

'Isn't the one at Djenné bigger?' I said.

Jack blinked and his head twitched from side to side as if a fly was buzzing round his ears. 'I meant the oldest,' he said. Then he waffled on for five minutes about the structure and how the wooden posts jutting out were for decoration and a whole load of other crap he made up as he went along. 'Why d'you want to go and see a pile of old mud?' he'd said when I'd suggested visiting the mosque.

Jack went to the bar to set up. The water was off and Fanta, the kitchen girl, helped me wash my hair in a bucket. I wouldn't recommend it but it was quite funny. Someone came to tell me there was a phone call for me at reception, a Madame Jill, and I went running down the corridor with my hair dripping. It was so lovely to hear my mum's voice. I managed to keep my whingeing in check. I put a nice gloss on it all. 'I'm so proud of you,' she said.

I could hear Jack talking in his Rasta voice in the bar as I went back down the corridor and I smiled because he does that for a joke. He must have perked up and I thought, oh, this holiday is finally beginning, it's going to be all right. I stopped because I had to get a hold of myself; I suddenly realised what a lonely few days I'd had, how not there Jack had been.

'She's very pretty, your girlfriend,' the Japanese boy, Tomo, said. He was the one who spoke the best English, the leader of their group. I smiled to myself.

'Hands off, dude. That's my moll,' Jack said.

'I think her name Leanne.'

'"Moll" means she belongs to me.'

Fuck, that annoyed me.

'Very big red hair she has,' the Japanese boy said.

'Yeah, and big red face too,' Jack said and they both laughed. My cheeks grew hotter and I leaned my face against the stone-cool wall.

'She like Africa?'

'She's a bit scared of it all. Culture shock, I suppose.' Jack tried out some chords to check the guitar was in tune.

'My girlfriend waits for me in Osaka,' Tomo said.

'You probably had the right idea, dude,' Jack said. I felt like the ground was slipping from under me and I put my hands against the wall, feeling its roughness with my fingertips. It was as though I'd stepped into a hall of mirrors, thinking I'd see myself made bigger or more lovely and instead had been faced with a distorted, mean version.

Then he told Tomo a hard-luck story about how we'd had some money stolen on the first day at the airport. I thought he was spinning him a line and then I twigged. It must be true. It must have been the guy that had disappeared after jostling us. How come he was telling this stranger and he'd never told me?

Jack started strumming 'On the Road Again', humming tunelessly along.

Two days later, we set off before dawn in a convoy of battered jeeps for Timbuktu. Four passengers to each vehicle. Jack went in with the Japanese boys in the first car because, he said, it was only polite, seeing as they were paying our fare. 'You don't mind, do you, moll?' he said. I was in the second one with some Spanish people who talked in loud, definite voices and took no notice of me.

A faint blush of rosy light low in the sky showed the sun was on its way and picked out the few people on the streets, painting them in softer colours than their daytime selves. It had rained during the night and there was an unusual, clean tang in the air, as if it wasn't just a new day, but a whole new episode in the town's story, and I felt cut off from it, like I was missing something important. The muezzin was wailing out through the mosque loudspeaker and the doleful drone accompanied us all the way through the town, past the early-morning women walking upright and purposeful to the river with orange buckets of laundry on their heads, past the little shuttered shop where they'd brought out the bench for me, past a man and a boy kneeling head down in a doorway, saying their prayers, and all the while the Spanish were jabbering away not noticing the amazingness of it all. I wanted to be out there, not strapped into this Toyota Landcruiser, with people who didn't care.

We stopped at a petrol station at the edge of Mopti to fill up. Our car queued for its turn as Jack's driver finished. The sun was half up by now and everything had sharp edges, each thing separate and distinct but at the same time like cut-out figures imposed on a background, not quite real. A late cockerel crowed feebly nearby. It seemed like a film set where everyone was running through their parts before the next take. I was an audience of one. There wasn't a role for me.

The driver of the first car made an impatient beckoning

motion into the semi-darkness at the edge of the road and Jack and Tomo came scampering up. Tomo ran in a knock-kneed way with his hands flapping at his sides. He ran like a girl. I wondered where they'd been and what they'd been doing. They might have been having a pee or sharing a cigarette. Jack held the door open for Tomo and boosted him up, playfully, with a push to the centre of his back. He was laughing. He glanced my way and caught me looking at him and he swivelled his head away and then quickly back again and kind of half smiled and gave a little wave as if to say everything was fine and normal. But it wasn't. He'd pulled my heart out and trodden on it.

Their vehicle took off and a young white guy came up and tapped on our driver's window. 'I'm looking for a lift to Timbuktu,' he said in an Aussie accent. '*Pas de place*,' the driver said. 'I can pay my way,' the guy said. The driver shook his head and went off to pay or whatever.

I got out of the car. 'You can have my place,' I said.

He looked at me like I was joking.

He gave me 30,000 CFA francs for my ticket and told me I'd saved his life, which was nice. I fetched my pack out of the back and hitched it on to my back.

'Tell Jack I changed my mind,' I said as the car pulled away.

The boy leaned out of the window and shouted back at me, 'Who's Jack?'

Spark

Exeter, Devon, 2004

One autumn afternoon, Adele came out of the library in the centre of town to find someone had locked their bicycle to hers.

A close look at the tangle of locks revealed that it was definitely the other bike owner who was at fault. He must have inadvertently included her crossbar in the embrace of his D-lock. She jangled the locks pointlessly.

A girl who'd emerged from the library just behind her and who was now sitting on the nearby bench, smoking a cigarette and tapping a message into her mobile phone, looked up. 'Someone did that on purpose,' she said.

'Why would anyone do that?'

The girl raised her eyebrows. 'A stalker?' she suggested.

Adele lifted her hand to her neck. She imagined Pedro crouching in the office building opposite, watching her through the slatted blinds. She swallowed and took a breath, patting her throat lightly as if to shift an obstruction. Her eyes dropped to the bicycle and she shook her head. Pedro wouldn't be seen dead on a bicycle. And Pedro had gone home to Spain.

'Not very likely,' she said.

The girl shrugged and shifted her weight on the bench, blowing smoke out through her nose. Her mobile phone bleeped in her lap. She stared at the message. Then she stood up abruptly, took one last vehement drag, dropped the butt on the ground and mashed it messily into the pavement with the point of her shoe. She wore open-toed stiletto shoes beneath her skinny jeans. Her toenails were painted lilac. They matched her eyelids. 'Been stood up,' she said, twisting her mouth to the side.

'Oh dear,' said Adele.

'Bastard,' said the girl and shrugged good-naturedly. She teetered away.

Adele went back into the library and settled herself in a window seat to wait. Waiting was fine. She wasn't in a rush. No one was expecting her. Joe was staying at a friend's. She had a newspaper open on her knee but her eyes were on the bicycle rack. For some reason she got to thinking about a man she'd seen on a bicycle one time. She'd been in the car with Pedro in the splintered-glass aftermath of some horrible, pointless row and they'd overtaken a rider on the main road. Something about him, the angle of his knee or the set of his shoulders, had made her turn to look back. He was just a man on a bike. Nothing out of the ordinary really. Darkish hair, long legs. He looked nice.

He'd caught up with them at the junction, so that before the traffic lights turned green and their paths diverged, she'd had a sidelong look. He was dressed in a dark grey suit and tie. His trouser ends were held against his calves with bicycle clips. He wore purple socks. His panniers had been of the padded kind for carrying a laptop.

At five o'clock the library closed. Outside a sudden autumn dark had descended. The two bikes were still locked together. It started to rain.

Down the road and round the corner, Richard's date entered the cafe where he sat waiting. As he watched her shaking the drops from her umbrella, which was the same bright red as her lips, tiredness enveloped him.

There was a section on the dating website to fill in what qualities you were looking for. Richard had laboured over this space, seeking something original and witty to describe his ideal partner. He'd ended up with some anodyne phrases in the end and made a virtue of his vagueness by implying he didn't have preconceived notions. He suspected the real reason was his lack of faith both in this dating process as a way of meeting someone suitable and in the very existence of that someone, but, like a child trying to go on believing in Father Christmas, he'd kept the suspicion at bay. The alternative – giving up and sinking into a lonely middle age – had seemed too grim. But this well-turned-out woman now eyeing him across the cafe in a way that made his neck itch was not the answer to his dreams.

The disappointment made him nostalgic for the moment five minutes earlier when it had all still been possible. The darkening sky outside and the now pelting rain had turned the cafe with its golden lights and gleaming chrome espresso machine into a beacon, a safe and snug place to ride out the storm. Through the porthole he'd smeared in the steamed-up glass, Richard had been aware of the envious glances of passers-by – the tug of the warmth and light, the promise of coffee and an almond biscuit to dunk – and of how they mostly resisted, fighting to keep their umbrellas up and struggle on to their buses or to their chilly parked cars. Richard had been happy to be in this warm and aromatic haven waiting for a woman called Miranda. Now he just wanted it over.

He thought of his bicycle, of pedalling quickly home and lighting the wood-burning stove. He had some courgettes, garlic and eggs in the cupboard. He could knock up a frittata and finish off the bottle of Pinot Grigio in the fridge. *University Challenge* was on at eight.

He stood up to greet her and they shook hands. His eyes slid away from her gaze, looking beyond to one of the large unframed black-and-white photos that decorated the cafe walls. A young woman on a bridge dropped tinted yellow rose petals into the river below while an enamoured cyclist watched her from the towpath. The word 'wistful' occurred to him.

It was in that moment that Richard was overwhelmed by a sense of the woman he could be with. He felt it most insistently between his shoulder blades as if a hand had trailed up his spine. He shivered.

Miranda sat down and smiled at him. Her lips peeled back over her top teeth. She was, he saw, rather glamorous with her lipstick and her glossy hair. But she wasn't the one.

In the queue at the counter Richard recalled an article

he'd read about the significance of facial characteristics. Upper-lip mobility denoted emotional openness. He wondered if his own was very stiff.

He glanced back at the table and was disconcerted to find Miranda contemplating him, her chin resting in her hands. He must not be unkind. He must be clear but, above all, not unkind. She gave a little wave, moving only the top joints of her fingers as if it were a secret signal they had. He should let her off the hook quickly. That would be best.

It was that transition time, after the shops and offices have closed but before the pubs and restaurants have opened, when city life is momentarily suspended. Adele, marching around the block to pass the time until the man came back to collect his bicycle and allow her to go home, sensed something else. This lull felt crammed with possibility and she held her face up to the rain.

On the high street she paused at the window of a brightly lit cafe, considering. She pictured a man striding long-legged through the empty rain-drenched streets. He would be approaching from the opposite direction as they both returned to their locked bicycles and there would be a meeting, a quiet unostentatious smile for her. There might be an awkwardness but she would sweep it all away and it wouldn't matter. She hurried on.

Richard was telling Miranda about his children. He didn't know why. Perhaps it was because she hadn't asked even though she'd plied him with eclectic questions as soon as he'd sat back down. Had he chosen to be a solicitor or was he a barrister manqué? He told her he was a layabout manqué but she didn't laugh. Where did he see himself in five years' time? 'Um, pass,' he'd said. She fired them at him as if she had a checklist and a time limit. Did he wear pyjamas? How did he feel about animal rights? Was he ruled by his heart or his head? 'My cat,' he said. 'She's the boss.'

Miranda made a little noise. She lifted her Diet Coke and swirled the glass around. There was a moment of silence while she looked intently at the bubbles in her drink. 'I have two sons,' he said. 'Adam has just gone up to Bristol to start a degree in electronic engineering and Josh is in his GCSE year.'

'I know,' she said, 'you told me in an email.' She sipped her drink.

'He's away for half-term, Josh,' he said and tipped his espresso down his throat in one gulp. 'Do you have any children?' he asked, blinking at the sudden caffeine rush.

She shook her head.

'Any animals?' he asked. 'I've got a cat, Enrica.' He knew he had already mentioned his cat and was faintly ashamed of his moronic chatter, but she was giving him no help. The time had to be filled until the drinks were drunk and he could say thank you but no thank you.

She put the half-full glass down on the table, pushed back her chair and stood up. 'This isn't working for me,' she said. 'Sorry. I can just tell. You know?'

Richard nodded. He tugged at his scarf. His neck felt hot and itchy.

Outside in the rain, Adele, on her second lap after finding the bikes untouched, hovered, tempted by the warmth and the thought of a hot drink. She had her rainproof jacket on but her jeans were soaked through and sticking to her legs. Again the thought of the other cyclist pulled her away. It might be a great gangly woman who rode a man's bike or one of those ancient Lycra-clad enthusiasts who were always overtaking her on hills but, then again, she had a feeling. She mustn't miss him.

'Come and have a glass of fizz.' A hand tugged at Adele's sodden sleeve and she recoiled in surprise. 'Be our very first customer.' A huge young man with fluffy pink hair was inviting her into a shop festooned with rosy lanterns.

'You were miles away, weren't you?' said the man. And he was right, she'd been indulging in elaborate fantasies as she tramped the dark wet streets. This time she had looped away in a different direction, although still with the bicycle rack at the centre of her wanderings, as if she were tethered to it by a long and stretchy leash.

'Didn't mean to shock,' said the man, gathering a bunch of tissues from the counter, 'although I usually do.' He sniggered. 'And amaze,' he added.

Adele took in the man's extraordinary appearance. He was dressed entirely in various hues of pink, including his boots, his middle section sheathed in a mini-kilt, complete with fluffy sporran, exposing a rugby player's muscular thighs.

'I can't stay. I have to be somewhere,' she said, feeling a blush coming on.

'No. You must come in. I need you.' He went over to a

spindly-looking table where rows of fluted glasses were displayed, filled two glasses from an already open bottle and brought them back. 'One little glass,' he said.

There was something fateful about this evening. 'Go on then,' she said, pulling off her gloves and stuffing them into her pockets. They clinked glasses.

'It's supposed to be our grand opening but everything, I mean everything, has gone wrong.'

'Are you on your own here?'

'Yes, my assistant's gone to drum up custom. She's handing out flyers. She went ages ago, and no one's even walked past. Until you.' He gave a little curtsy that made his skirt ride up.

Adele averted her eyes and looked around at the pinkness of the shop. The changing area was set back behind an opaque screen the colour of fingernails. She imagined the person trying on clothes would be silhouetted as they grappled with fastenings. This was a place for the young and trendy.

'Themed decor,' said the man. He had a way of popping his tongue out between his lips before he spoke and taking a breath, as if he were about to sing a sustained note.

'Is the shop called Pink then?'

'Fluff.'

'Pink Fluff?'

'No, just Fluff. I think we have the perfect dress for you.'

Adele allowed herself to be led to a rail of jewel-coloured garments. The man pushed three dresses in different shades of blue into her hands and ushered her into the changing area.

'Blue's your colour,' he said.

Adele perched her glass on a shelf and started struggling to wrench off her sodden jeans. The heavy material clung to her wet goose-pimpled flesh, and as she wrestled the trousers down, stumbling about in the confined space, her knickers were dragged in their wake. Chirpy whistling and the sound of glasses being rearranged made her wonder whether the fluffy man had seen her bare bottom pressed momentarily against the screen. She hastily tugged her pants back up. Her legs in the mirror were a wintry white, paler than her dingy underwear, the saggy knickers and bra of a woman who had no expectation of having her clothes peeled off by a lover. When had she become so dowdy?

She remembered Pedro's hands clutching at her breasts, scooping them out, mumbling 'Mine, say that they are mine' thickly into the nape of her neck, and the heat of his skunk breath, his wet whispering lips on her skin. She shook the image away.

'How's the dress?' the man called.

She looked back at herself. The dress transformed her. She smoothed its indigo swirls over her hips. It was perfect. She plucked her glass from the shelf. There was a blurred movement behind her reflection and for a split second it was as if Ellena were there again. It was only the man in the shop beyond the screen, but she raised her glass in a promise and toasted the memory of Ellena in the mirror.

She emerged from the dressing room and did a twirl.

'That's the one,' the man said.

'Not too mutton-dressed-as-lamb?'

'You,' he said, 'are *so* lamb.'

She left the shop, clutching her beautiful new dress, just as a small crowd of noisy young people was ushered in by a fuchsia-haired girl.

The rain had stopped and she retraced her steps with her hood down, breathing the chill night air.

The cafe that had been so bright was closed and shuttered, and as she passed in front for the third time, she was gripped by panic and broke into a run.

Her bicycle perched alone against the iron rack.

Richard switched on the central heating. He couldn't be bothered to light the stove. He looked in the cupboards and the fridge. The shrivelled courgettes had fused with the bottom shelf. He opened a tin of beans and tipped the contents into a pan, squeezing a teaspoon of harissa in to spice it up. The butter was hard so he poured the beans on to unbuttered toast and sat at the kitchen table, with the crossword in front of him. Rain was falling again, streaking the dark window. He thought of the note of apology he'd scribbled on his business card and tucked into the split in the saddle of the other bike. The words he'd written blotching under the deluge, the paper fragmenting and disintegrating.

The Other Girl

Dakar, Senegal, 1980

Once, when Adele lived in Africa, she found a girl in a sack at the back of the garage. The garage was big enough for two cars but Adele's mum didn't drive and that meant there was a space for George, the nightwatchman, and the dogs, Growler and Yowl. George had a rocking chair where he sat listening to the radio, turned low so that he wouldn't miss any intruders trying to scale the high walls or saw through the barred windows. He always looked comfortable and safe when they came back from somewhere in the evening, with the yellow kerosene lamp illuminating his quiet face as he rocked. Her father would pull up outside and George would come with the dogs to open the gates. Sometimes George opened the gates even before they'd beeped the horn, because the dogs knew they were coming and would run about yapping. Adele thought of the space at the back of the garage as George's room.

Other nightwatchmen hung around outside the gates in the evening. One of them used to bring a bench out and prop it against the wall, under the flowering shrub, and the others might wander along for a chat or to play a game of dominoes, but George didn't socialise. He had worked in security before in the country he came from and so was a real find, her father said. He took his duties seriously.

When the electricity went off, it was George who went down to the end of the garden with a torch to switch the generator on. The electricity went off quite often; all the fans stopped whirring and the silence would thicken. Then someone, Mum or Father, would shout 'George'. Five minutes later everything would suddenly crank back into life and the fan would stir the syrupy air into motion. The second fridge, where drinks were kept, which was in the hall outside Adele's bedroom because there was no room in the kitchen, would judder and then settle back into its usual hum. It was like the murmur of a low voice. It stopped Adele from feeling alone. She would fall asleep to its mumble. Adele didn't like the heavy black silence when the electricity went off; it felt like a blanket over her face. She thought of the African children who didn't have electricity in their houses and wondered how they could possibly bear it, smothered in the thick night.

Louis was going to school in England. 'You've got to tell them you don't want to go,' she said to him.

They were sitting in the tree at the end of the garden and Louis was carving his initials in the trunk. The oozing sap was orange like honey. 'I sort of do,' he said, without looking up.

'You don't,' Adele said. 'You're just saying that. It'll be horrible. Cold and wet and no colours.' Adele had been four when they left England and her memory was blurry. Louis had filled in the gaps with tales of constant rain and furry grey clouds that filled the sky and hid the sun.

'It's not really like that,' Louis said in a superior tone. 'There'll be loads of kids my age starting at the same time. We'll all be in the same boat.' Adele recognised the phrase as one of her father's: 'all in the same boat, all pull together'.

'Who'll I play with?'

'Dominic says the rugby is really good fun.'

'Really good fun,' Adele mimicked.

Louis ignored her. 'It's much better than the *lycée*.' All the expatriate children went to the *lycée* and Louis had been there for two years. 'I'll get a British education, which will stand me in good stead for the future. Dominic says I might be in his old house, the Yellows, which is very sporty so would suit me down to the ground.'

'Oh, it would suit you down to the ground, Louis my boy,' said Adele, affecting a pompous, grown-up voice. 'Stand you in excellent stead for the future.'

Louis stopped carving and looked at her. 'And,' he said quietly, 'I'll probably see my own dad. He'll probably come and visit me and I'll go to his house at weekends.'

Adele was shocked. Louis never mentioned his dad.

'I've got a new baby sister,' he muttered.

Adele broke off a dead twig. 'But what about me?' she said.

Louis shook his head and bit his lip, turning back to his carving.

'Don't go, Louis darling. Don't leave me all alone,' Adele said sarcastically.

Louis' face had gone red and he stabbed at the bark with

his knife. He spoke slowly and deliberately as if he were talking to an idiot. 'I'm going to school in England,' he said.

Adele wanted to bite and punch and kick him and push him out of the tree. She wanted to grab his floppy blond hair and tear a clump of it out at the roots. She jabbed at his arm with the twig in her hand and scratched it viciously up and down.

'Go then,' she shrieked. 'And good bloody riddance.'

Louis didn't look at her again and he didn't speak. He examined the scratch marks glowing white against the freckly gold of his skin, beaded with dark sequins of blood. He spat on his hand and smeared the blood away. New beads appeared instantly. Then he swung down from the tree and walked up the path.

Adele scraped the twig along the branch, flecks of disintegrating bark sparking, until it snapped in her hand. She faced outward then, not wanting to see the house any more, rejecting it and all its occupants. She looked out instead over the wall to the dusty wasteland beyond, which used to be bush but where new houses, like theirs but taller, were now being built. The workmen, who had been packing the lower part of the nearest building with concrete that day, were all gone now. Metal girders protruded from the half-covered shape, pointing jaggedly into the sky in crude imitation of the calligraphy of branches from the giant baobab tree beyond. Barefoot kids picked their way through the rubble, calling to each other in shrill voices. As darkness began to fall and the children dispersed, Adele stayed in the tree. She was a tree-dweller now. She gave a lonely tree-dweller's hoot into the warm air and another twilight creature replied, making her shiver.

Eventually her mother came out to fetch her. She said she was very disappointed in Adele. She'd been crying. Her nose shone red and her eyes had gone piggy. Adele's dinner had been put out for her in the kitchen because vicious little animals weren't fit to sit at a civilised table with civilised people. Adele stared at the mound of rice and fish on the plate – her mum had been trying to learn how to cook authentic dishes from Maimouna who did the laundry – while the rant went on. Her mum kept saying 'at a time like this' and 'how could you'. You'd have thought it was *her* arm Adele had raked.

Later on that night, or perhaps the next one, Adele woke up to a silent house and realised there had been a power cut. She lay there waiting for something to happen, but nothing did. It was as if she was the only person left in the whole world. Even though it was sweaty hot without the fans, her teeth started to chatter. She had a feeling that she was floating on a dark and bottomless ocean, all by herself. She sat up shakily and stretched her neck forward, straining to hear a sound, anything, but all she heard was her own breathing, panicky puffs instantly consumed by the pressing silence. Her torch wasn't on the bedside table. She swung her legs tentatively over the side of the bed, half fearing she would be submerged. Even when her toes touched the floor and she felt it was solid, the sensation of things being amiss persisted. She slid carefully down on to the strange night floor and felt her way along the corridor to Louis' room.

She paused just within the door, ears straining again, holding her breath in an effort to hear some evidence of her brother. When she couldn't, she started to cry, but the noise she made, a kind of raggedy whimper, was not like any noise she had ever made before so that she seemed strange to herself.

A light clicked on. She put her hands up and screwed her eyes tight shut.

There was an outlet of air. 'What do you want?' said a voice. And she stopped crying straight away when she realised that it was only ordinary Louis and he'd been holding his breath too.

'It's in my eyes,' she said, waving her hand, but he kept the torch shining straight at her.

'Go away,' he said.

'Can I come in with you?' Adele's voice came out squeaky. Louis didn't answer but he swung the torch away so it illuminated the edge of his bed and the shelf next to it where he stored bits of dismantled machines.

Adele crept under the mosquito net and positioned herself carefully, close enough to feel his solid presence but not annoyingly close. Louis seemed to be swallowing hiccups like pebbles caught in his throat. She wondered if crying was a sort of illness they were all catching and it would be her father next, though that was difficult to imagine. She patted the top of his back. The fan clicked back into life and the night light came on.

'It's all right for you,' Louis had said then in a thick voice. 'They're not sending you away.'

After Louis had gone, Adele kept going into his room and fiddling with his stuff. Tidying up and making it nice for him. Certain things were so alien she took no notice of them as if they were invisible, *Spider-Man* comics and the innards of unknown gadgets, but she rearranged his collection of interesting stones in a more eye-catching way. She decorated the edges of drawings in his sketch books and doodled on the blank pages, colourfully. Afterwards, she had a feeling he might not be that pleased after all, so she hid them under the bed, where she came across a stash of rescued tennis balls. She invented a new game, ball-wall, which she played endlessly in the driveway. It involved juggling two balls against the side of the house and carrying out a graded series of spins and hops in between every third and fourth bounce.

One evening, she got very close to beating her own record. Her father had just come home from work and was talking to George in the garage. 'So who's your money on then, Chief?' her father said. George wasn't a chief but that's what her father liked to call him.

'Heh, heh.' George's laugh was crackly like radio static. 'Let's keep the cup in West Africa where it belongs.'

'You reckon Ghana will hang on to the trophy?'

'Doctor Dom?'

'Do you think Ghana can win?'

In the pause before George replied, Adele did a hoppity-skip-jump and started the last round. 'Ghana isn't in the finals this time, Doctor Dom. It's Nigeria against Algeria.' George sounded like he was sorry about it not being Ghana.

'Yes, of course. I'm out of date. Nigeria then?'

'Sure they will win. Heh, heh. No problem.'

'Good, good. Enjoy the match.'

Her father came out of the garage but turned back to add a final word and so missed Adele's perfect double spin. 'Ask me next time though,' he said into the gloom and his voice was like a stone thrown into a pond.

When George didn't immediately reply, Adele flicked her eyes sideways to see what was happening, and that instant of reduced concentration was enough at this stage of the game to make her miss the second ball. It brushed the end of her outstretched fingers and bounced past her father's feet, trickling into the garage entrance. She pocketed the other ball and walked towards the open garage doors where her father was still standing, expectantly. He wore his usual work suit of light-coloured linen and had slung his jacket over one shoulder. Dark patches showed under the arms of his blue shirt. His trousers hung baggy and creased around his bottom. His black hair, so soft and loose compared to George's tight frizz, curled over his collar. From behind he looked like a boy.

The sun at Adele's back made her shadow stretch in front of her so that its elongated head extended into the garage before her real head arrived. George's laugh when it came sounded pinched and faint, a shadowy laugh, which may have been why she had the impression that her shadow, like an imagined other self, had seen something odd and indecipherable between the two men. Her shadow knew more than she did. Both men seemed to jerk backwards a fraction as if a wire binding them together had been severed and had twanged away.

George shook his freed head and looked down at the ground. 'I'm very sorry, Doctor Dom. It won't happen again.'

Adele picked up her ball and stood next to her father. 'Come on, Delly,' her father said, 'it's nearly dinner time.' He put his hand on her shoulder and twisted her out of the garage and round the corner towards the kitchen door at the back of the house. The smell of his sweat swirled about her.

Her mother was in the kitchen banging things about while Binata, the maid, was grinding nuts with a pestle and mortar. Sour, complicated smells wafted out of the oven and a vegetable mush of pale green was piled in the salad bowl. Adele had the feeling that her mum wasn't even asking Maimouna's advice now and was making it up as she went along.

'What's George sorry about?' Adele asked. Her father, bending to sniff the mush, recoiled as if a bee had stung his nose.

Her mother wiped her hands on a slimy tea towel and put them on her hips. 'He's taken the radio home to listen to the football and forgotten to bring it back,' she said.

'So?'

'Your father,' she said, 'thinks he should have asked first.'

Adele's father pressed his lips together, shaking his head. 'Beer,' he said and left the room.

'Your father,' Adele's mum went on but in a louder voice so he could still hear from the corridor, 'thinks it's not on. It's the principle of the thing. That's right, isn't it, Dominic?' she said as he came back into the room carrying a bottle of beer and two glasses. 'It's all about principle, isn't it?'

Her father poured the beer into the glasses, tipping them so there was less froth. 'I'm not going to be drawn,' he said. He took his glass with him into the living room.

Her mother snatched up the tea towel and flicked it fiercely in the air before wringing it in her fingers, breathing out loudly.

'George can have my radio,' Adele said.

Her mother sat down heavily at the table and picked up her glass. 'I don't think that's the point,' she said.

Adele put her head into the living room where her father was reading the paper. 'George can have my radio,' she said.

'That's not actually the point,' he said.

It seemed to Adele, however, that it might well be the point and after the disgusting dinner, when her father had gone back out to check on his cultures at the lab and her mother had disappeared into her room, Adele snuck to the garage with her radio.

The garage doors were open, awaiting her father's return, but George and his cosy yellow lantern were not there. Moonlight cut a diagonal across the threshold, creating a white-lit triangle near the doorway that extended halfway down one side and revealed the empty rocking chair, but left the other part obscure and shadowy. Keeping close to the wall, Adele stepped to the edge of the grey part and peered forward, feeling like she was trespassing. She detected a snuffle. 'Growler? Yowl?' she hissed, but neither dog replied. They would be with George, wherever George was. Her mouth was dry and she could taste the smell of paraffin, petrol and white spirit from the jars and bottles on the tool shelves. It made her head reel. She held her breath and took another step. Without warning, the moon was switched off and the garage plunged into absolute darkness. It was silly to be frightened. It was only an empty garage. She reached her free arm out to touch the wall and get her bearings, but the wall wasn't there. She must have moved further into the centre of the garage than she thought. She shuffled forward in the direction she estimated the rocking chair to be. Her foot stubbed against something. She thought she heard the snuffling noise again. She squatted down, placing the radio on the floor beside her. She reached out and patted the obstruction. Her fingers met the rough weave of sacking and she relaxed. It was only a sack of stuff for the garden or something. She rocked on her heels, patting the lumpy contours of the sack to reassure herself, and then, all of a sudden, shrugging her off, the sack moved.

Adele snatched her hands away and jolted back in alarm. She sat down hard on the concrete floor. Just as suddenly as it had disappeared, the moon emerged from behind its cloud and she found herself staring into the face of a girl. At the same moment, as if they had been rehearsing, both girls clamped a hand over their mouths to stifle a scream. The other girl had beads that glinted in the moonlight woven into the tight little plaits that covered her head, and her skin was so black the edges of her merged with the surrounding darkness. They stared at each other for a while and then the other girl, suddenly animated, spoke; a tumble of words in a hushed tone. Adele didn't recognise the language.

She shook her head. '*Tu parles français?*' she whispered.

The girl mirrored Adele's incomprehension. 'English? Do you speak English?'

The girl nodded guardedly. After that first flurry of words she seemed struck dumb, holding herself fearfully still inside her sack and shaking her head at all of Adele's questions about who she was and where she'd come from. When Adele asked where George was, the girl tipped her head back on her neck so that the whites of her eyes gleamed in the moonlight. She looked like Peter Rabbit caught in Mr McGregor's fence, as if she might end up as rabbit pie.

'I won't tell anyone you're here,' Adele said. She put her finger to her lips to emphasise the point. The girl stopped shaking her head and looked intently at Adele. 'No one would notice anyway,' she went on. 'My mum's always crying in her room and my father goes out a lot in the evenings. They sent my brother away.' She shrugged. 'So, there's no one here to notice.'

The girl nodded.

'Is George your father?'

The girl nodded again. Then she whispered something so softly Adele couldn't quite catch it. 'What?' she whispered back.

'Don't tell,' the girl repeated. 'My mother is sick.'

The clank of the gate being pushed open prevented Adele from replying. The girl made an urgent shooing motion with her fingers. Adele picked up the radio and scuttled back towards the garage doorway. George was facing the other way, pushing the bolt across. The dogs, held on a tight leash, were at his heel. Adele took one last glance back but the girl had disappeared inside her sack. Adele slid round the side and back into the house through the kitchen door.

She had to wait three days before she could visit her secret friend again because her father stayed home working on his results at the kitchen table every evening. Then, when her mother was in her room with a headache, her father out at the club, she heard George whistle to Growler and Yowl, followed by the creak of the gates. She shot out into the dark garage. 'It's me,' she hissed. There was no reply. She switched on her torch and swung it round the garage floor. The sack wasn't there. She heard a stifled giggle and directed the beam into the corner. The girl was standing inside her sack, one hand held over her mouth. Adele saw that the girl was quite big, nearly as big as she was. She quickly hid the old baby doll she'd brought as a present behind her back.

'What's that?' the girl said, shuffling over, holding the sack up to her chin. Her voice was muffled, as if she were used to talking in whispers.

'Just a doll,' Adele mumbled, swinging it by one foot.

'A baby,' the girl said and held out her hands, letting the sack drop around her feet. Adele handed the doll over and the girl cradled it in her arms, sinking to the floor. Adele sat down next to her.

'Watch this,' she said. She shone the torch inside her mouth so that it illuminated her face grotesquely from inside. She let out an eerie moan. She'd been practising this face. It was really scary.

'Let me,' the girl said. She shone the light up her nose, flaring her nostrils and snarling.

'That's a good one,' said Adele grudgingly. She thought she had the wrong kind of nose to make it work herself, but she would try later, in front of the mirror.

'My brother showed me.'

'Where's your brother?'

'Two brothers. Back home in Liberia.' She looked away from Adele and rocked the baby doll in her arms. Adele thought of her own faraway brother. 'God keep them safe,' the girl said. Adele nodded solemnly. She made the sign of the cross for good measure and the girl smiled. She had beautiful straight teeth. She wouldn't need a brace.

Adele was thinking that she had lived in Africa for six years but had never had an African friend before. 'What's your name?' she said.

'Delly, where are you?' Her mum's exasperated voice, calling from the kitchen door, cut across the girl's quiet reply, but Adele, scrambling to her feet, heard her say, 'Ellena.'

'Coming, Mum,' she shouted, shaking her head at Ellena who was mutely proffering the baby doll. 'You can have it,' she whispered, 'I've got lots of dolls.'

Adele stuck her head out from the corner of the garage so her mum could see her. Claire was leaning out of the kitchen door at the end of the house, her arms folded across her chest. 'I was looking for my ball,' Adele said loudly. To prove the point, she swept her torch from side to side on the driveway and then back into the garage, beyond her mother's line of vision. Ellena had tucked the doll into the front of her dress, like a mother feeding her baby.

'Isn't George there?' her mum said, frowning.

Adele supposed that George went out on the street to leave Ellena to get off to sleep in peace. She only discovered later, after they had gone, that he was out selling her father's tools and negotiating a good price for her father's radio. 'Just outside the gate with the dogs,' she said.

The next time Adele visited, Ellena was very quiet and so Adele told her one of the stories she invented against the thrum of the fridge at night. It was about a girl who could step through her mirror into another land. Ellena fell asleep before the end. Adele lay next to her, watching the rise and fall of her thin shoulders, wondering if Louis was lonely. She stayed until the hard garage floor made her bones ache. When she tucked the sack around the sleeping girl, Ellena opened her eyes. 'My mother,' she said.

Adele thought she was dreaming. 'It's me, Adele,' she said.

'My mother died,' Ellena said. She reached out her hand and Adele took tight hold of it, feeling the little bones under the skin.

Adele cried back in her own bed, as if they were both motherless.

Whenever Adele heard the clang of the gate that told her George had gone out, she would listen from her bedroom for a signal from Ellena. Two whistles meant he would be gone for some time. If Adele's parents were around she would press her lips between the window bars and send her own mournful night call to tell Ellena she couldn't come. Otherwise, she would sneak out, taking biscuits and fruit from the kitchen for midnight feasts. They played in the dark garage. They taught each other songs from their countries and sang them in hushed tones, inventing new words to the tunes and tiptoe dances to accompany them. They played a torch game, taking it in turns to spotlight each other's statue shapes. They were monkeys, snakes and swooping birds. They were monsters, angels and crawling creatures. Mostly, they sat close in the dark and whispered. They told stories: true ones about their lives and made-up ones. They parted with the beginnings of tales that had to be completed the next time they met so that their dialogue seemed to continue even when they were apart. They'd start each other off. 'What would you do if you grew wings?' 'What if you could make yourself invisible?' 'What if we were sisters?' By day Adele carried with her the sound of Ellena's husky voice, the feel of her hand, the kerosene smell of the garage.

Adele never did give George her radio. The excitement of her secret life with Ellena pushed it out of her mind. And then, when she heard that George had sold her father's radio and other things to the man who played dominoes under the bougainvillea, it was too late. Because, by that time, her father had already dismissed George and sent him away without a reference which was like 'throwing him to the lions', her mother said. And Ellena had gone without them even being able to say goodbye. This dreadful notion jostled for space in Adele's muddled waking thoughts with all the other things that happened at the same time. There was urgent packing to be done because, out of the blue, she and her mother were going to visit Louis in England. Her mother couldn't think straight and had to spend hours lying pink-eyed and motion-less on her bed, followed by shorter bursts of frenzied activity, plucking random books from shelves and throwing them into a suitcase, only to pick them back out later and shove them any old how, upside down, with the pages not the spine showing, on the shelves, sighing and muttering, 'What's the point?'

Her parents argued when Adele was in bed. Her father's voice carried more. His favourite words were 'soft touch', which he wasn't, and 'rules'. 'It's not one rule for them and another rule for us,' she heard him say one night. 'Can't you see how patronising that is, Claire?' He used her mother's name a lot. 'Please, Claire,' when he banged on the bedroom door. 'How could you?' was the phrase her mother used most often. The list of things her father shouldn't have been able to do was very long. It dripped on like a broken tap. Eventually, her father caught the crying bug and the arguments stopped. It was worse with him because he couldn't do tears. He made a honking noise that sounded like he was laughing until you saw his face, scrunched up with all the little veins trailing redly across his cheeks and nose like frayed ribbons. He did it in the living room where he slept now. Mealtimes were silent affairs but the food improved because her mother gave up any pretence of cooking and just slapped cold stuff on to plates or left Adele to do it when she was trying to think straight.

The night before she and her mother were due to leave, the electricity went off and the silence was worse than the shouting that had come before. Adele got up and put her flip-flops on. She switched on her torch and went down the corridor, past the closed doors. The key was stiff in the kitchen door but the bolts slid back smoothly. There was no moon outside. Inside the garage, Yowl was snoring and Growler whined but didn't wake up. She lay down inside the sack. There was a spongy lump beneath her toes. She pulled out the doll and then she knew that Ellena and George were on their own out there with the lions.

When her father found her, he shouted. They'd been going frantic when she wasn't in bed and what the hell was she playing at. He marched her into the kitchen where her mum was weeping into a tea towel. Her mum wailed and clutched her and called her 'my baby girl'. Her father was crumpled and smelt of whisky and sweat. They sat around the table and asked her what she'd been thinking, but words seemed far away, like fruit growing out of reach. 'This is your fault,' her father said to her mother. Her mother put her head in her hands. He went and stood behind her and put his hands on her shoulders, kneading them. Her mother shuddered. Adele went to put her washbag in her suitcase.

Adele left a letter for her father on the bed, next to the doll. You never could be sure how much adults knew and what they understood so she tried to be clear.

George's wife was poorly and he needed money for medicine and hospital. Then she died. His daughter's name is Ellena and she is nine years old. When you find her, please give her back the doll.

She tried to picture her father emerging fresh from a shower, jumping into the car and driving down the potholed streets to find them. It was difficult. Something more was needed.

PS If you don't save them from the lions, I am no longer your daughter.

It was cold in Britain but it didn't always rain. They stayed at Adele's granny's house in Cardiff until her mum got a job. Then they moved into a different house and Louis stopped going to the school with the yellow team and came to live with them. Just before Christmas her father sent a parcel. The present was a dress in the bluey-purple of the bougainvillea, unimaginably bright, and in its folds were a letter and a photograph. The picture showed a class of African girls in school uniform. He had drawn an arrow to indicate which one was Ellena. It didn't look like Ellena, but Adele had only ever seen her in the dark and the photograph was blurry. When her father phoned, she told him she was going to wear the dress to the Christmas party, but she didn't because it wasn't the sort of thing girls wore in Britain in 1980. Her great pockets of ignorance about music and television and her useless knowledge about who won the Africa Cup of Nations and what you could do with baobab tree bark were bad enough without adding unforgivable fashion crimes too. There was no room for her African life, its white light tree-climbing days and hot, black velvet nights, its impossibly sharp contrasts and its certainties, within the subtler shading and ambiguities of her British one. By the time the end of term came, she had a pair of stonewashed jeans and crimson Kickers and aspired to look like Debbie Harry who was a pop singer and sang in a group called Blondie.

Her father returned to the UK and got a job in London,

but he didn't come to live with them. Every other weekend she went and stayed with him in his hospital flat where large pipes gurgled through the night. Soon after her eleventh birthday, she sat some exams and started as a bursary girl at an independent girls' school where there were rules to cover every aspect of existence. She put the African dress away at the bottom of a drawer.

Africa persisted somewhere in her mind, endowing the distance she felt between herself and her life in England, her non-participation, with a kind of glow. In her teenage years, this Africa shot through her version of herself with a strand of unfathomable complexity and colour. It allowed her some-times to believe that her English life was just a tiresome game she was playing. Then, when she was twenty and studying languages in a cold northern city, her brother unwittingly snuffed out her African light.

Louis, a newly qualified engineer, had gone to West Africa to work on drainage at a camp for Liberian refugees fleeing the civil war that had erupted there in 1989, nine years after the People's Redemption Council's military coup. At first his letters home, long on figures and statistics but short on any description that might really evoke the place, didn't impact on her inner Africa, which remained intact by dint of its separateness. In her Africa, children didn't witness their mothers being raped and their fathers butchered.

When he sent a film for Adele to get developed, photos of the children in the camp, she saw that above the barefoot, hollow-eyed boy staring into the camera, hung a huge expanse of turquoise sky. The boy had an empty white plate on his head.

To one side of the gap-toothed girl in a grubby striped purple-and-grey dress, an ochre path of baked, compacted earth snaked away between two yellowy-brown huts with shaggy straw roofs. The girl's palms, raised to wave at the camera or at Louis operating the camera, were yellow too, from making mud pies perhaps. Another child with a pot belly and huge baggy shorts stood to attention in his flip-flops, his right arm held at a stiff salute and a look of abstracted concentration on his face. Behind him women sat on raffia mats tending a cooking fire, their skirts bunched around them. Beyond the women there was the dim hazy green of trees.

Her Africa hung on for a sputtering flicker, there in the turquoise sky and the packed earth and the hazy trees, and then it guttered and went out. Whenever it tried to return, sparked by the slant of the sun on certain mornings or the smell of woodsmoke in autumn gardens, she extinguished it, firmly, as someone putting away childish things. She invented other narratives to accompany her outward life but none ever had the staying power or force of the African one.

Later, when she lived with her husband and son in Exeter, before her marriage went wrong, the red Devon earth sometimes proffered a ghostly reminder of her imaginary Africa but, as her twenties passed, that receded and faded until it held the place in her mind of an exotic but long-dead relation who had forgotten to leave Adele anything in the will.

Halfway

Senegal and Mali, 2003–5

When the man came to collect me, I was wearing a new indigo wrap, a gift from my neighbour. My mother had plaited my hair and threaded it with glass beads the colour of the sea and with one cowrie shell that was a present from my brother. She told me I was going to a good respectable family where I would help with domestic chores. I would be able to continue with my education. I wanted to be a nurse. The man paid my mother and drove me away from my home in a smart car. When we were on the edge of the city in a yard behind a factory, I was helped up into a big truck with many other children. Twenty or more. Everyone had a little bag or bundle with them. In mine I had a T-shirt and my other wrap, an old pair of shorts of my brother's, some underwear and a picture of the Pope from my Christian grandma. The man who'd brought me stroked my cheek before he left. 'Someone's going to have fun with you,' he said. His gold tooth glinted. Then he drove away.

We were loaded into the back of the truck. 'Standing room only,' one of the bigger boys said. He was being funny, trying to talk like a conductor on the bus, but his voice wavered and no one laughed. The bigger ones of us stood next to the sides so we could hold the rim, up above our heads. The littler ones were in the middle. When the truck set off, some little ones fell over and they couldn't get back to their feet because of the motion of the truck. The ones nearest to us at the edge held on to us and in this way we swayed along, like the crown of a tree in the wind. None of us were tall enough to see over the sides of the truck. The sun climbed until it hung high in the sky above us, burning our heads and our faces that we tipped back to breathe. After a long time the truck stopped and we were allowed to get out and pee at the side of the road. Some of the little ones hadn't been able to wait that long. It was a yellow, parched place where the grass was high. They gave us nothing to eat or drink. They watched us all the time so we wouldn't run away but they didn't look at us. We might have been sheep or goats.

One little boy kept crying for his mam. A man picked him up by one arm and held him in the air. In the man's other hand was a stick. The man's arms glistened with oil like a wrestler's. He had a gold stud in his nose and a ring through his ear. He thwacked the boy on the back of his legs. 'I won't stop until you shut up,' he said. The little boy didn't shut up for a long time.

When the man had finished I went to the boy. He lay face down in the dirt. He smelt of urine and blood and the hot metal of the truck floor. I whispered to him to be strong. Then I was sprawled on top of him with bells ringing in my head. I pushed myself up and twisted round. Bright stars danced in front of my eyes. The man was standing over me, his hand raised to hit me again. 'Leave him alone,' he said. His words boomed and echoed as if my head were a cave and he was inside. I pulled myself up and stood in front of him. Then I looked down at my toes and I hung my head until he went away. When I put my hand to my right ear, it was wet.

They ordered us back into the truck but this time they made us lie down. There wasn't enough room for us. We were too many. Our legs were tangled, our feet in each other's faces. They covered us with a tarpaulin and rolled some heavy round things on top. We were crushed underneath in the dark. 'If you make a sound when the truck stops next time, I'll kill you,' the man said. Then they latched the doors. There was a boy with glittering eyes. I heard him say he had a knife hidden in his trousers. He was going to kill the men and run away. My legs were trapped under someone else but there was a space above my head and chest where I fought for my share of the dirty air. The only sounds in the truck after that were the rumbling wheels, the gasping and croaking of squashed bodies trying to suck air in and the whimpering of the littlest ones who didn't know they should save their breath. It was a music that rose and fell with the bumps in the road. It got louder each time we were jolted by a pothole and then faded as we got used to our new positions. Through it all I could always pick out the high note of the boy who was beaten. I was listening for it, just like you might listen out for the horns or the kora in a piece of music.

The pain in my ear was worse than a hundred bee stings. The buzzing became part of the music, like drumming. It got louder and louder. It was a swarm in my ear, drilling and thundering. It drowned the other sounds out. It bashed its way in, into a place in me where nothing had ever gone before, a place I hadn't known could be touched by an outside thing, a secret place that was unprotected. It was like a nail being hammered and hammered again. Then it died down. It dwindled to a metal hum, like a fork being rolled along a sheet of corrugated iron. With my other ear, my left one, I heard again the cries and groans of the children in the truck, our horrible song. With my right one I heard the tinny noise that seemed to be playing far away, in another room, but was playing only to me. I listened with my outside ear for the special note of the boy who was beaten, and it wasn't there. I listened with my inside ear and I seemed to hear his spirit fly away, singing his last song.

The truck hit a big pothole and tilted. I was thrown up so my face scraped the tarpaulin and came down again, landing on another child, my nose flattened against someone's ribs. I tried to kick myself clear but there was nowhere else to go. I wrenched my head round and my nose found a rip in the tarpaulin. Suddenly, I drew in a better air. Not fresh, but fruity. I remembered the plot of land beside Other-gran's house in the village, back before she came to live with us in the city. In my mind I lay on the grass under the banana trees with the leaves hanging down to the ground around, enclosing me. I brought my brother Boubacar into my green shelter and he lay at my side. He talked to me in my inside ear in a secret voice. He told me he was going to rescue me but I had to stay safe until he could come. Don't forget, he said, you're smarter than them.

The truck stopped and there were voices outside. We made no sound. They unfastened the back. We held our breath. 'Watermelons,' someone said. They shut the doors again and banged around underneath, rattling sticks against the bottom of the truck. We drove on.

Not long afterwards, the truck stopped again. The watermelons were lifted off and we could breathe. Children whimpered and cried but no one spoke. They left the tarpaulin so it was still dark but we could feel the sun through it. Later still, they stopped once more and opened the doors, told us to get out. We climbed down on wobbly legs and sat on the roadside. We were in an empty red dusty place dotted with stunted trees. They gave us pieces of melon and water from a plastic container. The men lifted five small bodies out and took them away. One of them was the boy who'd been beaten.

Without the load of melons and the littler kids, there was more room. The girls sat at the back and the boys at the front. A girl next to me kept muttering, 'We're going to get raped.' All the girls were crying, each one on her own. The knife boy climbed over the girls and crouched with his ear against the cabin. I pushed my way through and squatted nearby. He had thin white scars on his knuckles and above one eye. He was listening so hard to the men who were driving that his eyes had gone soft and unseeing. Then he turned his head towards me, his eyes snapped into focus and

I saw he was the sort of boy I would hide from on the way home from school. The sort of boy who shouted and threw stones, who snatched things from the market stalls and ran away. He might even be one of the boys that slept in the doorway of the market building. He stared at me. 'You've got blood down your face,' he said.

'That man broke my ear,' I said.

'That'll teach you,' he said and I knew that was how he'd learned all his lessons.

I asked him what he'd heard. He told me we were in Mali. The boys were going to work in a gold mine and the girls were going to be taken on somewhere else.

'Will you cut my hair off?' I asked. 'With your knife?'

He took hold of my plaits and yanked them, pulling my head to his mouth. 'How do you know about my knife?' he said into my left ear, the one that was tuned to outside things. His spit dribbled down my neck.

I reached my hand to his wrist and I dug my nails into his skin. 'I know many things,' I whispered.

We both let go at the same time.

He sawed my plaits off close to my head with his knife. The girls around us said nothing. I gave him the beads and he wrapped them in a hanky and put them away in his pack. He had the biggest pack of any of us. I kept the cowrie shell. I pulled on my brother's shorts and the T-shirt, put my wrap in my bundle and went and squatted with the boys at the front.

When the truck stopped again, they told the boys to get down and I went with them. The truck drove off with the girls crying in the back.

One of the men led us. He wore army boots and a baseball cap the wrong way round. We walked for three days across dry rocky land. My feet swelled up and my plastic sandals cut into them. The knife boy, Amadou, cut the ends of my shoes off so there was room for my toes. I tore my old wrap into strips and bound my feet inside. I made a turban with another piece of the cloth to protect my head from the sun. At night we slept where we were, huddled together.

We heard the mine before we saw it because it was hidden in high yellow grassland. It sounded like thunder, though the day was dry and the sky was clear. It was like the noise in my inside ear, hammers bashing rocks to dust. We followed the man to a place further on where a clearing had been cut in the bush and there were cone-shaped huts with roofs of dried grass. 'Find somewhere to sleep,' the man said. 'Tomorrow you start work.' Some men were cooking on a fire and gave us rice to eat. I went with Amadou because of his knife. We squeezed into a hut where adults were sleeping and lay on bare mattresses. I took out my wrap and lay it over us. I said a sura from the Koran and Amadou joined in, mumbling in the dark among the snores.

My first job was to steer the wheelbarrow full of dirt between the mineshaft and the place where it was pounded and washed. I walked carefully. I didn't hurry and I didn't spill my load. Voices spoke to me in my inside ear. At first it was often Other-gran, calling me home, or comforting me, but then she went away. Sometimes it was my mother, crying and wailing. I didn't listen to her. Once it was my sister

Husna and she told me she was working hard at school. Now and then it was Boubacar, telling me he would come, be strong, he would come. Most often of all it was the voice of a girl who lived in the room in my head and she gave me rules to live by. There were three: eat as much as you can whenever you can; tell nobody you're a girl; keep your head down.

I did all the jobs for children at the mine at different times. I pounded the dirt with a wooden post to make it fine. It reminded me of the women in my grandma's village, pounding the groundnuts, who sang as they worked, but we didn't sing at the mine. I washed the mashed dirt in a sieve and mixed the mud with mercury to pull out the gold. I heaved the rocks up from the mineshaft with a pulley and loaded the barrows. I fetched and carried. Amadou was sent down the hole to crack out the rocks, but they didn't send me. I was too small. I didn't like to look down the hole. It was a chimney sunk into the ground where men crept up and down the sides like ants in an anthill. Amadou hid small rocks in his pocket and later he would sit behind the hut scraping at them with his knife to see if they contained gold.

Cold nights followed hot days, with each one the same. We worked all day every day. After a few months my shoes fell apart and I went about barefoot. The soles of my feet became like leather. I wondered what Boubacar would say when he saw the state of them. My ear stopped hurting and some hearing came back. The girl in my head still spoke to me, but, as time went on, the other voices faded to the whisper of leaves in the wind. I missed them. Traders came and went in Land Rovers, delivering supplies and taking the gold dust to Bamako. Men on camels passed through sometimes, but they weren't good men. They had pointy teeth and guns. There were guards posted at night at either end of the village, both to protect the gold from raiders and to keep us there, but they said that no one escaped from the mine village. It wasn't so much the bosses as the desert that made sure of that. We heard stories of children who'd tried; their dried bones whitening under the desert sun, their skulls picked clean by vultures. I kept an eye on Amadou and his knife. I waited for Boubacar.

We were given rice to eat in the morning and more rice with sauce at night. Once, I had a mango. I'd just arrived at the pounding place with a barrowload. The man who weighed the gold, Rockefeller, was sitting in his open-fronted tent nearby, watching the boys pounding the dirt. Some men had arrived on camels the night before and were staying at the other end of the village. One of them with a nose like a bird's beak, a white cloth around his head and long blue robes, came walking past and with him came a sweet smell that made my head spin. He ducked into Rockefeller's tent and laid a box on the ground. 'Fetch water, boy,' Rockefeller called. It could have been any boy, but it was me. I dragged the water container across from the tank. I knelt on the floor packing charcoal into the burner so Rockefeller could make tea for his guest. Two fat mangoes lay in the stranger's box. I put my face close and I filled my nose and all the rest of me with the sweet smell, storing it. The robed man leaned down and plucked it out from under my nose. He put the mango in my hand.

I don't know when Amadou stopped talking about running away. He liked to talk about gold now. What he really wanted, he said, was Rockefeller's job: to handle the gold, sift it between his fingers into the scales. He talked about the feel of it and the colour, like powdered sunshine in your hand it would be, he said, yellow and warm.

Some of the children used to scrape the discarded dirt together and rub it with the mercury, trying to find a speck of gold that had been missed. 'The mercury will poison them,' I said to Amadou. 'We should warn them.'

'What else have they got to live for?' Amadou said.

'What do you mean?' I said.

He didn't answer in words. He just looked at me and then looked around at the place we were in as if to say this is the limit of our world and then he looked back at me, pressed his lips together, nodded.

I understood. That's how I would have felt if Boubacar wasn't coming to rescue me. Then I thought, how would Boubacar come? He was just a boy. He didn't have a car or a camel or even a bicycle. He didn't know where I was. I was lost. 'You have to meet him halfway,' the girl in my head said but I couldn't think how. So I went on waiting, following the rules, for two long years. Then one night something changed. I was sitting by the fire. My belly ached worse than hunger. I was looking into the flames and thinking about what to do with my trousers, Boubacar's old shorts. They were nothing but rags now and wouldn't last much longer. I was thinking that Amadou had another pair of trousers because he had lots of clothes. I looked at him across the fire and saw he was watching me with his black glittering eyes. He stood up. 'I'm going to sleep,' he said. 'Coming?'

I went with him and we lay in our hut, side by side among the other sleepers. I asked him about the trousers. 'OK,' he said. 'You can have them.'

'Thank you,' I said.

'What will you give me in exchange?' he said.

He knew I had nothing. 'I haven't got anything,' I said.

'Yes you have,' he said. He put his hand on my chest and he squeezed the new little mound of flesh there, pinching my nipple between his finger and his thumb.

I pushed his hand away. The voice in my head said 'careful'.

'If you don't,' he said, 'I'll tell everyone you're a girl.'

It was our secret, like the knife, but the knife was blunt and useless now. 'Tomorrow,' I said. 'I have to sleep now. OK?'

He moaned, but he left me alone. When he was asleep I felt for his bag. I wanted my glass beads back, but they weren't there. I found five specks of gold wrapped in a cloth. I put two in my pocket and returned the others. I took my bundle and crept out. The fires had all died down and the village was quiet. I filled my bottle from the water tank, drank it down and filled it again. I slithered on my stomach between the huts. I waited in the shadows until the guard had gone past and then I walked away past the mineshaft and into the bush. I walked all night under the stars, away from the camp and away from the track the traders used. When the first rays of the sun started to come up behind me I saw a pink dusty land covered in rocks stretching to the horizon. Not a tree or green thing of any kind. Not a living creature on the earth. Only big birds high in the sky. I lay in a hollow and drank half of the water. I took out my indigo cloth and covered myself with it. Then I slept.

When I woke the sun was blazing down on me through the cloth. The pain in my belly was worse. I was bleeding between my legs. I wedged a pad of my old wrap inside the shorts to catch the blood. I lay there in the hollow for hours waiting. My mind was empty and the voice in my head was silent. When the sun was lower in the sky, I got up and wound the indigo cloth around me as a skirt. I pulled a thread from the last strip and hung my cowrie shell on it. I fastened it around my neck as a necklace and tied the rest around my head as a scarf. I took one sip of water and held it in my mouth, swilling it round, making it last. I put my little bundle on my head and I set off again as a woman.

I walked towards the setting sun, going westward to my own country. I didn't come to a road or any path I recognised as a place where people might pass by. The ground became softer. My feet started to sink into it with each step. When it was dark I chose a star that hung above the place on the horizon where the sun had disappeared. I walked towards that star. I stopped often and rested. I heard my own breath coming into my lungs and leaving them again. It was the only sound. I took another sip of water and found I had drunk it all. My feet sank into the sand up to my ankles and each step was harder. The star disappeared from sight. Some big dark thing was blocking it: a mountain of sand. I climbed it on hands and knees, scrabbling through the soft sand, falling back and scrabbling up again. My breath scraped in and out. The top of the dune was a thin ridge. I toppled over it and rolled down the other side. I lost my bundle. I stayed lying where I came to rest. A wind blew up and lifted the sand, brushing me with it. I closed my eyes and hugged my knees to my chest.

When the sun rose I got up and started to walk again through the endless dunes that changed colour from brown to yellow to pink as the sun got brighter and found its strength. I tried to keep the sun behind me but it was impossible to walk in a straight line. The dunes dipped and lifted all around and I skirted their edges. The sand was soft and accepting of me when I fell. It seemed to fold me in like a blanket, to hold me in its boneless arms. The sun blasted into the back of my head as if it would burn through me and send its flames out the other side. It sucked the wet out of me so my tongue shrivelled and my breath scorched. It made my heart tremble and flutter like a trapped moth batting against the sides of a lamp. It punched into my head. It turned the sand under my hands and knees to a white-hot blaze. I cried, but I had no tears. I lay burning and my brother came. 'Ma wants to speak to you,' he said. My mother stepped forward. She knelt before me on a floor shiny like water. 'Forgive me,' she said. She disappeared. I pulled myself towards the water. It turned to dust.

I was on the edge of a dark and silent place. I heard the voices of men and there was nowhere else to hide. They had seen me and they were coming. The darkness called to me and I went there.

When I opened my eyes again, I was in a new place. The sky was red and it crackled. Water dripped into my mouth, as fresh as rain trickling down my throat. Then I slept. I woke and saw a woman, old and shrivelled, dressed in black, sitting by my side. She held my head up and fed me more water. I slept again.

Later, I woke again and tried to sit up. My head was banging and my arms were weak. I was lying on a mat inside a hut made of bent and woven twigs, covered in red plastic. A mud-cloth blanket that smelt of smoke and earth wrapped me. On the wall beside the mat hung a photograph of a man on a camel, dressed in robes the colour of my wrap. Through the doorway I could see the woman, sitting on a stool, preparing food. The smoke from the fire swirled around her. Beyond was a muddy river, shining brown and silver like glass in the rain.

The old woman turned and saw me. She came into the hut smiling and talking in a language I didn't know. I smelt the fish she was cooking. 'Am I alive?' I asked in Wolof and she shook her head, laughing. 'Am I dead then?' I said in French and she shook her head again. Then I heard a sound I'd forgotten. I was laughing.

I stayed with her in the hut on the riverbank and each day I grew stronger. I fished beside her with a line on a pole, gutted the fish and laid them out on the roof to dry in the sun. When she packed the dried fish in a basket and carried it to market,

I swept the hearth and sat watching the river. I was still and quiet and empty, washed through by the flowing river.

The old woman and I talked to each other in our own languages and we made signs. We drew pictures in the mud with a stick. I understood that Tuareg men on camels had found me in the desert. They had seen the blue of my skirt in the sand. The one in the photograph was her son or grandson and he had carried me here, to her, to be cared for. I felt that I loved this man and that I would stay there and wait for him to return.

One day I was cleaning out the hut and found Boubacar's old shorts crushed beneath my sleeping mat. When I washed them on a stone at the riverbank I found the specks of gold in the pocket. I remembered I had to meet Boubacar halfway. I didn't know where that was but it wasn't here.

I gave the gold to the old woman. She took it away. When she returned she had bought me sandals and found me a place on the boat that went down the river. She gave me a few banknotes and a parcel of food. Dried fish, tomatoes and dark wheat bread. Then I left her. I set off home.

★

When Boubacar told his sister where he was when he got the phone call, how he and Abdou were sitting at their sewing machines and he was making a shirt for a tourist in green damask with gold embroidery, he'd always say, 'No white boy can wear gold.' And then he'd laugh his tinny laugh. He never told her he'd all but given up on her. All she knew was that when she got to the Senegalese embassy in Bamako and told the staff she was Fatima Dieng, they had a record. 'Your brother's been looking for you,' they told her, and she said, 'I know. He's coming to meet me.' He took the train to Bamako and there she was. Taller, thinner, sunken-eyed. He never told her that when he got the call, his head spun and he thought he heard Other-gran singing.

Le Club Vingt-Cinq

Dakar, Senegal, 2005

They were almost at the top of the fire escape when the press of bodies above and below forced a halt. Adele was caught against the handrail, its metal edge digging into her ribcage. Her left hand was hooked in Napoleon's, two steps above. The position winched her arm up and through the gaps like an overhead pipeline. It forced her body aslant so that the side of her face was pressing into the back of the man on the next rung up. He smelt of warm hay. When she was able to take her face away, she left a damp patch on his fresh white shirt, the imprint of her sweaty cheek.

The person on the rung below, she supposed it must be a man but couldn't turn to see, was rubbing her bottom in time to the music coming from the nightclub doorway above. If she'd been on a bus in London or next to the photocopier at work, she might have protested, but here on a juddering fire escape in a backstreet in Dakar, it was different. She liked it. She worked her right hand, clutching the polythene bag of palm wine, up close to her mouth and sucked. The drink made her eyes water and she had the impression of swaying, although she was jammed tight. She imagined the stairway breaking loose of the building, buckling under the weight of all these bodies, the iron components along with their bones and flesh, the tangle of them as they fell. She took another sip. Her left arm was jolted higher and Napoleon's fingernails gouged the soft inside of her fingers as he firmed his grip.

There was an upward surge and she was hoisted, with a final pat from the unknown masseur, up to Napoleon's side. He slid his hand around her waist. They were nearly at the front of the queue. The sign above the doorway, a scribbled word in pink neon, flashed on and off, illuminating the chains at the bouncers' throats and turning their shades into opaque pools of light, like insect eyes glowing in the dark. *Vingt-Cinq*, the sign said. It blazed intermittently but insistently into Adele's eyes, as if sending a signal. She tried to decode it. Twenty-five. What did it mean? Twenty-five years earlier, when she was a child of ten, she'd left this country and returned to Britain with her family. She hadn't been back until now, when she'd come to search for her childhood friend, Ellena.

She hoped the number didn't refer to an upper age limit. She glanced at Napoleon, his sculpted jaw, the curl of his lashes, his uncrumpled youth. He turned and smiled at her. 'You've dazzled me,' she wanted to say, but was too drunk to think how to say 'dazzle' in French. He squeezed her waist and looked ahead again, trying to stare down the bouncer.

What if they let him in and barred her entry? She'd lie

if they challenged her. She'd claim to be under twenty-five. She'd say, 'I've had a shock. That's why I seem older.' It was true. She'd had a shock. She'd been told that Ellena was dead. She sucked hard on her drink.

Then without warning the bouncers slid apart like automatic doors and she and Napoleon squeezed through in a bundle of other people into a hot dark loft where the drumbeat reverberated.

Adele threw herself into the dancing, just as she'd thrown herself into all the evening's offerings: the beer she'd drained from green-glass bottles, the powerful weed that made her throat burn, the palm wine that tasted of the woods and coated her tongue in syrup, the stroking and the touching, anything to stop herself from thinking about Ellena and the sad young man who'd announced her death. They were packed so closely on the dance floor that she had to fit her movements to those around her. She imitated her neighbours, gyrating her pelvis and lifting her knees. The springy wooden floor played a part in the dancing. At first Napoleon was jumping exuberantly opposite her like a kid on a trampoline, but then she couldn't see him any more. She looked around. There were far more men than women. The men didn't seem to mind, dancing with or at each other, some of them holding hands.

The music changed and she found herself in a line congaing round the room, a pair of hot hands on her waist, her own hot hands clasping the steaming shirt of a shaven-headed boy. They danced around the bar where orange lights glinted off glass, in and out of the crowded trestle tables lining one wall and through the loops of cigarette smoke. They trooped across the dance floor, gathering up stray dancers and knitting them into the coil of their human rope. Like a foolish many-headed caterpillar, they cavorted the length of a mirrored wall and Adele saw herself, flushed and wild-eyed. Then she caught sight of Napoleon. He wasn't part of the line but was dancing to his own reflection, practising his moves.

She started to laugh. Bubbles travelled up her nose and down to her stomach. She was still swinging her leg out sideways at every third beat with the rest of them, keeping time, but she couldn't hold herself up straight. She was doubling over, helplessly headbutting the boy's bony back. It was only that and the clumps of his shirt she clung on to that kept her from falling. When the song ended, she broke free and staggered to the edge of the room, looking for a dark corner. The bouncing motion of the dance floor was making her feel sick. Her face was wet with tears. She wiped them away with the back of her hand.

There were three other white women near the bar. She went and stood nearby as if she were part of their group. She bought a bottle of water and drank it quickly. They were only girls, teenagers even, dressed in strappy tops and skimpy skirts. They provided some camouflage, but not much. A moment later they were whisked on to the dance floor and she stood exposed, horribly alone.

She plunged back into the throng, jigging up and down to a rap song with violent lyrics. Her head was throbbing along with the music, a drum beating behind her eyes. She was desperate to get back now, to the temporary home of her hotel room, the shabby brown sofa, the musty folds of the mosquito net and the door with a lock. The space between here and there was a vast unknown. She had no idea how to cross it. She kept dancing with everybody and nobody. She kept smiling. She didn't know what else to do.

Then Youssou N'Dour was singing 'New Africa', a song she played in her kitchen at home. She closed her eyes, swung her hips, mouthed the lyrics. The jostle of warm bodies around her was the swell and tug of a rising tide in which she was a small ripple. She floated her arms up in counterpoise to the rise and fall of her shoulders, loosening the ache in her head.

Someone was dancing very close in front of her. She opened her eyes to see a solid boulder of a man in a suit. The distance between them was a compressed duct of moist air in which particles of sweat and discarded skin cells swam. She took a step back, trod on someone's foot and stumbled. The stranger reached across to catch her by the elbow and steady her just as the tempo of the music slowed. He pulled her tight to him crushing the hot damp air between them, reducing it to liquid that trickled down between her breasts and gummed her skin to her dress, her dress to his shirt. The bulk of his body pushed against hers. He lowered his head, put his mouth to the bony bit below her ear. The movement of his lips against her wet skin was like the wriggle of fish. 'You were hiding,' he said.

'Pardon?' she said.

He didn't answer, concentrating instead on manoeuvring

her about in a cramped version of the tango. He was breathing heavily into her neck. One of his hands made its way to her buttocks. He must be the massage man from the fire escape, she thought. How ridiculous, a grown woman being groped at a disco. Yet she allowed herself to be tipped this way and that as if she owed him something. She was like a teenager, not knowing how much she'd promised or what would happen if she tried to withdraw.

The massage man bent her backwards, supporting the small of her back with one arm. He shuffled her a few steps one way and then another, kneading her with his other hand as if she urgently needed reshaping. She held tight to his bulging upper arms to avoid collapsing. Her feet scuffed along the boards. Her spine arched to its limit. It was as if he intended either to lower her to the ground there in the middle of the crowded dance floor or else to bend her until something snapped. The tendons in her neck tautened with the strain of holding her head up. It was an endurance test and she knew only that she must hang on. Otherwise, it would all come spilling out, the sorry mess inside. The dancers would gather round to see. 'Her friend died of Aids,' they'd say, 'she didn't even know about it. Dancing like that with her friend dead.' Something was at stake. Not just for herself, but for Ellena. She hung on.

Then, quite suddenly, the man let go. She reeled before finding her balance. Napoleon was speaking to the man, laying a hand on his shoulder. He towered over the squat stranger. The other man shrugged Napoleon's hand off and made to move forward to reclaim Adele, but Napoleon stepped in between, talking and gesticulating. He seemed to be inviting the man to go somewhere with him. The man shook his head and scowled. Only his jowls quivered. The core of the man was rooted and immovable as an outcrop of granite. From the fingers of Napoleon's raised hand dangled a little bag of palm wine. He pressed it on the man who stuck the straw in his fat mouth. Napoleon dug his hand in his pocket and reached out a cigarette, offered it to the man, produced a lighter, all the while lively with chat. The man's eyes kept flicking to Adele. Napoleon half turned to indicate her or something further away. It was his trump card. He leaned in closer, confiding. The man glanced again at Adele, hovering there behind Napoleon, and quickly lowered his eyes when he caught her gaze. She was suddenly conscious of her open mouth and shut it. The man pushed the cigarette between his lips, his head still down, his shoulders heaving in a snigger. Napoleon clapped his hand once more to the man's shoulder and they moved away together as if they were the best of friends.

A moment later, Napoleon was back. He smiled his dazzling smile, holding out another bag of palm wine. Adele took it and sucked hard on the straw. That was the problem. She'd been getting too sober, letting maudlin thoughts in.

'Napoleon to the rescue,' she murmured into his ear. His ear seemed a thing of great beauty, perfectly formed. She pinched out its contour between finger and thumb. She sucked up the dregs of the palm wine and felt it seep into her brain. She laid her head on his shoulder and they danced slowly.

She forgave him for finding himself more fascinating for a while. It was understandable.

She didn't know this man. She didn't know how old he was, whether he had a wife or wives, what the scope of his life was. He pressed his body against hers and she felt the stirrings of desire again and thought, what is it to know someone if it isn't this thing that crosses all boundaries?

They climbed down the endless metal staircase and got into the back of a shared taxi with a lot of other people. He jiggled her on his knee. His hands were trying to find a way into her clothes. She couldn't remember where they were going but she couldn't wait to get there. She whispered to him. 'It's OK,' he assured her. They dropped people off here and there, creating more space in the back of the cab, but she didn't move on to the seat. She hadn't sat on a man's knee for a long time. Napoleon's hand slid up inside her dress. His knees under her legs moved wider, parting her thighs.

They were in her hotel courtyard and she fumbled for money to pay the driver. There was hardly anything left in her purse. She emptied the coins into Napoleon's hands and he counted them out, tutting. He said something explanatory to the driver. 'You'll give him the rest tomorrow, yes?' he said to her.

They had their arms around each other all the way up the stairs. Napoleon was laughing, stroking her arm, reaching inside her sleeve and gripping her armpit while she got the door open. A shaft of moonlight fell over the floorboards and across the bed. She knelt to light a mosquito coil. He crouched behind her, lifting her dress up, tugging at her clothes. When they stood again amid the citron fumes, he pulled the dress over her head and stood back to look at her. She undid her bra and let it fall to the floor. She gloried in her moon-white nakedness reflected in his eyes.

He peeled his shirt off and began to unbuckle his belt.

'Where's the condom?' she said as he pushed her back on to the bed.

'No condom,' he said into her neck. 'I hate them.' His face clamped down on hers.

She struggled to free herself. She held his hands around the wrists and tried to still them. 'You said it was OK,' she said.

'Yes, it's OK,' he said, as if speaking to a child. 'I'm clean.'

She pushed at his chest with her hands, holding him off. 'No,' she said. 'No way.'

He lifted himself as if he were doing a press-up. 'It's OK,' he said. 'Look. I'm healthy.' He nodded down the length of his lean body.

She rolled out from under him on to the floor, snatched her dress up and stood quickly, holding it crumpled in front of her.

He lowered himself on to the bed and turned on to his back. 'I'll do it in a safe way,' he said. He patted the spot beside him.

'No way,' she said again. Her voice was shrill.

He looked her up and down. Then he swung his legs to the floor and reached for his trousers. He fetched a cigarette from the pocket, groped for the lighter.

'Don't start making yourself at home on my bed,' she said.

He lit the cigarette anyway and took a drag, staring at her.

She stared back. 'Fucking men,' she said in English. 'Fucking irresponsible fucking men.'

'Speak in French,' he said. 'I don't understand you.'

She crossed to the door and opened it. '*Va t'en*,' go, she said.

He got to his feet, came and stood over her. He could have picked her up and thrown her across the room. He turned away.

Later, when she was alone, she showered under the warm trickle from the cubicle in the corner. She drank glass after glass of water. Then she lay naked and damp under the gauze of the mosquito net, smoking her last cigarette. She thought of herself saying no to Napoleon and of how Ellena might not have had that choice. She thought of Ellena as she was then, all those years before, a little girl sitting cross-legged in the darkness of the night garage. Adele imagined bringing Ellena out into the light and running with her into the scrubland behind the house. They ran through the long yellow grass, away from the buildings, beyond the giant baobab tree to where the path sloped downwards towards the big, shimmering ocean. She tasted the salt tang, like freedom, on her tongue.

Twenty-five years gone by in a flicker, as if time had folded in on itself and she was hemmed into the edge of the pleat, as close to then as to now.

People's Redemption Council

Liberia, 1980

After the killings on the beach, George knows he has to get out. He knew it in his head before, but now he knows it in his gut. He can no longer stay holed up in the bush, imagining there will be some reprieve.

He emerges from the thicket to join the track he has walked every day for the last week, holding his head high, swinging his arms by his sides in imitation of the movement of an unhurried man. He is trying to call up the easy gait of his former self, back when sucking air into lungs, putting one foot in front of the other, were automatic. That man he used to be never thought about how he moved. He wore a smart uniform and polished shoes. George has had long days crouching in his hidey-hole to think about that man. He thinks he was a fool.

Every day at dawn, he has waited in the scrub by the junction for his wife and daughter to arrive from Monrovia. The American, Calvin, says today is the last chance, that George can wait no longer, that he will get him on the LAMCO train up to the border, but George can't leave without them.

Calvin has a wife and kids himself; he must know that. In other respects, George trusts the American; he's had plenty of opportunities to hand him over to the authorities.

Authorities! A bunch of wild-eyed illiterates. No discipline. They won't last. George was lucky he was in Buchanan when the guns started cracking or he'd be a dead man too, like all the others.

He's late getting to the junction today because of watching the beach executions on television this morning in Calvin's back room. The programme is still playing inside George's head.

If Miata doesn't arrive today, he doesn't know what he'll do. He hitches up his ill-fitting trousers to squat in the elephant grass, behind the straggly hibiscus that is his chosen lookout point. Calvin is a short, stocky man, where George is tall and lean. Calvin's old trousers hang loosely from George's hips but end above his ankles; they burned George's uniform the night President Tolbert was assassinated. The shirt fits well enough though and is very good quality.

George parts the leaves and peers through. A woman and a child are standing with their backs to him on the edge of the road and his heart jumps like a baboon before he realises it can't be them. The child's a boy and the woman wears traditional clothes and carries a heavy pack on her head. Miata wears Western-style clothes in African cloth. She has her dresses made by the Kpelle tailor in Matadi. She has done so for years, since George was promoted and she got the teaching job. She owns a collection of shiny handbags and no longer carries things on her head.

An army jeep rumbles into view and he squats down, holding his breath. Let them pass by.

Men in fatigues hang out the sides of the jeep; they are armed to the teeth, literally. One of them grips a grenade in his mouth, another a hunting knife. All hold rifles at jaunty angles to their bodies, conscious of the figures they cut in the morning glare. The woman pulls the child close to her as the jeep screeches to a halt, the man with the knife in his teeth jumps down and George fights not to hide his face in his hands. The man shouts in a language George doesn't understand and he's shocked by this new reminder that the whole order of things has changed. The language of command in this country he thought was his is no longer English. The woman's reply is low, unhurried, respectful. It is all he can do to keep himself still. His heart swells. Miata's worn a disguise. She's a good woman. A clever one too. She speaks Krahn as well as her own mother tongue and English. She nods at what the soldier is saying and gestures back along the road with her free hand.

The man jumps on to the running board and the jeep screeches into a U-turn, stirring up clouds of dirt with its spinning wheels. As it sets off back where it came from, George gets a glimpse of the driver, hunched over the wheel, hat pulled down over his brow, sweat glistening on his cheeks. It is David Farley, who served under him in the presidential guard. So they aren't all dead. Had David been with the rebels all along or had he turned, trying to save his own skin? When George had last seen him, ten – or was it eleven? – days before, he was joking outside the Executive Mansion in Monrovia. He'd been trying to find out what George's increasingly regular trips to Buchanan were all about. 'The president's business,' George had said to shut him up but, if truth be told, George didn't know what was in the messages he took to Calvin. He'd imagined they were to do with the iron-ore trade. Now he wonders. They'd been sealed with the foreign minister's stamp: Cecil Dennis, dead on a beach, without his shoes.

George calls softly through the leaves, his breath stirring the orange flowers and making them tremble. 'Ellena,' he calls, but his voice is a croak, stuck in the back of his throat, and doesn't carry. Nevertheless his daughter half turns and, when he rustles the branches, she tugs on her mother's dress and the two of them, after a quick glance around, walk towards him, as if they had all the time in the world. They duck beside him and he pulls them close. Nobody speaks.

Quickly, quickly, he leads them back along the path, past the quiet houses. When they are far from the road, the hush lifts. Children are playing outside and it feels more normal. George slows his pace and realises his wife is far behind. She's been slow in her movements since Ellena was born. Too old for babies, she said she was, but blessed. He controls his desire to shout at her to hurry up. His daughter, in her boy's clothes, reminds him of his older children, his two grown sons. He hopes they'll find their way in the new order. For the first time, he's happy that neither of them wanted to follow him into the army.

When Miata catches up, he steers them across the clearing

beyond the fish-rot stink of the dump, through the undergrowth to his hiding place. Only once they're inside does he speak.

'Did you get the money?'

Miata lifts the bundle from her head and places it on the ground, bending to retie it. She shakes her head. 'They tore up the house,' she says.

He's glad she's busy with the bundle; it gives him a moment to compose himself, to try and mask his fear. 'Calvin will help us,' he says, reaching out to touch her arm.

She looks at his hand against her skin. 'They were smashing up buildings,' she says quietly, 'setting fire to cars. You could hear guns booming all the time. People were dancing in the streets. In our own street, people came out and danced.'

George pats her arm. 'You're safe with me now,' he says.

Miata pulls Ellena in close to her side. 'They say they're going to end corruption and that they had no choice. They're bringing redemption, they say.'

'Redemption!' says George and spits. Miata bites her lip and doesn't speak again.

They leave on the night freight train, wrapped in blankets from Cora, Calvin's wife, who has become suddenly helpful and almost jolly, pressing a package of 'useful things' into Miata's hands and clucking over the silent child. Until now, when he's finally leaving, Cora has been twitchy with George, unlike the groomed person he has met before on official visits. She never looked him in the eye when he slipped into their house on Silver Beach after sunset for a beer and some chicken and rice. She would stay in the room while he ate, her small blue eyes fixing on anything, the TV in the corner, the cupboard where photos of their sons on graduation day are displayed, the bright new sofa under the window, the masks and carvings on the wall, on anything except George. Her presence made him push the food down fast, swallowing it lumpy and half chewed, always agreeing to seconds. All he could give them in exchange for hiding, clothing and feeding him, was this hunger. It was supposed to be different when Miata arrived from Monrovia with the money. He would have paid his way.

The train rattles away from the ocean, away from Buchanan and up into the hinterland. As they leave the city behind and the buildings give way first to vegetation and then to rubber plantations, the trees close in around the track, enfolding the train and its huddled human cargo. George takes a deep breath, as if he hadn't breathed properly for days. The night-birds cry, invisible overhead, insects thrum around his head and the train clatters on, carrying them north, towards Yekepa and the border beyond. Whatever comes next, to be on the move, to stretch after days of being cramped, to have his wife and child lined up beside him, is a gift.

He unwraps the parcel and a torch rolls out. This might be a very useful thing. He switches it on and examines the other contents: dried fish, bananas and bread, a plastic bottle of water, a ball of string, a packet of American chewing gum, two safety pins and a roll of toilet paper. He flicks the light over to Ellena but she's already asleep, slumped against her mother, her eyelashes flickering. Smiling, he turns to Miata and sees she's watching him. Her face in the torchlight looks bruised, the skin under her eyes the colour of scorched aubergine. His smile suddenly feels false and foolish. He reaches out his arm to slide it around Miata's shoulders, but she pulls away.

'What have you done, George?' she asks.

He takes his hand away and looks at her, this woman he has shared his life with for a quarter-century, who seems not to know him. What does she think he's done?

'They didn't tear up our neighbours' houses,' she says.

George can't bear her gaze and looks down at the pile of useful things again, poking at them with the torch as if the safety pins or the chewing gum might provide an answer to her questions. What is it he's done? He's done his duty as a soldier. He's served the elected president of their country. In the previous century his great-grandparents came over from America with other freed slaves to found Liberia. But he can't be blamed for being, by an accident of birth, a member of the ruling class. He can feel his life, his history, the sense he has always had of himself and his place in things, slipping away from him, like feet unable to get a purchase on mountainside scree. He doesn't know what to say. 'Why did you come?' he asks eventually.

She shrugs and looks at the sleeping child. 'You're my husband,' she says.

He keeps seeing the face of Cecil Dennis, the foreign minister, as he was on the TV programme at Calvin's house, staring back at the screaming soldiers who kicked away his shoes before they shot him. Howling crowds cheered them on as they fired hundreds of rounds into the bodies. A hundred years of oppression avenged, the commentator said. 'It's been broadcast round the world,' Calvin said.

'And your people?' George asked.

Calvin shook his head.

'Champions of democracy?' George nudged.

Calvin stared up at the ceiling fan a moment before replying, plaiting his fingers across his big stomach, choosing his words. When he eventually spoke, saying something about democracy being a fluid concept, especially in Africa, George felt his insides loosen and he had to grip the back of the chair and tighten his buttocks not to shame himself. The Americans have accepted the new regime, it seems. 'Why are you helping me?' he wanted to ask, but didn't dare.

They alight in the early morning, before the train reaches its destination, in the place Calvin has described, a scraped-out clearing where ore bins are stacked. The thick jungle presses in on either side of the track ahead, the canopy meeting in a high green arch, but here they are exposed. George jumps first. Ellena leaps into his arms. Miata throws the bundle to him and then throws herself too fast, panicking. She lands heavily but she will not allow him to help. The hollow of George's back arches inward in anticipation of an accusing shout or shot as he forces himself to walk at Miata's pace, a painful hobble, across the open space into the shelter of the rainforest. The train chugs on to Yekepa. Miata rips a scrap of cloth from her wrap and ties it tightly around her swollen ankle. They wait, as they have been told, just within the forest. They keep still and quiet. They eat the food. George watches over his wife and child who doze and then wake and talk in whispers. They seem thinner and less solid than before. Monkeys rustle and jabber up in the trees and birds squawk. An ant bites like fire, deep inside George's shoe. They wait.

Just as Calvin promised, a man comes to find them as the sun goes down. He puts his finger to his lips and they follow him silently along the railway track, around the edge of a shanty town. The man keeps stumbling and tripping in the dark, and every time he does, he turns and hisses at them to shush although they haven't made a sound. George wonders if the man's drunk or dim-witted. They skirt an open space, clinging to the forest rim, then climb a hill and emerge facing a row of white bungalows, some of them with lights inside. 'Is this Area F?' George whispers, because he knows that's where their contact, Bob Edsholm, the mining engineer, lives. 'Shh,' says the man and leads them round the side of a dark and empty house and in through the garden door. George can hear the man's rasping breath as he fumbles for the light switch but fails to find it. 'I have a torch,' he says. 'Shh,' the man says and goes on fumbling, his hand making slapping sounds against the wall. The yellow electric light reveals a storeroom, containing garden tools and furniture, a folded-up sun umbrella, a rack of tennis rackets. A single bed has been pulled out into the middle and blankets laid out next to it on the floor. This is where they're to sleep.

'Is Bob here?' George asks.

The man shakes his head, backing towards the door. George sees that he isn't drunk, but scared. 'Thank you for your help,' he says.

Miata and Ellena share the bed and George lies next to them on the floor. Miata hums a lullaby to soothe Ellena to sleep and George listens too, fighting the encroaching heaviness in his own eyes, then dreaming he is awake and watchful as sleep creeps up and kidnaps him.

He awakes with a shout of pain, his eyes popping open into total darkness. A hand slaps across his mouth to silence him. He tries to twist away from the vice-like hold on the flesh of his left cheek, moaning.

'Quiet,' Miata hisses, letting go of his cheek but keeping her hand firm over his mouth.

He waits for his breathing to slow. 'Was I snoring?' he mumbles between her fingers.

'You were *sleeping*,' she says.

'I'm sorry,' he murmurs into her palm. He starts to form soft little kisses with his lips against the inside of her fingers and she snatches her hand away. She lets her breath out in a fierce puff, as if through gritted teeth. He props himself up on his elbows, alert now as he should have been before and waits for her to speak. The only sound in the hanging silence is the rasp of her breath; laboured breathing like someone with a wound who's trying not to cry out from the pain. The bed creaks as she rocks to and fro.

He whispers, 'You are my darling.'

Miata suddenly finds her voice. The words explode from her in a furious whisper. 'Your darling?' she spits. She takes another shuddering breath. 'And have you asked your darling how she survived the killing in Monrovia? Have you asked where your darling was while you were swilling beer with your American buddies in Buchanan? Where she hid, how she fed your child with no money, how she got past road-blocks and barricades and trigger-happy boys fresh from the bush with big guns in their hands?'

George shakes his head. 'What could I do?' he says. 'I'm sorry.'

'For what? For not asking? For not coming back for us? For being one of Tolbert's henchmen in the first place?' There is a silence while she waits for him to speak. 'I heard,' Miata continues, 'all the bad things your men have been doing. Extortion. Yes. Stealing. Yes. Beatings.' With each repeated 'yes' she prods him in the sore place on his cheek again.

'Not me,' George whispers.

He can feel her stare in the darkness. 'But you knew,' she says in a cold, accusing voice. 'And you say what could I do?'

George daren't reach out to her. A feeling of utter black dread such as he hasn't known since the night of Ellena's birth clutches at him. He sees again the dark red of Miata's blood staining the sheet, an impossible amount of blood to come from one ordinary-sized woman, and Miata herself a shrunken caricature; her skin without its sheen, her face grey as dust. That night too he thought he'd lose her.

He gropes for the right words. He can't think clearly with the deafening pump of blood in his ears. He knows things got worse after the rice riots, but he can't remember the exact moment when the rot set in or when brutality became the norm among the presidential guard. 'Sometimes,' he says carefully, 'there's the devil in front of you and another devil at your back.'

In the silence that follows, a mosquito whines around George's head and Ellena calls out like a little bird in her sleep. Eventually, Miata lets out a sigh. 'I know,' she says and George's heart surges.

'I couldn't come back for you. I would be recognised. I can't disguise myself like you can,' he says.

'I know,' she says again. Her voice has softened.

He reaches for her hand and she lets him take it. He strokes her fingers. 'Did someone help you?' he asks.

'A neighbour.'

He thinks of the people they've met since they left the military compound to move into the new neighbourhood. He'd like to go and thank the good Samaritan who was brave enough to help his wife and child. 'Which neighbour?' he asks.

'Idriss,' she says, naming the fat Lebanese trader who lives in the big house behind theirs.

George is puzzled. Idriss shutters his shop and lies low when there's trouble. He squats sweatily behind a barricaded door, counting his money. He can't easily imagine him sheltering a destitute African woman and child when bullets are flying. Idriss seems like someone for whom everything has a price.

George blinks into the darkness as if he's trying to make something out in a deep black hole. 'But you couldn't pay him,' he says slowly.

'No,' Miata says.

'Why would he help?' George asks, thinking, for some reason, of the dense thicket of palms and vines between their two houses. Yellow hibiscus grows wild there, starlike flowers with red-stained centres.

Miata shrugs and pulls away from him to tuck the cover closer around Ellena. George presses his fingertips into his aching eyes. Yellow flowers burst behind his eyelids. A wave of nausea rises in his gullet. He swallows it and lies back on the floor. Miata reaches down to stroke his forehead. He is surprised at the evenness of his own voice when he speaks. 'Why do you think these people are helping us?' he asks.

She takes a moment to think. 'Because Mr Top-Man Calvin told them to,' she replies. 'And Calvin's your friend.' George nods. 'As far as these people are ever really our friends. It's not because you could get him in trouble. They'd have got you out fast and hush-hush if that was the case. You didn't know what was in the documents you were carrying, so it's not that.' She pauses, as if waiting for him to say something. 'You didn't, did you, George?'

'No,' he says.

Miata sighs and makes a tutting noise just as she does when Ellena's schoolwork isn't up to standard. 'Guilt,' she says eventually. 'That's why Calvin's helping you. When they're all together, they're like one big machine, they can do anything they want, no questions asked, but when they're just one man, like Calvin there, they feel guilty.'

George ponders this.

'So I suppose,' Miata adds, 'it's because Calvin cares about you.'

George is happy to rediscover Calvin's friendship in this

way. They are 'brothers under the skin' Calvin had said one time.

'We're just little people. We don't count,' Miata says.

'Except to us,' George says. Miata reaches for his hand again and clasps it.

'Can't we stay here?' Miata asks in the morning when she joins him at the garden fence. George has got up early, found the hose curled outside and watered the garden as recompense to their hosts. These lawns the Europeans love so much return quickly to scrub if they aren't doused twice daily. George would use the water for vegetables if it were his yard. The wet earth gives off a fresh, peppery scent. It's a new day. Between the slats of the fence they watch women walking by on their way to market. They are Guinean women from across the border. The turmoil in the south of Liberia means nothing to them. They are dressed in their market-day best and the enamel bowls on their heads are packed high with green oranges, butter pears, mangoes, papayas and pineapples. A small boy walking next to his mother is carrying carrots, arranged like the spokes of a wheel, on a blue plastic plate on his head. Here it's as if they're already in a different country. George imagines a simple life. He could garden, Miata might find work in the school.

The Swedish man, Bob, whistles from the veranda. 'It's better if you're not seen,' he says and they retreat to the storeroom. 'What's your plan?' he asks George, sitting on the wooden chair opposite the bed, pushing his floppy grey hair away from his face and slicking it back with the sweat of his hand.

George shakes his head. He thought Bob would have a plan.

'I was hoping to take you across the border in a LAMCO truck. We cross all the time with core samples, but they're checking everything and everyone.' He sighs. 'Do you know people in Guinea or the Ivory Coast?'

'In Senegal. I know people in Senegal.'

Bob drops his head into his hands, rubbing the heels of his hands into his eyes. 'Senegal's a very long way,' he says eventually. 'You need a plan, man. You can't stay here.'

He leaves them a newspaper and they look at the pictures of looting in Monrovia. There's a list of eighty-three former officials, judges, army and police officers who have been arrested and are to face trial for treason. George knows some of these men. Others wanted for being 'inimical to the interests of the people' are on the run and will be hunted down on the authority of the new leaders, the People's Redemption Council, the paper says. Their pictures are to be printed tomorrow so the people can help bring them to justice. Cold fear shivers in his belly.

Bob's son, Lars, comes with food. He is as tall as his father and even skinnier. His white-blond hair falls past his shoulders and is scooped back in a black band. He shows Ellena the scaly skin of a green mamba he caught and she smiles. 'Want to come and meet my friends?' he asks her and George looks at Miata in time to catch her assenting nod.

Miata packs the leftover food into her bundle while George paces. They have no papers, nothing. They have no plan.

Lars and Ellena return an hour later with a group of

children, mostly Swedes but with enough local ones for Ellena not to stand out. 'I'll take you to the border,' Lars says. 'I know a way through the forest.'

George keeps his face blank. 'I'm a scout,' the boy explains. 'How soon can you be ready?'

'Let's go,' George says.

They scuttle across the road with George and Miata bent low in the middle of the group. Then they plunge into the rainforest which is right there on the other side of the road and walk in single file. Miata is limping badly and after a few minutes they stop at a little hut so that she can tie the cloth more tightly around her ankle. The hut has a banana-leaf roof and smells of the dank forest floor. There's a pile of comics stacked in the corner. 'This is our HQ,' Lars says and there's a part of George, a little part not tainted by the fear, that's able to smile at the gaggle of white kids who are at home in his jungle, who are trying to lead him out of danger in his own country.

Lars buckles a belt hung with lizard skins and a hunting knife around his waist. He sends the other children home. 'Good work, guys,' he says. 'Cover for me.' George shakes them each by the hand and thanks them before they leave, repeating their names, the strange and the familiar. Sven, Heidi, Björn, Trond, Doris, Karl, Joko, Bendu and Saye. 'Is it true that you were the president's main man?' one asks him, before Lars shoos them away.

Lars leads the way through the thick, wet green of the forest. Miata walks behind him, leaning on a stick. George brings up the rear, Ellena on his back. Lars follows no discernible route, but presses through the undergrowth, forcing it to part for them, stopping occasionally to gaze around, to finger the bark of certain palms as if greeting them. George sees marks on the trunks, notches made by a knife, and understands that this strange white boy cuts his own path. They move slowly, at Miata's pace, picking their way over giant roots between the towering trunks of ebony, mahogany, irokos and other trees whose names George doesn't know. Occasionally they emerge into grassy clearings where the sun breaks through the canopy and George sees it's past its zenith now. This is the pattern of their progress, from dark to light and back again, until they come to a sort of path, a trodden route, and movement becomes easier. Ellena grows heavier on his back and snuffles into his right ear. His shoulders ache and he can't wipe away the sweat dripping into his eyes because his arms are holding Ellena's legs. Monkeys, too far up in the leaves to identify, swing along above them, chattering. George had thought the border closer to Yetepa but they seem to have walked for hours. Time, like democracy, is a fluid concept, he thinks, consciously, effort-fully, twisting his mind away from the border: guards, soldiers, dogs, men with guns and unanswerable questions.

All of a sudden, Lars stops, swivels and motions them back. They retreat into the trees. A man is approaching. A shaft of sunlight shooting down through the treetops glances hot-white off the blade of the machete he carries. Lars waits, bouncing on the balls of his feet, his hand close to the knife at his belt. George swings Ellena down from his back and takes her hand in his. Miata shrinks back into the foliage. He looks into her eyes and knows she can't run.

If the man's surprised to see a white boy in his path, he doesn't show it. There's a muttered exchange of words between the two, which sound like ritual greetings, and then Lars pulls something from his pocket and passes it to the man, who tucks it in the cloth tied across his shoulders. They nod at each other and shake hands.

Lars turns and beckons them from the bush. 'It's OK,' he says.

George doesn't want to move, fears a trap, but Ellena tugs at his hand. 'Come on, Daddy,' she says. 'It's OK.'

'This man,' Lars says, 'will take you to the bus stop.'

George doesn't understand, thinks 'bus stop' might be a code. 'Bus stop?' he says stupidly.

Lars nods. 'We call it bus stop. The place on the road where you can get a ride. This man will take you there,' he says again.

George considers this. He knows his wife and child are watching, waiting for him to say something and make a decision. 'There'll be a bus?' he asks at last, looking at the man with the machete who, he now notices, has a stack of firewood on his back.

The man shakes his head, puzzled.

'Sooner or later, there will be a bus or another vehicle,' Lars says. 'It'll take you to the town north-west of here, I forget the name, and there you'll find another transport on to Senegal.' He smiles widely at the three of them, pats Ellena on the arm. 'Hey, little sis,' he says, 'safe now,' and she grins back. Lars's teeth are too big for his face and George remembers that he's only a boy, thirteen, fourteen at most. Just a few years older than Ellena. He can't imagine what he was thinking to put the fate of his family in the hands of a child.

'But we need to cross the border and we have no papers,' he says sadly to Lars, sorry to puncture the boy's pleasure. 'I thought you knew a way to cross.'

Instead of replying, Lars does a little dance, hopping from foot to foot and flicking his fingers in the air so that they make a clicking sound. He says something to the machete man in a language George can't speak but recognises as French, and the man laughs wheezily, his toothless mouth gaping.

'We *are* in Guinea,' Lars says eventually, when he has got his mirth under control. 'We crossed the border hours ago.'

The old man nods.

'I cross all the time,' says Lars.

'Do your parents know?' asks George, mustering his dignity.

Lars raises his eyebrows. 'Parents,' he says, 'what do they ever know?' and he bestows his special grin on Ellena again.

'Why do you cross?'

Lars spreads his arms wide, palms up, sweeping them out in a grand, all-encompassing movement.

Waiting with his family by the dirt road where the man leaves them, George feels a surge of energy and hope. The world around him seems made anew in the light of the sinking sun. In an hour a lorry will stop and give them a lift as far as Nzérékoré and the countryside they pass through, so like his own and yet not his own, will move him almost to tears. Later that night, he'll buy bus tickets with a few of the Guinean francs Lars pressed into his hand and they'll eat hot yam and meat from the stalls at the bus station. In a week they'll make it into Senegal and he'll find the Dakar office of his Senegalese contact, a trader turned businessman, who'll help him get a job, despite his lack of papers. In five weeks he'll start his life again as a nightwatchman for a British doctor and his family. In six months Miata will be dead from a wasting sickness. He'll find himself branded a thief and cast out with Ellena. One day, ten years down the line, he'll switch on the TV to watch Samuel Doe, the man who killed his president and forced him from the country, being tortured before he is shot. He'll see the executioner sipping a beer as Doe's ear is cut off and it will be the turn of his sons back home to run from soldiers invading their village.

All of this is inconceivable right now, his daughter and his wife beside him. As the sun sinks into the earth, he can almost smell the sap rising in the trees that line the dusty road. It's rising in him too, as if he could start afresh, put out new leaves.

No Sleep before Bamako

Mali, 2004

The girls back at the hotel made me a cup of tea. Three glasses of tea in fact. I sat in the yard on the packing crate with the silent, staring baby on my knee, surrounded by fish heads and bones while they boiled the pot on the brazier and poured frothing glassfuls back and forth. The first glass was dark green and murky like pond water with a strong, sour taste, 'as bitter as death' they said. The second was sweeter 'like life', and the third was a golden colour and thick with sugar. That last one, Assetou told me, was supposed to be 'as sweet as love'. All the sugar couldn't disguise the underlying bitterness though.

I counted my money. As well as the 30,000 francs I'd got for selling my place in the car to Timbuktu, I had about 9,000 in change and three twenty-pound notes my mum had given me 'just in case'. It added up to about eighty quid to last me three weeks until my flight back. Jack had been looking after our money. Assetou came with me to the bus station to buy a ticket. She held my hand all the way and then gripped me tighter when we arrived and the ticket touts and sellers started calling to us and jostling. I didn't know where I was going, but the opposite direction to Timbuktu was south so I bought a ticket for Bamako, the capital. It only cost 8,000 CFA francs so that was all right. Assetou wouldn't take the 500 I offered her for helping me, but as I watched her walk away, with her basket balanced on her head, I had the feeling that I'd accidentally given her something else I was going to need, that I'd popped the image of myself as an adventurous heroine into her basket and she was taking it away, leaving me on my own in a crowd of strangers.

There seemed to be hundreds of people sitting waiting outside the bus, far more than the bus could possibly hold and they had mountains of luggage, ridiculous things like flowery mattresses and baskets of live chickens and bulging plastic holdalls in every possible size. After a while, a man in a peaked hat and a sort of blue uniform came over to me and asked to see my ticket. For some reason I was convinced he was going to say it wasn't valid and I started to feel really panicky and scared. I couldn't understand what he was saying to me and I tried to explain that it was a bona fide ticket that I'd bought from the ticket office, but he was taking no notice of that and kept pointing to the bus and jabbering on. Eventually a man from the queue, an old gent with a bony face like dark wood and a little silver beard on the end of his chin, spoke quietly into my ear in English. 'Ascend the autobus,' he said.

I climbed aboard and sat in a seat halfway back. That's the safest place on planes so it's probably true of buses too. Then I sat there for about two hours all on my own with the sun bashing through the window in full view of the other passengers who waited outside in the shade of a rickety lean-to shelter, chewing nuts and laughing and drinking mint tea. It was like I was being punished but I didn't know what I'd done wrong. I pretended to read my book and drank my bottle of water which tasted foul and smelt worse, like swimming-pool water. I hadn't wanted to waste money on the proper bottled stuff so I'd filled it up out of the tap and put a purifying tablet in. I had to drink it though. It was that or die of thirst. I kept thinking I should get off and buy more water before the journey began but it seemed too difficult and then it was too late because everyone piled on. They squeezed into the seats and I was squashed tight against the window by a big fat warm mamma with a toddler on her knee. All the luggage got tied on to the roof, little stools were put down the aisle and people crammed on to them too and the man I thought was the driver walked away and another one with a Rasta hat and a spliff in his mouth climbed into the driver's seat and we were off.

Soon we were out on the main road going south and hurtling through the darkness, and although it was cooler, a dust-filled wind came rushing down the bus through the front door, which didn't shut, and it was difficult to breathe. My nose clogged up straight away and my hair went flying about wildly, whipping the woman next to me across the face and I had to tug it into a wad on the window side and lean my head against it. People put their heads down and wrapped cloths over their noses but I didn't have anything like that. I breathed through my mouth, salty grains of dust, thinking I was going to suffocate. I thought of Jack, on the road to Timbuktu, and I couldn't remember why I'd left him. I was wearing one of his shirts over my T-shirt, a big baggy one. I pulled it up over my head, wriggled my arms out of the sleeves, and inside there, where it smelt faintly of him and with my hair as a pillow, I drifted off.

I woke up because my legs had gone to sleep and there was a heavy weight on them. When I got my head out of my shirt tent, I saw nothing much had changed; people sat quietly in the swirling gloom, heads nodding on to their chests, and the bus rumbled through the night. The little boy belonging to the woman next to me was lying across both our laps, his head lolling on my knees, his eyes open a white slit. There was nothing to see out of the window. No lights anywhere and no other traffic on the road. Now and then we passed some smudge and a movement that might have been a huge animal rearing up. I had no idea how far Bamako was or how long it would take to get there or what I would do when I did, but it felt like I'd never arrive anyway and that's how my life was to be from now on, an alien white girl squeezed inside a dark bus going nowhere.

After hours and hours, the bus stopped on a long dark stretch of road and then backed up a bit. There was a white guy standing on the verge, with a cloth wrapped round his head in the Tuareg way, but on him it looked more like a bandage. He climbed on the bus as if it was perfectly normal. There was nothing there, not a twinkle of a light, not a building, not even a mud hut, just trees and shadows. It was the middle of nowhere but it was obviously somewhere to him. And it should have comforted me, that here was someone like me, of my own kind, but it didn't. He seemed so at home that it made him as foreign and weird to me as the Africans. The easy way he swung himself on and settled into the seat nearest the door – someone must have got off somewhere but I couldn't grasp how because we hadn't stopped – and joked with the other passengers crammed up there at the front, made me feel small, as if I'd got no right to be scared and lonely and little, as if he was mocking my fears.

Then we were rolling through the night again and the brief chatter and whispering that greeted the white man died down. I wriggled back inside the shirt and tried to sing the words to 'All That You Have Is Your Soul' in my head. If I'd had my iPod I could have listened to that but we hadn't brought any electronic things; Jack said it would get in the way of our authentic African experience and we wouldn't be able to charge them up. I really wanted something to get me away from the authentic African experience. My mosquito bites were itching and I couldn't bend down to scratch them. I had twenty-three bites on the right leg, nineteen on the other and they'd all erupted into crusty boils as if I'd got leg acne. My stomach was hurting and I couldn't get the idea out of my head that I'd poisoned myself when I drank the water. It felt like I'd actually drunk the contents of a dirty pool where hundreds of people had gobbed and peed and really I was just waiting for the other symptoms to appear. I don't know why but I got to thinking about the people at Woolworths and wondering if they'd be sad when they heard I'd died of poisoning on the road to Bamako. I even missed old Jim calling me college girl; at least a college girl was a someone.

Then came an awful cracking noise and the bus started careering from side to side and people were screaming and shouting. My head was jammed inside Jack's shirt so I couldn't see what was happening. The bus skidded to a stop, and in the deathly silence that followed, I fought my way out of the shirt, ripping my head through the hole that had become too small. The bus lights came on and I saw everyone still in their places but some of them had glinting fragments sticking out of their heads and arms and there was blood trickling everywhere. People looked round at each other wide-eyed and then they were all laughing, shrieking with laughter and talking in high, excited voices as if they were delighted with their new piercings.

There was fog in my head and a sick taste on my tongue. My stomach heaved and I clutched one hand over my mouth, scrabbling over bodies, pushing and being pushed, wedged in a confusion of arms and legs, flailing and falling, caught and manhandled, jostled, passed like a parcel, my neck squeezed, my head pulling against a tug on my hair, a grip that would not let go, and I was out on the road, bent double and drenched in the smell of sweat and terror and I was vomiting up the whole dirty swimming pool until I was empty. Whoever was holding my hair out of my face let go and told me to sit down with my head between my knees. He gave me a bottle of water and went away. Later, when he brought me out a blanket and put it over my shoulders, I saw it was the white guy. In the light from the bus his eyes were fiercely blue. He had a brown, weather-beaten face and needed a shave. He looked about forty. I took a sip of the water. It tasted of earth. I spat it out.

My teeth were chattering despite the blanket and weird clicking noises came from the bushes behind me. Even if the bus was full of laughing hyenas, I didn't want to get left behind here. I went and stood near the doorway.

The windscreen was shattered but still in place and there was a hole in it where the wing mirror had smashed through to fly down the bus flinging its sharp fragments into people's flesh. They were picking the pieces out of each other and dabbing at the cuts, pressing torn-off bits of bandage the white guy and another man were doling out against their skin to stop the bleeding. People kept getting on and off the bus, disappearing into the bushes for a moment. The old man who had told me back in Mopti to ascend climbed down with the help of a cane. He had a piece of white bandage stuck above his eye. He walked slowly and carefully, tapping his stick, to the side of the road. He stopped on his return journey. '*Ça va mieux*, young lady?' he asked. He was old. Much older than my nan. I tried to imagine my nan coping with a journey like this one and I couldn't. I followed him back on to the bus and clambered over the people in the aisles back to my seat. I kept my head down, embarrassed at how I'd trampled on them in my stampede for the doorway. 'Sorry,' I kept saying when I stepped on their toes and their fingers. 'Sorry.' They squeezed their bony knees to one side to let me through.

'Drink the water. It'll make you feel better,' the white man said as he worked his way back to the front. 'It's not poisoned,' he said, as if he'd read my mind.

'It tastes funny,' I said.

'That's the iodine,' he said.

'Right,' I said.

'It works as a purifier,' he said.

I drank the water and I did feel better. It tasted like medicine. I took the child on my knee while his mother went off to do a pee. It was hard work for her getting down the crowded aisle but people manhandled her along, the same way they'd done with me earlier.

The bus set off again, very slowly. There was zero visibility out of the broken windscreen but another guy hung out the window next to the driver and called out instructions in a hoarse voice so we didn't go tumbling off into the scrubland or jungle or whatever was out there in the limitless dark. The driver seemed unfazed by all the kerfuffle. He still had a spliff in his mouth and his eyelids were drooping heavily so he probably couldn't see much at the best of times.

Soon we stopped in a place where there were lanterns burning and women cooking on braziers on one side of the road and everyone got off. I realised I was starving hungry. I queued up at the same stall as the old man and was given a tin plate with some mush and meat that only cost eighty francs. There were little plastic tables and chairs, like the ones they use in infant schools, set out under an awning held up with stripped tree trunks. I sat at a table on my own but then my bus neighbour and her kid came and joined me. I copied what they did, putting out my hands for water to be poured over them and rubbing them together under the stream. They ate only with their right hand, patting the yellowy mush into a shape and scooping up the meat with it, popping it quickly into their mouths. I couldn't get the hang of it and dribbled sauce all over the place. Someone brought me a spoon and I got on better but I couldn't eat it. My stomach seemed to have shut down. It was very rich, spicy and nutty and there were fatty lumps in the sauce. The woman hoovered up what I left.

People drifted off after they'd eaten. I wandered over to a stall where they were selling hot drinks and I bought something delicious and creamy that tasted like Ovaltine, served in a plastic mug. I thought I was beginning to get the hang of things. There are worse things than milky drinks by lamplight. I looked around for somewhere to sit and suddenly realised I couldn't see anyone from the bus. I stared at the people sitting about in the darkness and I didn't recognise any of them. And then my hollow stomach did a flip as I saw that the bus had gone too. It had vanished. My teeth started to chatter again and sweat broke out all over me. I could actually smell myself. I smelt like a camel.

Then the white guy appeared. That was his trademark, appearing out of nowhere like an African. I leaned against a fence post and sipped my Ovaltine. 'Where d'you get that drink?' he asked and I pointed nonchalantly at the stall as if I always went there for my night-time beverages. He bought two and took one over to the old man, who I now saw was sitting on a stool nearby, almost invisible in the dark. The white guy squatted down next to him and the two started chatting in quiet voices.

In the darkness around me soft yellow lamps lit up the people cooking and chatting on the roadside. Up above, thousands of big juicy white stars hung in the black sky. It was like magic to have arrived somewhere at last, wherever it was, where there were people and activity and bustle, after all the hours of sameness and dark. I wanted to share it with someone. I missed Jack. Not Jack as he was but Jack as he might have been, as I'd imagined him. I didn't understand what had happened, why, or even if he'd changed, but I missed the idea of him. Although the mirror shards had flown past me, I felt like one of them had lodged itself in my gut and was making me bleed inside and because it wasn't really there, there was nothing to be done. It was a sad and lonely feeling.

'I love this stuff. They use condensed milk. It reminds me of boarding school.' It was the white guy who'd come and stood next to me, creamy drink in hand.

'Mmm,' I said. I hardly seemed able to talk to this weird man with the Tuareg turban wound round his head and blond stubble pushing through on his sunburnt face.

'Give us your cup,' he said. 'I'll take it back for you.'

I handed him my empty cup. 'Um. Do you know where the bus is?' I asked. I could hear the tremble in my voice, but he didn't seem to notice.

'Being repaired,' he said. This seemed so unlikely in the middle of the night in a little place lit by kerosene lamps where there weren't even houses, just temporary shelters made out of plastic and sticks, but I thought, he knows stuff.

'You came from Mopti?' he asked.

I nodded again.

'Is that how they're wearing their shirts these days in downtown Mopti?' he said. He laughed, not unkindly, and turned away to return the cups.

I looked down at myself. I'd got my head through one of the sleeves. That was why my throat felt so constricted. The shirt was ruined. I bit my lip and pressed my fingertips into my eyeballs to keep from crying.

'Take this water and drink it.' The man was next to me again. 'You need to rehydrate yourself after you've been so sick. You need to keep drinking. Have you got any rehydration salts?'

I shook my head. He held out a few crumpled sachets and smiled. Creases appeared in his cheeks when he smiled, almost like they'd been cut there with a knife. 'If you get dehydrated, you'll get very weary and dispirited too,' he said. I thought of Jack slumbering for hours, wrapped in the pink sheet in Mopti. And me, there on that roadside. I could have lain myself down in those shadows and let them swallow me up. 'It can creep up on you,' he said.

I was definitely going to cry if he kept looking at me as if he was my concerned uncle or something. 'Are you a doctor?' I said. He didn't look like a doctor.

He shook his head as if that was a really weird idea. 'No, I'm an engineer,' he said.

'Bridges and things?' I said. Sciency subjects were never my strong point.

'Not exactly,' he said. 'My background was in engineering but now I work in the field of appropriate technology.'

'That sounds interesting,' I said, which wasn't strictly true. I was just being polite.

'Yes,' he said. 'We adapt and develop techniques and technology to local needs.'

I nodded in a 'please tell me more' kind of way. He didn't really need any encouragement though. He was off. He talked in the sort of language that can be hard to get the meaning out of when you don't have the background. He'd seemed exotic in his desert garb materialising out of the dark but now he was on his thing he came over as a bit of a geek. I let him chunter on. The stallholders were packing up. A woman who'd been cooking over a little stove stood up and stretched. She bent low with flattened back and untied the cloth around her middle so that her baby, curled asleep on her spine, was exposed. Then she flapped the cloth back over him, retied it tightly and straightened up. She flipped the stool she'd been sitting on upside down, balanced a bowl of leftover stuff on top and hoisted the lot on to her head. She made it all look easy.

There was a whining noise somewhere far off. It sounded like one of the screechy little mopeds that teenage boys back home screech about on. I realised that all this time we'd been on the roadside not a single vehicle had gone by. The whining got louder and sure enough a moped came screaming along. The driver was a full-on Tuareg: blue robes, white headgear wrapped round so that only his eyes showed, silver glinting at his throat. The white guy shouted and waved at him and he pulled up further along, glanced over his shoulder at us, turned the bike round, scooted back and turned the engine off.

'Two minutes,' the white guy said. The Tuareg inclined his head and sat waiting in a majestic way as if he were astride a camel.

'Have a good time in Bamako,' the guy said, holding out his hand.

'Aren't you coming?' I said dumbly.

He shook his head. 'No. I'm going with my friend here.'

He pressed a card into my hand. *Louis Hendrick*, it said. *Environmental Engineer*. There was an address on it too. 'Come and visit the project if you're in the Djenné area,' he said.

I hung my head, fingering the card in my hand. I couldn't speak. I didn't even know the guy and here I was on the verge of bursting into tears because he was leaving.

'You have got somewhere to stay in Bamako, haven't you?' he said.

Before I could answer there was a great trumpeting blare that made me jump, and the bus roared back into our midst with a techno beat blasting out. People started to emerge from the stick shelters, smoothing themselves down.

'You're in luck,' Louis said. 'They've fixed the sound system too.' He was grinning. 'No sleep before Bamako for you,' he said.

I looked at his smiley face and then at the people queueing up to get on the bus. 'No,' I said. 'I haven't got anywhere to stay in Bamako.' Then I blurted out the whole story about leaving Jack on the way to Timbuktu and not having any money and all that.

I didn't really want to come to Africa. I hadn't even heard of Mali six months before. I could never have imagined myself living with an African family in some out-of-the-way village with no running water. That's what I ended up doing for the rest of my time in Mali though, thanks to Louis. The charity that employed him had a sort of office-cum-base in a village on the banks of the Niger River and that's where I worked for a couple of hours each morning, typing up Louis' notes on fuel-efficient cooking stoves and the like. He was elsewhere, travelling round all the villages he was responsible for. He'd got a four-wheel drive but it had broken down and he was waiting for the spare part to arrive. In the meantime he found other ways of getting about. I'd had enough of trekking around. Louis said you learn more about a place by keeping still and watching anyway.

The people of the village, their life was all work, from when they got up in the morning before it was light, until it got dark. The women treated me like an extra daughter. They didn't let me help and so I spent a lot of time playing with the children. Wherever I went children came with me, holding my fingers, stroking my skin and hanging on to my arms or bits of my clothing. I taught them to play grandmother's footsteps and they showed me a game like chequers they played with stones.

The villagers were waiting for the rains. They couldn't plough the land otherwise. The men hung about under the central tree, a giant baobab, leaning on their sticks or their hoes, muttering and then falling silent, looking at the sky for signs. The rains should have come by now. Louis had told me about desertification. The desert was creeping up on the village. The grasses were receding. I sat basting in my hut typing up his notes on 'Greening the Sahel'. When my hands got slippery with sweat on the keyboard I'd look out at the dry red expanse of land, wrinkled like decrepit skin. Good luck to him, I thought. How could anything besides the thorny bushes and blackened trees that were already there ever find the strength to push up through that hard earth?

When we ate, it was so dark I couldn't see what I was putting in my mouth. I was always hungry and then quickly full. I was on the outermost rim of the world, a place not forgotten but never known. The world was turning and turning about us, and I sat among these people on the edge, tucked into the big dark as if it were a cosy blanket.

One afternoon, me and the kids were playing hide-and-seek in the long grasses and trees near the riverbank. I crouched with two toddlers in a hollow behind a mango tree. I was watching the child who was the seeker, Kadi, head sunk in her hands so she couldn't peek. She'd only got to twenty or thereabouts, when she dropped her hands, stopped counting and raised her head. I was going to rise up from our hiding place and tell her off but something stopped me. She sniffed the air. She tipped her head to the sky and I followed her gaze. There were clouds moving in fast from over the hills.

A little wind swept my face. No more than a breeze. I stood up, pulling the little ones in to my side and holding them there. The women were coming back from the fields.

The wind got up and I leaned into it, the children clasped against my legs. The returning women started to run, the rain splattering their unprotected bodies, the bright fabric of their clothes flapping about them and slapping the air, their bare feet sinking into the quickly forming mud, babies bouncing on their backs.

Small mangoes from the upper branches started to fall around me. The other kids came hurtling through the frothing air to scoop the fruit up in their shirts and the little children let go of my legs and ran about in the drenching rain, laughing. I stood in the torrent as the rain plummeted from the darkening sky. My skirt and T-shirt were plastered to my skin. It was as if I were naked in the huge wet and I cackled like a demon among the cavorting children. Then I ran for cover. The office was one of the few buildings with an intact roof. It was packed and steamy. We watched from inside the shelter; the wind tore branches from the trees and flung them down.

After an hour or so, the weather calmed and fires were lit. A soft rain fell throughout the night and into the next day. In the morning the men began ploughing the fields.

Dakar

Dakar, Senegal, 2005

Adele spotted her man leaning against a pillar. The piece of
cardboard he'd scribbled her name on dangled from his hand
and he had a peaked white kepi, pulled down over his eyes.
When she tapped his shoulder, he snorted, pushing his hat
up his forehead.

'Were you asleep?' she asked in French. She hadn't been
in a French-speaking country for so long that it felt strange,
like play-acting. The man raised his eyebrows so they disappeared under the brim of his hat. She smiled at him to
show she was making a joke because no one could sleep in
the midst of the hullabaloo of Dakar airport.

'Yes,' he said. He sighed and made a tutting noise. 'I was
sleeping.' He spoke as if his rest was well deserved and Adele
had woken him for her own selfish purposes at an unseason-
able hour. He rubbed his eyes, rearranged his hat, indicated
with an inverted beckoning motion that Adele should keep
close and elbowed his way into the crowd. By the time she'd
picked up her bag and slung it on to her shoulder, the flow
of people had already closed behind him. She joined it, trying

to steer herself in the direction of his bobbing white hat, resisting the guides, porters, taxi drivers, money changers and more porters.

Someone grabbed her arm and held her. 'Elephants and snakes,' he hissed into her ear. 'I'll take you to wild elephants.' She came to a halt, overwhelmed by the press of people. Her throat constricted. There were fingers inside her pocket.

Then the man with the white kepi was at her side. He reached for her bag and swung it on to his head, simultaneously flipping the back of his hand against the elephant man's ear and batting the pickpocket away. 'Come on,' he said. 'Stay with me.' He pushed off into the crowd again, one hand held up to steady the bag, swivelling every now and then to make sure Adele was behind him. Each time he found her still there, he gave an encouraging nod and made a slight inclination of his torso, a half-bow as if commending her for playing her part. They might have been dancing an ancient ritual dance.

He led her through the melee and out into the blinding afternoon sun. She followed him like a blinkered horse, keeping at bay the colours and the smells, the noises of music and revving machinery, the shouting like someone with a megaphone and all that confusing jostle, his upright presence her only focus. They came to his car, an old grey Peugeot guarded by two small boys whom he paid with a shining spin of a coin. Someone had hand-painted a word along the side of the car, in slashes of black and red, but she couldn't read it. It wasn't the name of the hotel.

He was watching her. 'It's mine,' he said.

She nodded.

'"Safarika". It's my business.'

The black paint had run into congealed trickles, adding extra tails to the 'a's so they looked like 'g's. 'What does your business do?'

He looked up at the sky for guidance, tutting in the back of his throat. Adele's face felt hot. 'I take tourists on safari in my car,' he said eventually.

'That's a really good name,' Adele said. She nodded enthusiastically. 'Brilliant.'

'I'm Napoleon,' he said, touching his hand to his chest. He wore silver rings on two of his long fingers.

'Adele,' she said.

He took the hand she held out but, instead of shaking it, he did some complicated high-fiving, thumb-pressing, finger-entwining routine. 'That's how we do it in Senegal,' he said.

'Things have changed since I lived here then,' she muttered as he swung her bag into the back of the car.

'To the hotel?' he asked, when they were seated, a look of genuine enquiry on his face, which was now wide awake under the squashed hat.

Adele imagined being whisked away to a vast savannah, led to a shelter in the shade of a giant baobab. She swallowed, her throat constricting again. 'Yes, the hotel please,' she said.

'Is it your first time in Senegal?' he asked as he pulled out. His mobile phone rang before she could protest that she'd lived here for six years as a child. She wasn't just a tourist. She was here to find a friend and to make amends.

Napoleon drove fast one-handed, his mobile phone clamped

to the side of his head. He let go of the wheel to change gear, then jerked the veering vehicle back on track, all the while making complicated arrangements to meet someone to pick up a delivery. He spoke in fast French with the odd phrase in a language she didn't recognise thrown in. Adele sat bolt upright, her hands clasped around the sides of her seat, staring wide-eyed out of the streaked windscreen.

A minibus was struggling along in the fast lane in front of them, belching black smoke. It was one of Dakar's *cars rapides*, the Renault vans that coughed their way around the city transporting passengers. Their blue-and-yellow colours threaded the fabric of her memory of the city. This one was obviously a survivor from that time. The metal bodywork had been dented and banged back into shape so often that it had a tin-can consistency. Mostly, when she was little, her father drove them about. If he was away or the car at the garage, they got taxis. There was no call for her family to suffer the discomfort and danger of the *cars rapides*. She remembered only one occasion when she had to squeeze on to her mum's knee although she was too big and her head was pressed against the van's ceiling. Louis had crouched next to them in the space beside the side door. People shouted out when they wanted to get off. Then the conductor, the apprentice they called him, would signal to the driver to stop by banging on the bodywork. When it was their turn their mum had let out a squawk and Louis had rolled his eyes.

Napoleon drove right up behind this one. He wedged the phone between his ear and hunched shoulder so that he could jam his hand on the horn, all the while keeping up his conversation. The apprentice, a young man in purple trousers and a yellow T-shirt, balanced improbably on the running board at the back of the swaying bus, made shooing gestures and wagged his finger like a schoolteacher at a naughty child. Napoleon nudged the car very close and then let it drop back. The apprentice slapped the chassis, like a rodeo rider urging his steed to greater effort, and the bus rumbled on, neither faster nor slower but with more of a lurch. Napoleon repeated his manoeuvre. The people crammed in the minibus started trying to turn their heads to watch what was going on, lifting their arms to create room to twist round in the cramped space. There was a wailing noise within the car like the yowl of a trapped cat. Napoleon clicked his tongue against his teeth gleefully as he drove the car close again. The minibus was higher off the ground so that the boy on the running board appeared suspended just above them. He lifted one leg in a threatening gesture as if he would stamp through their windscreen. His purple trousers billowed.

Napoleon held the car's position, mirroring the pitch and roll of the minibus, his head at a sharp tilt with the phone still clamped into the side of his neck, driving like a possessed gargoyle. The boy, his mouth wide open in laughter or a scream, drummed urgently with his fingers and the palm of his hand on the bodywork. Suddenly they were jamming up too close and there was a slight jolt of impact before Napoleon stamped on the brake. They skidded, the squeal of the tyres joining the other noise which Adele now identifed as coming from her. She clamped a hand over her mouth to stifle it.

Napoleon's phone flew out sideways, hit Adele's arm, fell to the floor and smashed. He wrested control of the wheel and they dropped back to a safer distance. He glanced over at Adele who quickly bent to retrieve the bits of phone. She composed her face before she sat back up. There were grooves across the palms of her hands where she'd been hanging on.

The minibus had shifted into the other lane and they were finally overtaking. The passengers crammed inside laughed and waved as they shot past. Adele twisted in her seat to look back. Across the front of the bus a word was painted in white capital letters. ALHAMDULILLAH, she read. In God we trust.

'He's a madman, that apprentice,' Napoleon said, shaking his head.

'Not the only one,' she said.

'You're right. This country is full of madmen,' he said, making his percussive noise.

Adele slotted the battery back into the phone and handed it back. 'In my country it's against the law to talk on a mobile phone while you're driving,' she said.

'It's the same thing here,' he said. The phone rang. 'So sorry,' he said, 'I lost the connection.' He resumed his negotiating.

The city as they approached was much more of a metropolis than she remembered, a conglomeration of white high-rise buildings shimmering in the heat haze. They passed the square tower of the central mosque's minaret and turned into a wide tree-lined boulevard, Napoleon still talking on his mobile. Boulevard de l'Indépendance, she said to herself. They turned down a narrower street where, amid the stop and start of the traffic, the cacophony of horns reached a climax. She closed her eyes against the hubbub. She smelt acrid fumes laced with sweet spicy cooking, smoke, rubbish and something underneath it all, more pungent and visceral, a hot and anarchic aroma.

Napoleon finished his phone conversation just as they turned into a yard halfway along a road of dilapidated tower blocks and warehouses. Adele had booked her room online. It was one of the cheaper of the budget hotels in Dakar. She'd had an extended email conversation with Madame the proprietor in which Madame had promised to give her a welcome '*à l'africaine*'. Adele had imagined a little home from home. In the contact information she'd left with Joe and his dad, she'd given the hotel telephone number. 'My base in Dakar' she'd called it. She took in the unfinished two-storey concrete construction partially painted in pink and orange geometric blocks, the earth yard bare but for a dusty palm tree, the pile of grey rubbish in the corner like the spilled contents of a giant Hoover bag. There was a sweet farmyard-and-rot smell and a humming noise in the air. She inhaled through her mouth.

Napoleon had set her bag down and was running on the spot next to his car, pumping his bare, muscly arms and lifting his knees comically high like a cop chasing a robber in a silent movie. His trousers hung dangerously low on his hips, the gap between them and his vest alternately widening and shrinking again, revealing his torso, the skin sleek and black as if it had been French-polished. His crumpled hat hung off the back of his head.

'Is this it?' Adele said. Her voice was shrill.

Still pumping, he looked at her questioningly.

'This is my hotel?' she said. She extended her arm, palm open, to indicate the debris, the pall of disuse and neglect.

He stopped running, hitched his trousers up and looked around in a bright, quizzical way. 'Yes, yes,' he said. He nodded at the dusty tree. 'This is the hotel garden,' he said. 'You can sit under that tree when it's hot.' He turned back to her and smiled. 'OK?'

Adele pressed her lips together and nodded.

'OK, I'm off,' he said, opening the car door.

There was a tightness in Adele's chest. She didn't want to be abandoned in this abandoned place. She cast around for something to make him stay. 'Could you recommend anywhere nice to eat near here?' she said in a voice so high it bordered on a squeak. He looked out of the gates towards where she was flapping her arm at the warehouse opposite, as if it might conceal a row of bistros and other eating establishments.

'Nooo,' he said, stretching the word over three syllables. 'You don't want to go out.'

'Yes I do,' she said, consciously lowering her voice.

He looked at her very directly then, appraising her. 'Madame has cooked meat for you,' he said, nodding in the direction of the shuttered reception area.

'I'm a vegetarian,' Adele said.

He sucked air in through his teeth. He nodded slowly as if he'd thought as much. His phone rang. 'I'm coming now,' he said into it. To Adele he said, 'She's cooked vegetables too.' He laid his hand on her arm briefly and looked at it, admiring the effect of the contrasting skin tones. He let go and swung back into his car, pulling the door to and holding the phone to his ear. The heat of the imprint of his hand lingered on her arm. 'Tomorrow, I'll take you out. We'll go dancing,' he said. Adele wasn't sure if he was speaking to her or not. Then he drove off.

Madame was nowhere to be seen. The sulky girl who took her details didn't make eye contact. Adele's room was on the first floor. It had a shut-in smell of cigarettes and dirty fabric and old wood. The window was set too high for her to see out. A piece of torn linoleum lay in the middle of the concrete floor. The walls were painted dried-blood brown. As well as the bed and some hooks, there was a small wooden sofa with brown cushions, the stuffing protruding. The place made her want to run amok.

Instead, she dragged the sofa across the room, climbed on to the arm and grappled with the window which gave on to the courtyard. The window had been painted shut. She resisted a desire to smash her fists against it. She got down and fished out the birthday present Joe had given her from the bottom of her bag. Although she knew already it was a Swiss army knife, because they'd gone together to buy it with his saved-up pocket money and a donation from Granny Claire, she unpacked it carefully. He'd wrapped it in a picture he'd drawn: a boy in shorts on a hill waving at a plane. *Come back soon, Mum*, the speech bubble said. Three weeks. She had never been away from her boy for such a length of time. She sat back on her heels smoothing the picture out on her knees. In the bottom right-hand corner he'd written something in tiny letters. She held it up to her face. *To the best mum in the wold*, it said. Was that a joke or was his spelling really that bad? She stood up, smiling.

The knife had a corkscrew attachment, a bottle-opener and a nail file as well as a range of blades and other devices with less obvious functions. She selected a suitable-looking one and chipped away at the paint for ten minutes until she was able to shove the window open. It wouldn't stay so she propped it ajar with a pen. The air outside was as hot as the air inside, but at least it had some movement and a faint salty tang. To celebrate her handiwork, she lit a cigarette and smoked it through the gap. In the yard below, the girl from reception was sweeping dirt towards the pile. In a smaller yard off to the side, a tin-roofed shelter housed three small goats and a generator. Her cigarette was one of the rare delicious ones that made smoking worthwhile. She was glad she'd decided against using this trip to have a go at giving up. Between the big building opposite and the smaller one next to it, a block of flats with different-coloured balconies, she caught a glimpse of darker blue. The sea. She blew smoke in its direction.

She turned and surveyed the room, looking for other things that needed mending. She was humming the tune of *Bob the Builder*. 'Can she fix it? Yes she can,' she sang sotto voce. The air-conditioning unit was half hanging off the wall. She'd tighten that up before she went down to dinner.

Later on, she ate as much as she could of a plate of omelette and chips in the murky dining room. The other guests, all men, all African, had just finished and were leaving as she arrived. They greeted her with respectful nods. The meal was fine, although there were no vegetables, but her stomach baulked at the notion of food. She bought a big bottle of water and asked about beer. The hotel didn't stock alcohol. 'But it's my birthday,' she said to the man who was serving. He shook his head with great solemnity. Then he wished her a happy birthday and much joy in the coming year for her and her family. He offered her a banana.

When she sat back down she wondered if she'd offended him by asking, if he was, perhaps, very devout or a member of some sect. She knew it wasn't Ramadan but it might be some other religious festival where the mere mention of alcohol would cause offence. The man wore a long white boubou over baggy trousers. On his head was a black-and-white skullcap. There was something monkish in the way he flowed silently in and out of the room collecting dishes and laying tables. She couldn't crash into other people's culture in this unthinking way. She made up her mind to apologise but he had entirely disappeared.

She stepped out into the deserted courtyard. Night had fallen while she was eating. A yellowish moon hung low in the sky. Someone hissed at her from the stairwell and her heart raced. She made out the man's pale clothes, luminous in the darkness, before she saw his face. He had a carrier bag in his hand. He held it open to her. Inside were three bottles of beer. They both laughed. His teeth gleamed in the moonlight. She handed over a wad of CFA francs and headed upstairs.

She sat like a castaway on the ruined sofa in the small

yellow circle of the overhead light, her legs drawn up underneath. The low-wattage bulb melted the edges of the room away into shapeless semi-darkness. She smoked two cigarettes in a row and took a photo of herself surrounded by empty bottles. She toasted her wan image on the screen.

She thought she would never get to sleep. She lay ghostlike and outwardly still beneath the white mosquito net while her heart pounded as if in a hurry to get it all over, hurtling at double time towards her end. At some point, though, she must have slept because she awoke in the darkness, parched and, for a moment, ignorant of her whereabouts, unable to decipher the meaning of the monstrous groans and puffs that the air conditioning emitted. Like sleeping with a snoring giant in the room, she said to herself. It reminded her of the comforting hum of the fridge in her childhood home. Here I am again, she thought. She drained the water from her bottle and after that she slept very soundly, as if the giant was keeping watch.

Over the next few days Adele embarked on the purpose of her visit: the hunt for Ellena. Her days in the city assumed a pattern. Every morning she'd set off into the Dakar hubbub that started at the end of the eerily quiet street on which the hotel was situated. She'd clamber into *cars rapides* and taxis or pick her way along crowded streets, clutching her bag to her chest and saying 'no thank you, no thank you' to the street sellers and potential guides that dogged her every step. She made her way to the places on her list: the Methodist church her father said George had frequented, Ellena's old school, the Liberian consulate, asking questions and receiving blank faces in answer. Back in England, despite the lack of response to all of her exploratory letters, the list had seemed full of promise. Any one of its locations might have generated a whole new list. But on the ground in Dakar each avenue turned out to be a dead end. Perhaps her father, who'd tried to dissuade her from coming at all and warned her it was a wild goose chase, had been right. She didn't feel like a veteran returning to a place she had once lived. She felt surprised and disconcerted by how poor and dusty and shabby it all was, by the gulleys choked with rubbish she glimpsed up side streets, the tumbledown accumulation of shacks in between more solid buildings squeezed along the roadside, some of them pushed out and spilling almost into the road for lack of space. The school was the most shocking. There seemed to be hundreds of children in each class and the teacher shouted to be heard above the noise of rain on the tin roof.

Every afternoon, before the sun went down, she would return to the hotel and fling herself sweatily on to the bed. She would have it in mind that after a shower and a rest she would at least make herself go out and eat at a restaurant on the seafront, but the bench under the palm tree with a bottle of beer had acquired a strange attraction. It wasn't that she was waiting in for Napoleon, it was just nice and quiet there under the tree. She watched the comings and goings of the other guests. They were all construction workers employed to build a new banking headquarters downtown. They rose early and went to bed early. Their voices and laughter from the dining room when they ate their evening meal together would ring out into the yard, but she couldn't decipher their words. That was how it was. She reached for understanding and she missed. When the teacher she spoke to at Ellena's old school shook her head and then gave a sidelong look, there might have been meaning in her look but Adele couldn't interpret it. The teacher had examined the photo and agreed it was indeed the same school, but there were no records from that time.

Adele would catch a glimpse of something down a side road, a tall woman in red swaying with a full bowl on her head, men playing cards under a tree at the dusty edge of the pavement, and think that there was the Africa she remembered, but then it slipped away and she was a stranger again. She thought of the feel of his hand on her arm, the smoothness of his skin, his hat at the airport, a white beacon to follow.

On the fourth day she set off for the island of Goree. She left much later in the day than she intended for no good reason at all. But, as soon as she was on the ferry, the sea breeze wafting over her, hope surged in her stomach, as if the city had stifled her and now she was on track again.

She had the Goree address from her father. He had been reluctant to part with it for reasons she couldn't fathom but, when pressed, he'd dug it out. He said it was the last place where George had worked and she had written letters both to the occupants and to George himself prior to setting off from England, explaining what she was doing and giving all of her contact details. She'd had no reply. It was fifteen years since her father had heard from him, he said, but still, walking up the hill, the hopefulness persisted. Bright painted houses with sky-blue shutters on narrow cobbled streets swept clean. Everywhere there were trees, palm trees lining the wider walkway near the jetty and trees with feathery leaves dipping over her, dappling the paths she walked along. In the spaces between houses and over roofs, beyond the green fuzz of the wooded areas was the sharp blue glitter of the ocean. The air had a freshness and the sounds were birdsong and the sea. There were no cars on the island.

Goree gave scope for fantasy. If I moved back to Senegal, Adele thought for the first time since she'd arrived, perhaps I would live here on this island, and in the morning I would stop at this little shop and buy a bun and a coffee and eat my breakfast sitting on this bench, waiting for the ferry to take me to the mainland to work.

The house was a colonial-style villa on the crest of the hill. The woman who answered the door had no knowledge of George. She was a scarily smart Nigerian, purple-red lipstick, high heels, a skirt so tight it squeezed the curve of her buttocks, gold chains round her neck, fingers and wrists, eyebrows plucked into a perfect arch, her hair straightened into a stiff dramatic bob. She and her husband had lived there for five years, she said. They'd inherited staff from the previous people, a British family, but they'd had to sack them all bar the garden boy because they were very lax and overpaid. Spoilt. The nightwatchman they'd dismissed had not been called George, however. She was unable to supply the name of this family but said she thought they'd gone back to the UK.

'You British don't know how to handle your staff,' she said. 'Not like you used to in the old times. You've lost your spirit, my husband says, always apologising for the wrongs of colonialism.' She dipped her head in a kowtowing gesture.

Adele recognised some of her own and her family's attitude in this description. 'Where's he from, your husband?' she asked, keeping her voice neutral.

'Brighton,' the woman said.

Adele nodded and smiled apologetically. 'Would it be possible to speak to your gardener?'

The woman curled her nose in irritation. 'You won't get any sense out of him,' she said. 'He only speaks to plants.'

Dieudonné, the garden boy, a man somewhere way beyond sixty, was crouched behind his hut at the end of the garden, dribbling water from a handleless teapot on to tiny yellow shoots. He wore a yellow T-shirt with the words 'Key West' emblazoned in orange across his back, and baggy shorts. His knees were wider than his thighs, like knobbly nodes on thin branches. He didn't look up as Adele approached as if he were lost in his work, absorbed to the exclusion of all else in concentration on the life of these sickly saplings. Perhaps it was this dedication that had saved him in his job when all the others had been sent packing.

With the mistress of the house standing at her side, Adele greeted the old man in Wolof and then in French. The woman beside her let out a long-suffering sigh. The gardener turned his face up and looked vaguely in Adele's direction, like a blind person directing his eyes to the place from which a voice emanated, before dropping his gaze back to the earth again.

That way of being simultaneously looked at and not gave Adele an insubstantial feeling, as if she existed in a different dimension to this man. While Adele explained about George and how he might have been working here in the house when he, Dieudonné, had started, he placed the broken teapot gently down and pushed his fingers into the earth, wriggling them down like worms. When she paused, he shook his head.

'Did you know George Barthes?' she asked. The man shook his head again, wiggling his planted fingers so the earth erupted around them.

'I told you,' the woman said and went back into the house.

'You might have known him by a different name,' Adele persisted.

He made no response to this suggestion at all. He seemed to be in abeyance, waiting for her to exit his domain and leave him alone. Adele reminded herself that she was running out of leads. She crouched down, consciously pressing herself into the man's space. She fetched out the ancient, creased photo of Ellena at school and held it out. He freed one hand from the earth, wiped it laboriously on his trouser leg and took the photo.

Adele became hopeful again. 'This is his daughter, taken a long time ago,' she said. 'George was tall with a broad face.' She faltered. How to describe an African to another African she didn't know. 'He was quite light-skinned,' she said tentatively. 'Not like you,' was what she meant. 'He would have been in his forties I should think when I knew him so he would be an old man now and his daughter is about the same age as me. She is about my height and she wears her hair in little plaits sometimes.' Adele stopped. It was his silence that was making her prattle senselessly on. She could be describing half the women in West Africa. 'They are from Liberia,' she threw out.

The gardener creaked upwards to his feet and Adele was obliged to do the same. He held out the photo to her. He was shorter than Adele. When she looked into his face, it was like looking down into a dark well, trying to make out if there was water at the bottom, expecting a glint of light on a ripple, but finding total blackness. She took the photo and put it back into her wallet.

'Go home,' he said.

'Pardon?' she said.

'Go home,' he said in a louder voice, then he bent and picked up his teapot, and Adele, dismissed, made her exit around the side of the house and out the front gate so that she didn't have to see the Nigerian woman again.

Her legs felt shaky on the walk back down the hill and the sun was beating down on her head. She stopped to look round and back up towards the house to check that she was following the lane down to the place where the ferry docked. She had thought on the way over that she would explore the island after her business was done; she would go to the *Maison des Esclaves* where slaves had been held before being dispatched across the ocean. She had been there once as a child with her father. There was a door that opened straight on to the sea way down below. The door of no return. She retained the image of that doorway framing a rectangle of perfect innocent blue.

She stopped at the little kiosk where she bought and drank a bottle of sickly Orange Fanta and ate two soft cakes that came in a twist of polythene. It was the kind of thing that never passed her lips when she was in Britain, but she needed a shot of sugar to give her strength, to stop her from crying. The sweetness on her tongue and then the fizz up her nose took her back. She pictured the entrance to their house in Dakar, the blue-painted garden doors with the iron bolts and the explosion of purple flowers tumbling over the fence and down to the ground.

It had been her intention to visit her old home. It was on her list. But she'd made the list when she was back in England, before she'd learned what hard work doing anything at all was in the heat, with the torpor and the ever-changing retinue of helpful assistants, and, at some point, she'd mentally crossed it off.

The taxi passed a sign for her old neighbourhood but she wouldn't have known the way. The world she'd explored independently as a child was limited to the network of streets where they lived and to the wasteland at the bottom of the garden. Even of the regular journeys she'd made to destinations further afield, to school or church or the clubhouse swimming pool, she only retained snatches – a tree that grew at an angle, a green tin roof, a shop with mattresses piled in front of it, a Shell garage with palm trees in the forecourt – and had no idea how these places were connected. In the intervening years businesses must have come and gone, buildings been removed and erected, new roads built and flows of traffic altered, but she found herself trying to believe that there was something familiar about the slope of a side street or the configuration of a set of stalls and the low-slung loop of the telephone wires above. And then, without her realising when it had happened, she saw that it really was the main road near her old house. She had to resist an urge to lean forward and say 'Right at the lights' to the taxi driver to show she knew this place and to claim it as hers. They turned into her old road and it was exactly the same. It was so very much the same that, as she stepped from the taxi, she spun with vertigo.

The road was just a track between high concrete walls broken up by iron and wooden gates, but the pink, purple and red bougainvillea dripping over the walls, softening the edges, creating different shapes and patches of shade, turned it into something lovely, and it was this loveliness that she remembered and that caught at her. There was even a table set against the wall further down where a group of men were playing cards just as the nightwatchmen used to do when she was a girl. She walked along the edge of the track, trailing her hand along the wall. When she came to her old gates, she didn't pause. She wasn't ready to look yet. She went straight past heading for the end of the road where the wasteland was. She half expected her own child self to come running out to meet her. The men at the table went quiet for a moment as she swept by.

Around the corner at the end of the road where sandy paths had criss-crossed a wilderness of scrub and where tall grasses whipped at your legs as you ran, an estate of one- and two-storeyed houses had sprung up. They didn't look new. Suddenly, the years that had passed weighed down on her. There was a hollowness in her chest. She was bereft, as if those years had been snatched away, not lived.

She turned and walked slowly back along the road. She stopped at the card table and the men looked up. There were five of them. Three wore a kind of uniform. Behind them another man, younger and dressed in T-shirt and jeans, leaned against the wall, one knee bent, talking into a mobile phone. She greeted the men and they returned her greeting. The man on the phone raised his voice, gesticulating with his free hand. Adele saw that he was watching her. He'd upped the volume for her benefit.

She addressed the oldest of the men at the table. 'I used to live here,' she said.

'*Soyez la bienvenue,*' he said, welcoming her back. The others nodded in assent, welcoming her too.

She pointed to the house. A Saudi family was living there now, they said. She told her story. None of them knew of George and Ellena. They had never heard of them. '*Désolé, madame,*' they said.

As she took her leave, the man who'd been on the phone peeled himself out from under the bougainvillea. He was a slight young man, with a lopsided smile. His teeth were chalky. They looked breakable. 'Can I help you?' he said as if she'd just walked into his shop. The older man at the table glanced up at the boy and then at Adele. He gave an almost imperceptible shake of his head. Adele deduced that he was warning her off.

'No, thank you,' she said and walked on. The ground at

the road edge was soft underfoot. Tall trees growing behind the walls cast their shadows out in black wavering bands across the hummocked surface to the other side and up the opposite walls. She saw now that there were patches of tarmac pocking the surface of the track like scabs. It must have known a grander period at some point in the intervening years before it had reverted to dirt again. The young man fell into step beside her. He had a restlessness about him, a pent-up energy as if he wanted to move much faster. 'Boubacar can help you find the person,' he said.

'Who?' she said, not turning to look at him, wishing him away.

'The man you seek,' he said.

She slowed as they approached the wall that hid her old house. 'You used to live here,' he said. They had both come to a halt outside the gates. The blue paint had peeled away in patches revealing the metal beneath. The hinges were heavy with rust. 'Boubacar remembers you.'

'What?' she said. She turned to look at him. He nodded at her, making little twitching movements with his scant eyebrows. She shook her head. 'Who is this Boubacar? I don't know Boubacar.'

'I'm Boubacar,' he said. 'Me.'

'Oh,' she said. She considered him. He screwed his nose up and drew his chin in. She didn't know what to make of his facial expressions. They communicated nothing to her. 'You're too young. It's twenty-five years since I lived here.'

'Boubacar is older than he looks,' he said. He laughed and she saw his fragile little yellow-and-white teeth again. 'My mother worked in one of the houses. I used to play down there after school.' He waved his hand towards the end of the road where it had been scrubland. 'I waited for her to finish work.'

Adele recalled the gangs of children playing football behind the house. Their shrieks and calls in the afternoon sun. She recalled as if out of the corner of her eye little kids sitting waiting in the dust against the wall or under the table where the watchmen played cards. She hadn't paid them any mind. It sounded plausible but he did look too young. 'Do you remember our nightwatchman, George?' she asked.

'George?' he said, narrowing his eyes as if questioning her memory.

'He was Liberian. He didn't work here for very long.'

'Ah yes. George. The nightwatchman,' he said. 'He returned to Liberia, I think. Now that there's peace.'

This fitted with what her father had suggested. They walked on and turned the corner at the far end of the street, going towards the main road. Boubacar busied himself with his phone, getting it out of his pocket and examining it, pressing some keys, sighing, returning it to his pocket. 'I'm waiting for a call,' he said.

'When did George go? Did you see him?' Adele asked.

He shook his head. 'I'm thirsty,' he said. They were outside a shop.

'Can I offer you a drink?' Adele said. She followed him into the store, past shelves of rice in bags and tinned fish and out the back through plastic strip curtains to a yard where there was an upturned oil drum and four stools. A bright green fishing umbrella attached at an angle to the wall provided some shade. A girl in a tight yellow dress appeared and Boubacar asked for a beer. 'I'll have beer too,' Adele said.

The girl came back with two cold bottles of *Gazelle*, two glasses and a spoon. Boubacar poured his beer vertically so that the froth half filled the glass. He added some powder from a sachet in his pocket and stirred it in. The froth and the liquid below it turned red. He ate the froth quickly with the spoon before sucking up the remaining liquid. Then he emptied the remainder of the beer into his glass and repeated the process. The girl brought him another bottle. He poured it out as before and set it back down on the oil drum in front of him. He looked across at Adele and nodded. 'So you didn't see George before he went,' she said.

He took another slurp and licked his lips. 'I don't know this man George but another old man who watched the *toubab* houses a long time ago. George said goodbye to that old man.' He nodded and spooned more froth into his mouth.

'Do you know where I can find that old man?' she asked.

'He's gone,' he said. His face closed down. He took another swig of his drink and rallied. 'I was going to Europe once. To Spain,' he said. 'They all drowned but I knew how to swim.'

'Oh dear,' Adele said. 'That's awful.'

They sat in silence for a while. She couldn't think what else to say. 'What about George's daughter, Ellena?' she said eventually.

He waved his frothy spoon in front of his face and licked

his lips thoughtfully. 'In my opinion,' he said, 'that girl married a Senegalese man.'

'In your opinion?'

He took his mobile phone out of his pocket. It hadn't rung. 'No,' he said into it. 'I'm very busy with an important client. Don't disturb me.' He put the mobile down on the table and they both looked at it.

'And did she go back to Liberia with her father?'

He picked the phone up again and shouted into it. 'Didn't I tell you?' He blew air out in a pantomime of extreme exasperation. 'She's married to a Senegalese man so she stays in Senegal,' he said to Adele. His voice was thickening and his eyes seemed to roll in his head.

He stood up and gave himself a body-popping shake. He moon-walked around the table and then positioned himself under the umbrella and began again. 'If a foreign woman marries a Senegalese man, then she follows him wherever he goes. She no longer belongs to her father but to the man she's married. She no longer belongs to her birth country but to Senegal. This is how it is.' He slumped back on to his stool and drained the dregs of his drink.

'I understand,' Adele said. She glanced around to see where the girl had gone. 'And where did Ellena and her husband go?'

'To Ziguinchor,' he said, naming the main town in the south of the country, in the region of Casamance. 'She was a teacher.'

'And they live there now?' she said, her voice rising.

He ran his finger thoughtfully round the inside of his glass to collect the last traces of froth. 'Yes, they live there,' he said.

Adele drew her notebook and a pen from her bag. 'Do you have their address?'

He stuck the frothy finger in his mouth and shook his head.

'Do you know her married name? If they're working?'

He kept shaking his head, more as if he was enjoying swilling it about than in response to anything she was saying. He'd drifted away.

The girl came to collect the glasses. 'He's drunk,' she said to Adele. As if her words gave him permission, Boubacar laid his head on the table and shut his eyes.

'What's that red powder he put in his drink?'

'It's wine,' the girl said.

'Powdered wine?'

The girl nodded.

'I've never heard of such a thing,' Adele said.

'You don't have powdered wine in your country?' the girl asked, amazed.

Adele shook her head.

'And don't you have motorways either?' the girl said.

'We do have motorways,' Adele said.

The girl tilted her chin up and regarded Adele from an angle, the green beer bottles dangling from the fingers of one hand. 'That's nice for you,' she said.

'How old is he?' Adele asked.

The girl shrugged. 'Twenty?' she said.

'I thought he was too young,' Adele said.

'No, no. I mean thirty,' the girl said. 'Or maybe more. Who knows?' She tapped her temple and made a gesture towards

Boubacar's slumped form, indicating that he wasn't right in the head.

'What happened to him?'

'Bad things.' The girl put the bottles down and counted the bad things off on the fingers of one hand. 'Father died. No job. Shipwreck. Lost all his money. Lost his sister.' She picked the bottles up again.

'How did he lose his sister?' Adele said.

'She got trafficked,' the girl said.

Adele thought she'd ask what 'got trafficked' meant, but was suddenly overwhelmed with a feeling of hopelessness and couldn't speak. She paid the bill. She tried to think. If Boubacar was in his thirties, his information might well be accurate. Eyes shut, his head cradled on his hand on the tabletop, he looked no more than a child. The sight of him made her want to cry.

When she scraped her stool back, he raised his head. She took out a 5,000-franc note and handed it to him. 'Thank you for your help,' she said. 'I'm going to go to Ziguinchor to look for Ellena.'

He stood up unsteadily and gave himself another shake, an eel-like motion quivering through his body. He pushed the money back. 'Boubacar will take you to Ziguinchor,' he said.

'No thank you,' she said firmly.

'I know many people in Ziguinchor. You don't need to pay me.' He shook his head and widened his bloodshot eyes at her. 'No, no, madame. No payment because me, Boubacar,' he pressed two fingers to his collarbone and swallowed, 'I'm your friend.' He waved his fingers in the air.

'Very kind. But I will make my own arrangements.'

He picked up his phone and held it up. 'I know a good driver.'

'I'm meeting up with my brother. We'll go together.' She took out another note and laid it next to the first. 'Do you know what he was called? The man Ellena married,' she asked.

He took a step towards her. He looked at her and then his gaze swivelled away. The whites of his eyes were yellow. 'It was Abdou,' he mumbled. 'Abdou Ndiaye.' He picked up the banknotes and stuffed them into his pocket, a defeated look on his drunken face.

Adele wanted to leave quickly now. She wanted to shake off any responsibility for this man's sadness, his failed attempts to better himself, all the doors closed to him. She couldn't bear to see him mouth into his dud phone again.

He took another step towards her and breathed fumes. Adele stood her ground. She wondered where the girl from the shop was. He did smell of wine.

'I'm going now,' she said.

'That woman Ellena,' he said. 'She's dead.'

'What do you mean?' Adele said.

'She died. Long time ago.' He staggered to the barrel and sat back down.

Adele shook her head. 'No,' she said. 'She can't be dead.'

Boubacar shrugged. 'Dead,' he said. 'Aids.'

Adele turned away. She walked through the shop and out into the street. A man greeted her from a doorway. 'Hey,' he called.

She kept walking, didn't look at him.

He fell into step beside her. 'Hey, my friend. You've got troubles. I can take you to a healer.'

Adele ignored him. She wasn't far from the main road where there would be taxis.

'Do you want a taxi? Stay here, I'll call you a taxi.' He put his hand on her arm and she shook him off.

'Go away,' she said.

They were at the main road and she raised her arm to flag a cab.

'Taxi,' the man shouted as one came to a halt. He ran to the door and spoke to the driver. 'Come here, white lady,' he called to Adele. 'Come here, my friend. I have a taxi for you.'

She turned away from him and set off in the opposite direction along the uneven, obstacle-strewn pavement. Cars and buses thundered past, honking their horns. A dirty urban wind picked up some greasy paper and pasted it to her shins.

Resettlement

Ethiopia, 1985

Each night the gunfire is closer. He sleeps in tortured snatches. In his dreams he crawls through an underground tunnel; earth fills his fingernails, the roof presses down on his head, heavy with the weight of the recent dead.

By day he treats the war-wounded. He wasn't meant to get involved with the military. He was supposed to be strictly neutral. He was here to work with the displaced, victims of famine and of the government's resettlement programme. He should be weighing malnourished children, inoculating and medicating their mothers, but the charity evacuated its staff because of the insecurity and the army has taken over. He has stayed on. In the face of danger, Dr Dominic Healey has remained to tend the sick. It was decided in a split second. He'd looked into the face of the man with the helicopter and he saw home. I'm going home, he thought, and with that came a picture of home as he wanted it to be and of his wife waving him off, the look on her face, a kind of shine as if she'd been polished, how she'd held him in her arms and said she was proud of him. It wouldn't work if he slunk back after only a month away. He wouldn't have secured his hero status. He heard himself say, 'I'll stay.' The pilot, before he spun away, looked at him as if he were a madman. 'You're on your own then,' he'd said. Then they'd gone and he was blasted into this bleakness. It exploded around him like dynamite.

The medical staff had had their own compound within the camp, guarded now by government troops in their bright green, Soviet-style uniforms. The officers have taken over the aid workers' bar and he's no longer comfortable drinking there. He spends the evenings in his hut listening to the World Service on a portable radio, pinching his nose against the stench of the latrine just outside. Asrat, the boy detailed as his official helper, who takes his clothes away somewhere unspecified to wash and returns them filthy, the blood ironed and starched into their fibres, who brings him cups of tepid murky liquid he calls tea in the early hours and watches him drink, like a mother watches a baby or a poisoner his victim, sits with him in the half-light from the hurricane lamp. He hates the gloom but at least it hides from Asrat's curious eyes the sight of his indiscriminate weeping when they listen to the news from out there in the world where he once lived. The miners' strike in Britain has ended with defeat for the miners. The new leader of the USSR wants disarmament talks with the Americans. A British journalist is taken hostage in Beirut. The weeping catches him in gusts as if he were a lone sailing ship out in the ocean, tossed and buffeted by unpredictable winds.

In the blasting heat he stitches wounds with shaking hands,

digs out shrapnel, carries out unanaesthetised surgery. There is more than one insurgency across the country, but in this part the rebels are the Eritrean People's Liberation Front, fighting the Ethiopian army for the independence of their land. The doctor uses his skill to patch together the bodies of those his country's enemies support while the refugees he came to help are out of bounds, languishing and starving. Their horns ring out in the early morning as they carry their dead to be buried in shallow graves they scratch out.

Planes occasionally make it through, bringing supplies. When they take off again, he can hardly bear to watch, but can't look away. They are leaving and he's still here. He sees himself running after them, catching hold of the tailboard and hauling himself aboard. He sees the soldiers gunning him down. The imagined reflection of himself as brave and impressive in his wife's and daughter's eyes, the story he might tell them about being the only doctor, the only white man remaining, has faded like a photograph left in the sun, its colours bleeding into the dirt.

He lies on his camp bed. In the whitish columns of dawn light falling through the holes in the corrugated roof, specks of matter and small flying creatures eddy and flutter. They seem to him the outward manifestation of the flutter and gripe inside his body, as if he's been unzipped and has started to leak. He is unsurprised. It's logical that it should be a two-way exchange. He pats his chest as if he could locate the source of the leakage. It's somewhere to the left of his heart, but the hole isn't quite tangible. Today he feels a hollow, a dip he hadn't noticed before, as if his bones are caving in.

He gets to his feet, steps over Asrat's sleeping body and lifts the flap of hide that serves as a door. Beyond the barbed-wire fence surrounding the inner compound, the tent city stretches out on the arid plain. He hears a click and turns. A soldier stands to the side, his AK-47 rifle cocked. They watch him all the time, but they don't touch him. He is their prized possession, not only a doctor, but a British one. That still counts for something, even in the back of this hellish beyond in the midst of their unfathomable war. 'I'm going to check the medical store,' he says, even though he knows this fellow can't understand English. The man follows him across to the green canvas tent. 'Stay outside,' he says, pointing to the man's hands and miming washing. 'Hygiene,' he says. He ducks inside. He splashes water noisily from the container inside the doorway. He kneels among the boxes, finds the ampoule, cracks it open and draws the liquid into a syringe. He can hear voices outside. Quickly, he shoots the morphine into the side of his thigh muscle and drops the syringe back in the box. There is a small pile of used syringes there. He will dispose of them later, when no one is watching.

The Colonel bursts in. 'Doctor Dom,' he exclaims in his clipped Oxford-educated tone, at the same time as Dominic, keeping his head down to hide the rush, says, 'We need painkillers urgently now. And we need more saline solution. When is the next delivery due?' in a voice made bold by the drug. He speaks as if he were in a surgical ward in England and this were a reasonable request.

'Go and eat. There are casualties coming,' the Colonel says. A village has been strafed. 'Your rebels are bombing innocent children now,' the Colonel says in a humorous tone as the wounded are carried in on makeshift stretchers. Dominic attempts a laugh. The Colonel is unfailingly affable to him but likes to joke that the war is all Dominic's fault. The United States is arming the rebels, according to the Colonel, and without that they would have been quelled long ago. Thus, by the Colonel's logic, by dint of his Britishness, the doctor is culpable. Even though they're on opposing sides, he knows the Colonel rates him highly and is grateful for his skills.

All the suffering causes Dominic pain, but it is the children that hurt most. There used to be a distinct line between him and others, especially African others. His first patients, beyond saving, back when he still had qualified staff to work with, were a mother and child. She was emaciated, her eyes dulled, her leg gangrenous. The child, a little boy with a pot belly and spindly legs that no longer bore him, naked except for a rag tied round his middle, clung to her. His hair was the colour of rust. It lapped his cheek in little waves in the same way his daughter's curls framed her face. Dominic remembers the green of the mother's robe. It was the colour of grass and new shoots growing. Their faces are part of his mental landscape. They crossed the line as if it weren't there and they opened the hole in him so that now they all crowd across and their pain is his. They are his people and he loves them. He blesses them. With the morphine in him, he keeps stitching and patching, cobbling broken people together as if there was a life for them to live. Sometimes, he leans down and whispers to them, speaking into their dead eyes and their unknowing ears, saying, 'Don't worry, this is the place we all come to.' Sometimes, when no one's looking, he presses his lips to their foreheads so they don't go unkissed from the world.

He is sitting on the edge of the camp bed. The lamp gutters and flares. Asrat has taken the dishes away to wash. On the radio they say that the British government is phasing out red telephone boxes and Dominic weeps. He clutches his knees to his chest, hugging them there, bone against bone. He rolls off the bed. He must check the medical supplies. They haven't been checked at night before so it needs doing. He scuttles to the doorway, flips it open and pauses, taking shallow breaths so as not to take in the stench. A shadow closes in on him, knocks him to the ground. He tries to stand but a hand holds him down. 'Who's that?' he says, his face pressed into the earth, eating dirt. 'Get off me, man. It's the doctor.'

Blows batter his shoulders and legs. A hand grips his wrist and twists one arm behind him, pushes it beyond where it's meant to reach. The pain is intense and tears come to his eyes. A foot presses into the small of his back, grinding him further into the dirt. The dust fills his mouth. He shifts his face a fraction to the side and sees a booted foot. He concentrates on breathing. They stay like this, he and the booted one, both breathing heavily. Out on the plain the funeral horns start up in high-pitched blasts. 'Colonel,' he says. 'Get the Colonel.' The boot on his spine presses harder, kneading its way into the small of his back, pinioning him. He lies still.

His ear to the ground, he feels the pulse of approaching feet.

'Doctor,' says the Colonel in a gentle voice and his heart gives a leap of gratitude, a thrill of fellowship.

The pressure on his back is lifted, his arm released. He struggles to turn over. He is too weak to get to his feet yet. The Colonel stands over him, black against the lightening sky. Dominic can't make out his features. He holds a rifle in his hand. He is flanked by two more soldiers. 'Your man must have thought I was an intruder,' Dominic says and tries a little laugh.

At a nod from the Colonel, the soldiers step closer. Empty ampoules and syringes rain down on Dominic.

'You said there were no painkillers left,' says the Colonel.

A boot connects with his kidneys. The doctor writhes. 'I'm a British citizen,' he tries to say. 'I demand –'

Someone stamps on the hollow in his chest.

Twins

Ziguinchor, Senegal, 2005

On a bridge upstream, a bunch of excited boys were taking it in turns to fling themselves from the white posts that marked the side, chirruping and squawking like hoarse birds. They perched atop the fencing with arms flapping and heads thrown back, throats stretched and offered to the fading light, before throwing themselves in spinning abandon, legs powering like pistons through the air, over and down into the silver water.

The Casamance River and its banks were coloured with a pearly radiance, a soft and enclosing vapour that blossomed out and down from the sky, wrapping the line of trees, the upturned carcass of a fishing boat, the swell of water. It hid the imperfections, heightened Louis' other senses. He smelt the wet mangrove plants, the sludge of stirred silt, the fish. It was nice to stop. To relax into the wicker chair on the terrace of this riverbank hotel and breathe it in. 'Le Pelican Volant' the hotel was called but he hadn't seen any flying pelicans, only the bedraggled bird tethered here on the terrace, standing on one leg and fixing him occasionally with a malevolent yellow eye.

'Will you be eating here tonight?'

The barman's voice woke Louis from his reverie. He looked up at the man, in his pressed blue shirt and trousers with a shiny buckle at the belt. 'I'm not sure.'

'Tonight the cook's preparing mangrove oysters,' the man said. 'We have rice and green beans with cashew nuts. Or we have prawns.'

'It sounds good. The thing is, I'm waiting for my sister.'

'Your sister's coming too?'

'My sister,' Louis said. 'The woman who's already staying here.'

'Adele is your sister?' the man said.

He nodded.

'Same mother, same father?' the man said.

Louis smiled. No one ever thought they were siblings. 'Same mother,' he said. 'My name's Louis.'

'René,' the man said and held out his hand. 'Here it's more common same father, different mother,' he said.

'I know,' Louis said. 'I've got another sister like that too. Will you join me for a beer while it's quiet?'

René went to fetch them both drinks and Louis fell back into his contemplation of the river, shimmering away into the distance on either side. The longer he stayed in Africa, the more he craved the sight and sound of water. In neighbouring landlocked Mali, his home was in a village on the banks of the River Niger. When he'd been out on fieldwork in the vast dry outlands, he needed to return to its rumbling passage or he would suffocate. The dust would clog his nostrils.

René returned with the beers. 'My father,' he said, continuing the conversation from before, 'is a Muslim. He has two wives. My mother is wife number two and she's a Catholic.'

'In some parts of the world people are killing each other for that,' Louis said as they clinked glasses, 'and here you marry each other.'

'Here we find different reasons to kill each other.'

'They've signed a peace agreement, haven't they? The separatists?' Louis said and instantly wished he hadn't. Even though he'd lived in Africa on and off for most of his life, Louis was wary of talking politics. Somehow, somebody would inevitably mention the legacy of colonialism and borders drawn by rulers with no respect for tribal allegiances. They would lay the blame for Africa's ills at the feet of the former colonial powers, or the modern equivalent, the multinationals. They'd talk about the lack of nationhood in Africa and they might go on to bring in the curse of oil and the stifling effect of protectionism and subsidies in the West. In Mali, someone would start to shout about cotton, how the growers couldn't export their crops for a living wage, and here in Senegal, they might decry the cheap rice imports killing indigenous production of their staple food. Louis had seen the bags of easy-cook American rice in the stalls when he was walking to the hotel from Ziguinchor's little airport. And the problem with these discussions was that the somebody who created this clamour was nearly always him. It was as if he were trying to pre-empt any criticism, as a representative of the oppressor by dint of his freckly white skin and his background of plenitude, by getting there first. It didn't endear him to anyone, least of all himself. No African he'd met had ever blamed him the way he blamed himself. There was a kind of egotism in thinking everything was his responsibility. He tried to do his bit, he reminded himself. Sometimes, he didn't know if it was any good, if when one life improved because of his efforts, another, somewhere else, deteriorated.

'Yes, three months ago, but they've done it before,' René was saying. 'The problem is the people who sign these deals don't have authority over the fighters. The president came, tra la, blow the trumpets and bang the drums. We sang and danced in the street and then the day afterwards someone was shot, just down the road from here. This conflict has been going off and on since 1990 and it's not over yet.'

'How's business?' Louis asked.

'It's been bad. When we get the ferry back, things will pick up.'

Someone came into the bar behind them. René stood up. He lit the lantern on the table and the one hanging from the rafters. Then he lit two mosquito coils, one to either side of Louis' table. 'Even with these you'll be eaten alive if you stay out here,' he said.

'I'll come inside in a minute,' Louis said.

'Shall I bring you another?'

'No thank you.' The two he'd already drunk were gurgling in his empty stomach. René disappeared inside. There came the sound of voices and the clatter of crockery. There was a splash somewhere nearby, the plop of a big fish jumping. Maybe it was a barracuda. Out in the dim stretches of the sodden paddy fields on the other side, little lights moved.

The pelican unfurled its other leg and flapped its huge wings. There was a rush of warm air.

He sprayed mosquito repellent on his ankles, wrists and neck and pulled his shirtsleeves down, buttoning the cuffs. He took out Adele's note from his pocket. '*Dear Louis, great hotel. Well done for sorting that. I hope you don't arrive while I'm out but just in case . . . I've nipped out to see someone who might be able to help, a sort of wise man. I'll be back by five.*' He looked at his watch. It was half six. Help with what? he wondered. He'd understood that she'd come to Senegal to visit an old friend in Dakar. The pelican paced towards him, pulling at its tether. When it could come no closer, it let out a piteous wavering cry. He picked up the remains of his beer and went inside.

A French family with three blonde children were sitting at one of the two tables. They had a basket of bread in front of them and their places were set for dinner. Good cooking smells, garlic and spices and sizzling peanut oil, came from the kitchen. He nodded at them, went and stood at the bar where René was washing glasses.

'Did my sister go with anyone, do you know?' he asked.

'I don't know. I didn't see her go. She might be with Vincent,' he said.

'Who's that?'

'He's OK. He's a guide. He hasn't had much work recently. She said to me, your sister, people were following her everywhere, not leaving her alone, hassling her. I said, pick one that seems trustworthy, take him on and then the rest will leave you alone. So she picked Vincent.'

'Good,' said Louis. 'Perhaps I'll have another drink after all.' He sat at the empty table.

A young man came in and went up to the bar. He spoke to René who pointed Louis out to him. He marched across, hand outstretched. 'I'm Vincent,' he said, 'your sister's friend.' He had a wide, open face, big round eyes. The tip of his nose and cheeks glistened.

Louis stood up, grasped his hand. 'Where is she?'

'She's not here?' Vincent said, looking at the empty chair opposite Louis. 'I don't know. I saw her this morning. We went out again looking for her African sister.'

'Her what?'

'Her African sister,' the young man repeated with a rising intonation. He wasn't so sure of himself now.

Louis eyed him, keeping very still to conceal the sudden turmoil inside. It was as if the past had been unfurled like a worn carpet but the colours and the pattern were different from the one he'd thought he'd trodden. Had his stepfather fathered another child when they were living in Senegal? Did that explain something, give coherence to the blotchy pattern of his family life? Did it even, he wondered for a hopeful moment, slot something unresolved about his own life into place? No. It made no sense.

'*Comme qui dirait sa gemelle?*' Her sort of twin, Vincent suggested, and something in the way he spoke, a kind of lilt to his voice, let Louis know he was quoting Adele. He could hear her saying it, 'my sort of African twin'. He didn't know what that meant.

'She was supposed to be back by five.'

Vincent looked at him seriously, with a sweet and steady gaze. He was waiting for Louis to take the lead. 'Will you help me find her?' Louis said.

'Of course,' the young man said.

They went out into the Ziguinchor night, down soft sandy streets, between little yellow-lit houses, past people padding along quietly, around the edge of a clearing where some ceremony with drums and chanting children was taking place, past women sitting on doorsteps who hailed them as they went by. They went in and out of bars and lit places. Louis let Vincent ask the questions. Had they seen the white woman, the one who was looking for her African sister? Everyone seemed to know who he meant, but either they hadn't seen her that evening or their information seemed not to convince Vincent. Occasionally Vincent updated him. 'She hasn't been in this bar today', 'She was at the cybercafe this afternoon', or 'She bought cigarettes at this stall earlier'. Soon there were others in the search party, a ragamuffin posse roaming the streets of the sleepy town. One boy volunteered to go and ask in the bars down near the port. Another was dispatched to the Lindiane neighbourhood where the marabout, the holy man, lived.

They emerged on to a main road, a tree-lined boulevard. Louis noticed and memorised little details as if someone might ask him about it afterwards and call on him to bear witness. He made mental notes. A flag with a blue star flapping from a rooftop, tyres used as ballast on a tin roof, a road sign pointing in three directions: 'Town Centre, Bus Station, Guinea Bissau'.

Vincent disappeared behind a privet hedge topping a white

242

picket fence and they crowded in after him. Tucked behind it was a tiny bar, a wooden shed with a high fold-down bench in front. The woman behind the bar launched into a long explanation when she was asked and Vincent listened, asking questions and nodding at the replies. The woman, brown wrap, green T-shirt, kohl around her eyes, plaited hair, three chins, Louis noted, raised her voice and her hands and started expostulating. Louis couldn't follow. He didn't even know what language they were speaking. It had clicks in it. Diola, he supposed. The woman made a gesture with her thumb and forefinger, wagging her hand and nodding knowingly sideways at Louis.

Vincent looked to the side as they came out, tilted his head down as if someone were trying to shine a light in his eyes. He avoided Louis' gaze. 'She was seen with Modibo,' he said.

'Not a good man?' Louis said, striding beside Vincent as they plunged off the road down a path between patches of land like allotments where maize grew.

'It's OK,' Vincent said, 'I know where he goes.'

'What was she shouting about?'

'African women, they like to shout.'

'Tell me,' Louis said.

Vincent gestured. 'I know Madame Adele is a good woman. She came for tea to my father's house yesterday.'

They were crossing a kind of wasteland now. The path between tall grasses and rambling weeds was narrow. There was only just enough room for them to walk side by side. Louis glanced behind. The others were following. He counted nine of them, tramping along quietly in the starlight.

'Watch out for snakes,' Vincent said. 'Keep to the middle of the path.'

'You don't want to tell me what the woman said?' Louis said.

Vincent threw his hands up. 'She was saying what's all this fuss about one white woman? Why are we searching in the night when it's obvious. She's gone off with Modibo. She was saying this is what white women come here for, to taste a bit of sweet black bamboo.'

Louis was sorry to have pushed the point. He said nothing. Foreboding dried his mouth and stilled his tongue. They traipsed along in silence.

They came to an open area where a building loomed, a concrete block of flats with missing windows. They stopped at the doorway.

'You lot stay here,' Vincent said to the search party.

'What is this place?' Louis said.

'*Un coin*,' Vincent said and led the way inside.

'A corner? A corner of what?' Louis followed him into the hallway, past the bare, concrete stairs. It reminded him of the council flat in south London he'd lived in for a while where the stale stench of urine and stewed cabbage on the stairway was a constant. But here, instead of that echoey silence, there was hubbub ahead, somewhere out of sight; women's voices and laughter, the thwack of wood on wood, the thrum of a machine, the soft strum of a kora and a bleating noise like a child in distress.

They turned the bend beyond the stairwell and it opened out into a lamplit corridor that stretched the length of the building, full of people and bustle. The doors along one side kept opening and shutting, sending shafts of yellow light into the space and then withdrawing it so that the people were brought into focus and sunk into semi-shadow again with the creak of a hinge. Raucous laughing women came in and out, adjusting their clothes, admiring each other, preening. Some had feathers in their hair. Little tables where people sat drinking and chatting and chewing nuts were set higgledy-piggledy down the middle. Three men at the foremost table were playing aggressive dominoes. One slammed a piece down on the table with a bellow of triumph. Vincent went to speak to them, but even before they replied and turned to point further down the corridor, Louis had caught sight of his sister at the far end and was pushing his way towards her.

Arms raised above her head as if chained to the ceiling, she stood in an attitude of surrender, draped in crimson cloth. A man knelt on the floor beside her, pawing at her legs and her hips. A woman stood behind reaching around Adele's breasts and his sister stood passively, like a sacrificial lamb. Louis fought his way through the muddle of tables, hefting a wandering goat out of the way, squeezing past a musician in voluminous saffron robes, tuning his kora. He narrowly avoided treading on a pair of babies, nestled in each other's arms, asleep on a mat. Their mother at a nearby table shouted a warning. Louis paused, put his hand to his chest in a gesture of apology. Then he gazed ahead, bewildered.

Adele had disappeared. The man who'd been kneeling was getting to his feet. He had pins in his mouth. Louis stood there blinking. He had a feeling he'd been here before, not in this place, but in this situation, whatever it was. Vincent caught up with him. 'Where'd she go?' Louis said.

The man took up his seat at a trestle sewing machine against the far wall. There were three machines in a row but the other two sat idle. The man spat the pins delicately into a small round tin. He fixed a head torch around his forehead and switched it on. A door opened and the woman who'd been standing behind Adele emerged carrying the crimson cloth and a tape measure. She handed the cloth to the man who fitted it under his needle. The whine of his machine resumed, his sandalled foot pumping the pedal.

'She's having a dress made,' Vincent said.

The door reopened and Louis caught a glimpse of rolls of fabric behind his sister, who was momentarily framed in the doorway against the yellow electric light, before she stepped out into the corridor. Louis watched her, his anxiety turning to fury. How old was she? Thirty-four or thirty-five? And still she'd run off into the night without making sure someone knew where she was going. She picked up a half-filled glass from a table and went across to the sewing-machine man, leaning over him, examining his work. As Louis moved towards her, he saw in the light from the tailor's head torch the bangles around her wrists and ankles, the beads threading her curly black hair, and the desire to pick her up and shake her fell from him. He hadn't seen her for three years. She'd never come to visit him in Mali even though he always asked. She couldn't, she said. And that last Christmas in Cardiff at their mother's house had been awful. He'd taken Joe out to the pictures and down the park in the freezing cold to get him away from the oppressive atmosphere. Adele had been so reduced, so stricken and uncommunicative, so stuck in a dead-end tortured relationship with some Spanish toerag that he'd thought the wild child gone forever. And here she was again.

When he tapped her shoulder, she turned and flung her arms around his neck. 'My darling Louis, I didn't expect you until tomorrow,' she said. She smelt of strong spirit, hooch or whatever they called it here, but she didn't seem drunk. She looped her arm through his. 'Hey, Vincent,' she said, grinning. 'You've met my big brother then.' She led them to her table and introduced them to Sylvie, who'd been taking the measurements for her dress. 'Drinks, everyone?' she said.

'Let's get back to the hotel and have some dinner,' Louis said.

'OK,' she said lightly and bent to embrace Sylvie. 'Thanks for today,' she said. 'You saved me. The dress will be ready tomorrow?' she called to the tailor, who nodded, without raising his head from his work.

Outside, the gang of helpers greeted them with a cheer. 'Who are all these people?' Adele said.

'Your search party,' Louis said.

'But I wasn't lost.'

'We didn't know that,' Louis said quietly.

'Oh, I'm sorry. I didn't realise,' she said.

He put his arm around her shoulders and faced the little crowd. He raised his voice to address them. 'Here's my sister fine and well, as you can see,' he said. 'Thank you for your help.' He inclined his head and put his hand again to his heart.

'Welcome. You're welcome,' they called back. As the search party dispersed into the darkness, Louis wondered, not for the first time, whether generosity of spirit was in inverse proportion to material wealth.

The three of them stood on the threshold of the big house. 'Thank you so much. I can find the way back,' Louis told Vincent.

'I'm going the same way,' Vincent said solemnly.

'Then please come and join us for dinner.'

'I think you and your sister want time alone.'

'No. Come and eat with us. My brother's just going to tell me off as soon as we're alone. Please do, Vincent,' Adele said and Vincent laughed. Louis could see he was already half in love with her.

They set off across the wasteland, Vincent in the lead. 'How's Joe?' he said.

'He's on really good form. I had an email from him yesterday. He's been kayaking with his dad. I can't wait to see him. Hang on. Let me say something to Vincent.'

She ran ahead, almost skipping to catch up with Vincent's lope. She made a musical jingling noise as though little bells were hung about her body. Louis followed them, listening to their voices in the warm night air. 'I didn't like that Modibo friend of yours much,' she said.

'He's not my friend,' Vincent replied.

'Oh good. I'm glad. He said he was and that's why I went with him. I ditched him after we'd been to the marabout's house.

He just wouldn't go away and kept wanting money and do you know what I did? I went up to a woman who was sitting outside her house shelling maize and I said, this man is bothering me and she shouted at him. "Shame on you," she said and then he slunk off.'

'Women help each other,' Vincent said.

'That's right,' she said. 'I'll remember that. And the marabout was very interesting. I told him about Ellena and he wrote out a text for finding what is lost. I had a pouch made in leather.' She turned round, flapping something that hung at her neck at Louis. 'Look,' she said, 'my grigri.'

'What's that?' Louis said.

She fell back beside him. 'It's magic,' she said.

Louis took hold of her hand. She seemed so fey he felt a need to hold her, to stop her from straying further. They walked like that, hand in hand, as they'd done when they were children. There was no reason to lift her on to his back and carry her to safety like he used to, but he felt an urge to do so. Unseen creatures rustled in the high grass. The vegetation swayed and dipped, twinkling.

Adele leaned into his side. 'I love it here,' she said. 'Don't you love it? I just love it.' She made an ululating sound.

Vincent half turned and then resumed his stride.

'Oh, for goodness' sake,' Louis said.

'Why are you cross, Louis? I'm so happy to be here. Africa and you. It's like coming home.'

'I'm not cross,' he said.

'And something's about to shift. I can feel it.'

'You're going to have to start at the beginning with this Ellena story. I just don't get it.'

They were at the boulevard again. 'I'll tell you all about it when we've got a moment,' she said. That moment came later, after Vincent had gone, when the two of them sat on the hotel roof under a clustering of bright stars, but over dinner, she talked about the marabout. He was a shrunken old man who sat cross-legged and barefoot on a woven mat in his mud hut, but you could tell that he had immense power and insight. He knew what she was seeking before she even spoke. He had touched his hand to her forehead and she'd felt blessed. Africa was her spiritual home, she said.

When Vincent went to the toilet, she said to Louis, 'I finally get it. I understand why you've chosen to live here.' Her eyes were shining. 'You know when I was in Dakar I couldn't make sense of it all. I was on the outside looking in. The poverty and squalor, it was too much. I nearly gave up. I had some weird encounters.' She broke a piece of bread and crumbled it between her fingers. 'And then I came here and I feel like I'm starting to understand.'

'What do you understand?'

'You need to surrender to it.' She opened her arms, palms up, and held them there. 'Embrace it!'

'Don't embrace it all. Some of it's not that nice,' Louis said.

'When did you get so cynical?' she asked, picking up her fork again and spearing a piece of fish. 'You sound like my father.'

'What a really horrible thing to say,' Louis said, just as Vincent returned.

She gave him a look and turned to Vincent. They started to discuss arrangements for the next day; a boat trip down the river to visit some villages. Louis nodded his assent when they looked at him, drank more beer. He wasn't really paying attention. A long-buried memory had surfaced.

He is three years old and he is with his mother, Claire. They are going to meet someone special. He is wearing his new blue coat and his mum has brought a comb in her handbag to slick his hair down. It's made of metal and scratches against his scalp. He knows the special person can't be Santa Claus because it isn't Christmas, but he thinks it will be someone like that. It might be Jesus or God because she has talked about him in a whispery way, like she does in the church she's started taking him to, when she tells him to stop fidgeting. It is a secret. The person is waiting in the upstairs cafe in a department store. He is tall with curly black hair and a red face. He bends down to shake Louis' hand and Louis sees himself reflected in the man's glasses. He smells like cod liver oil and his hand is slippery. 'This is Dominic,' his mum says. No one has ever shaken Louis' hand before. He sits on his mum's lap, her hand on his tummy, and the man talks to her across the table. He wipes his hand on his mum's skirt. They bring Louis an ice cream in a silver bowl and he scrapes his spoon across the bottom to get the last bits up while they go on talking over the top of him. His mum leans forward, resting her chin on his head. The scraping noise makes his teeth squeak, but he keeps doing it even when there's no ice cream left in the bowl.

'He's a bit big to sit on your lap, isn't he?' the man says. He raises his cup and makes a slurping sound. Louis watches him, safe on his mother's knee. She hates slurpers. His mum doesn't say anything. Then she lifts him off and sets him down on another chair, by himself, and they go on talking. They hold hands across the table. Louis closes his eyes and becomes invisible. He slides off his chair, goes under the table and crouches. Blah, blah, blah, they go above him. He opens his eyes. There's a gap between the man's grey socks and his grey trousers where a bit of hairy white leg shows. It's like a sandwich. Grey bread with a white filling. Louis sinks his teeth into the soft part of the filling.

'I'm not cynical,' he said to Adele, when Vincent had gone and they'd retired for a cigarette on the terrace. 'I'm full of hope. But I'm a realist. Just don't compare me to that fuckwit.'

'Are you talking about my father?' Adele said.

'Is that the one who's a fuckwit?' he said. He didn't wait for an answer. 'I asked Mum once why she married him and do you know what she said?' He didn't look at Adele. He was staring at the pelican, still tethered by one skinny brittle leg, uselessly flapping its wings. Two dogs were slumbering behind it in the corner. '"I did it for you." That's what she said. She did it for me.'

'Mum married my father for you? I don't get it.'

His own father was feckless, she'd said. He wouldn't settle down and earn a proper living. He wanted to go on manning the barricades, living life in a state of perpetual revolution.

Dominic was a doctor. Established. He could offer them a better, more comfortable life. 'She broke my dad's heart, you know.' His voice was thick. He felt like he was going to cry.

'Come off it, Louis. He married again about five minutes later.'

'That doesn't mean he didn't have a broken heart. What you don't realise Del –' he started and then stopped. What was the matter with him? Was he going to tell his sister his theory that she'd only been conceived so that their mother could lure Dominic into marriage?

'You're exaggerating,' she said. 'OK, he's not the easiest of men but he loves us in his way.'

Louis pulled himself back. 'Well, he loves you, at least,' he said. He patted her hand. 'As he should.'

The next morning Louis went for a walk while Adele was still sleeping. They had stayed up half the night talking, sitting outside their cell-like rooms on the hotel roof, but still he'd woken early, when the cocks started crowing. His head was full of Adele's stories. He knew now that she'd come to Senegal to search out a woman she'd known long ago when they lived in Dakar as children. He remembered George but not the girl herself who turned up after he'd been sent away to school. She had some notion of paying this woman back because, in a way that wasn't clear to him, Ellena had helped Adele, when she was lost. A man in Dakar had told her Ellena lived in Ziguinchor so she'd come here. The man had also told her Ellena was dead but she didn't believe that part. She had at first but now she thought he'd only said it because she refused his offer to help find her. And he was a lost soul. He'd say anything.

People greeted Louis as he wandered along the leafy lanes. He'd only arrived the evening before but already he was known. 'How's your sister?' they called out to him. 'Very well thank you,' he replied, although he wasn't sure it was true. It seemed unhealthy to him, this obsession with Ellena, this belief that she'd appeared in a mirror, that they were twin souls. 'You're not making any sense. It's completely irrational,' he'd said.

'But that's the point,' she'd replied. 'Things don't work rationally here.'

'So you went to see a witch doctor.'

'A marabout.'

'And he gave you a magic charm.'

'It's no more superstitious nonsense than the religion we were brought up in. And it's relevant to here. It's not that I believe it. It's that I don't *not* believe it, if you see what I mean.'

'Not really,' he'd said. 'I don't get what you're trying to achieve with all this.'

'Redemption,' she'd said.

He walked to the port to look at the memorial to the people who had died when the *Joola*, the ferry that plied between the capital and the Casamance, had sunk in 2002. Through a green iron archway at the embarkation point, a model of an anchor was set into a white-painted block. Beyond that was a wall with a mosaic image of the ship and beyond that the river. The area was freshly painted green and white, surrounded by palm trees and white wrought–iron lanterns. A new ferry was to be launched soon.

'Nearly two thousand people died in that disaster,' a voice behind him said. It was René, out with his dogs. 'More than the *Titanic.*'

Louis took this in. He lived in Africa. He should be used to shocking facts and figures.

'It was licensed to carry 580 passengers and crew. It's still down there on the bottom of the ocean with a thousand bodies inside.'

Louis thought of them, beating their hands at the portholes, clamouring to get out, screaming for help that never came.

Adele was sitting on the terrace waiting for him when he got back to the hotel. She was facing out to the river. It was glittering in the morning light, rumbling on its journey to the westernmost tip of Africa where it would open out into the Atlantic Ocean. A jug of orange juice, a Thermos of hot water, some sachets of coffee, a baguette and pots of jam were laid out on the table. He pulled the other chair round so he was sitting beside her. Sometimes it was easier to speak if you weren't face to face.

'You're not going to find her, you know,' he said.

She tore open the sachets and tipped the coffee into cups. She took the lid off the Thermos and poured the hot water. 'It's a sort of quest,' she said quietly.

'But why her? You don't really know her. If you want to do something to help, there's a million deserving cases. It seems so arbitrary.'

She bit her top lip, stirred sugar into her drink. Far out on the water two pirogues sped by. The smell of their fish catch wafted across. 'You remember Pedro?' she said. 'He was HIV-positive. I lived in absolute terror of contracting it myself. I can't tell you the fear. It was like this iron fist that clutched my insides. And the guilt.' She blew into her coffee.

Louis didn't speak. My little sister, he thought, gazing blindly out at the river.

'I thought I was such a shit exposing myself to that risk when I was a mother, a daughter, a sister. When it wasn't just me who'd be hurt. I felt like I was paralysed.' She took a sip of her coffee. 'Yuck,' she said. 'Why don't they give you proper coffee? Don't they grow it round here?' She poured some orange juice. 'Then one night,' she continued, 'Ellena appeared. I know it sounds mad. But after that, somehow I found the courage to get a grip on myself. To go and get tested.'

Louis put his arm around her shoulder. That was why she'd come to see a witch doctor. She was searching for some wacky miracle cure. His cheekbones throbbed.

She turned to face him. 'It's all right,' she said. 'The test came back negative.'

Louis blew out pent-up air. He took his arm away and turned his attention to the breakfast table. He tore off a large chunk of bread and smeared it with jam.

'It took me a while to get myself back together, sort myself out,' she said.

'And you're sorted now, are you?' he said and took a bite. It was delicious.

'Ish. Anyway, I realised I wanted to do something in return. Dad said he was in touch with George for about ten years after we went back to the UK. I know he helped them out, sent them an allowance, I think, but Ellena was my friend and I never even wrote to her.'

The almost impossible-to-assimilate thought of Dominic as selfless benefactor was so distracting that Louis missed some of what Adele was saying. He looked up at the river. Vincent was chugging towards them in a long yellow boat. He waved.

'Listen, Del,' he said. 'Stop beating yourself up. It doesn't matter who you help. What matters is that you don't turn a blind eye.'

Adele had caught sight of Vincent too. She stood up and stepped forward to the edge to catch the rope Vincent was coiling ready to throw.

'There was this girl from Cardiff who worked on my project last year. She only came to Mali for a holiday,' Louis said.

Adele half turned. 'From Cardiff?' She laughed.

'What I'm saying is it's just to do with making a connection,' he said. 'This girl was wandering round Mali on her own. A bit lost. A bit self-obsessed. I took her to my village and she did some useful work.' Louis thought of the girl with the flame-red hair waiting at the riverside, children clustered around her. She'd told him she didn't want to go home, that she'd come back as soon as her exams were out of the way. She'd made it happen. She was going to work with him during her gap year and he was expecting her later this summer. She'd just written to say she and her mother were having a double celebration – her A level results, her mum qualifying as a maths teacher.

Adele missed the rope and it slithered back into the water.

Louis stepped beside her waiting for Vincent to position the boat so he could throw the rope again. 'What I mean is, you've been here two weeks. Haven't you come across someone else, someone real, that you could do something positive for?'

He caught the rope and hauled Vincent in, aware of Adele watching him. Then he tied the boat up to the balustrade.

Vincent stepped ashore. His face glowed in the sunshine. '*Bonjour, Madame Adele, Monsieur Louis,*' he said. 'Are you ready for our day out? I'm going to collect our picnic from René and we'll leave in ten minutes. *Ça va?*' He disappeared inside.

'You pulling on that rope,' Adele said, 'reminded me – do you remember? I was stuck on a rope swing and you rescued me. You were always rescuing me.'

It wasn't quite how Louis remembered the occasion, but he accepted the compliment. '*Plus ça change,*' he said and grinned.

Over the next few days, they went on outings and drank tea with Vincent and his little brothers in his father's compound. They hired bicycles, ancient old boneshakers that made your bum ache, and cycled to a nature reserve. Children ran out shouting '*Toubab*', or the Diola equivalent, at them as they passed. They drank beer in all the '*coins*' they could find and listened to music in a downtown bar. Wherever they went, Adele asked about Ellena, but she didn't hang her days on the search. 'I might as well ask,' she said, 'you never know.'

On their last night, before he went back to Mali and she returned to Dakar for a couple of days before catching her flight home to Britain, they went to a nightclub and danced like crazy. They tried to recreate the twist that they'd won a prize for back when she was six and he was ten and ended up giggling in a heap on the floor.

They sat the next dance out. 'I went dancing in Dakar,' she said. 'To a nightclub at the top of a fire escape.'

'Sounds suitably dodgy,' Louis said.

'That wasn't the dodgy part. I nearly slept with this guy afterwards. But he wouldn't use a condom. So I said no.'

Louis really didn't want to hear about his sister's sexual exploits. He looked at Vincent, strutting his stuff in the middle of the dance floor, glancing across at them to check if Adele was admiring him. She wasn't. She was staring down into her drink.

'That was good, wasn't it?' Adele said.

'What was?'

'Saying no.'

'I'd expect you to say no in those circumstances,' he said.

'But I didn't always. Not with Pedro. That's the thing,' she said.

He looked at her then. So ineffably precious. 'Yes, that was really good,' he said. 'It'd be nice to see you with a good man.'

She nodded. 'Chance would be a fine thing,' she said. 'What about you and this Cardiff girl?' she said.

'I'm old enough to be her father. Do you want another drink?' he said.

'What?' she said. 'What aren't you telling me?'

'Nothing,' he said. When he got back from the bar she was looking thoughtful.

'I know what I'm going to do when I get back to Dakar,' she said. 'First, I'm going to buy Boubacar a mobile phone and enough credit for a year.'

'Who's Boubacar?'

'The guy who told me Ellena was dead.'

'The crazy one?'

She nodded. 'More sad than crazy. Then I'm going back to the school I visited. And I'm going to see about twinning it with my school.'

'Twins!' he said.

In Between

Nimba County, Liberia, 2007

The late sun slants in a yellow bar across the paddy fields. Women at the sharp green edge crouch low in a line, wide-brimmed hats covering their faces, gathering and stacking the rice seedlings. He can hear the squelch of their feet in the mud. It has oozed between their toes, sloshed up around their ankles, painting their legs with wet brown boots. He focuses on their sinuous bend and stretch, lets his mind and breathing be soothed by the repetitive movement.

George turns his attention back to the crumpled letter laid out on the table in front of him. It is an airmail letter that has taken three months to arrive via several government offices in Monrovia. People have scrawled notes on it. '*Not known here*' and '*George who?*' It has been opened and not resealed. It bears the round brown stain of a coffee cup. Over the top of the stain, in a splash of red ink, someone has scribbled a note. '*Try Nimba County*' it says, and they have written the name of the village where he lives.

When he first saw it he imagined it might be the president herself who'd written this directive. He saw her striding past the cluttered desk where his letter had come to a halt on top of a pile of other documents, stopping to exchange a word, perhaps about the rice self-sufficiency project. Her massive headdress cast a shadow over the official sitting there. Then she spied the letter addressed to 'George Barthes, c/o Executive Mansion, Monrovia, Liberia, West Africa'. 'George Barthes,' she might have said. 'I know George.' It is not beyond the realms of possibility. When he returned to Liberia after twenty-five years in exile, he wrote to her. He congratulated her on her victory and told her of his hopes for lasting peace. He reminded her that they had served together under President Tolbert all those years before. She was the minister of finance then. They had passed sometimes in the corridors. They had both had to run from their country after the coup in 1980. They had both lived in exile. She didn't reply to that letter, but she might have taken note, because here is this one, which has been given a helping hand and has arrived at his doorstep all the way from England.

Two photographs fell out when he unfolded the letter. One is of a white woman, wearing strange baggy clothes standing in the sunshine next to a boy with straight brown hair falling to his shoulders. '*Me and my son Joe*' it says on the back. The other is an old one with faded colours of a class of schoolgirls in uniform. An arrow points to one of the girls. On the back it says: '*Dakar, Senegal, 1980. The arrow is pointing at Ellena.*' He turned the photo back over and scrutinised it again. He recognised none of the children. The one indicated was certainly not his daughter Ellena.

It was a long letter that twice forced him to his feet to

pace the length of the room, fists tightened, tears in his eyes, and once made him laugh out loud in unholy glee. When he finished reading, he scrumpled it into a ball and threw it away from him as if it were a poison-pen letter. Now he smoothes it out and begins again. '*Dear George,*' he reads, '*I don't know if you remember me.*' He does. He worked for her father as a nightwatchman when he first arrived in Dakar. Adele, the doctor's daughter. She used to play ball by herself in the driveway and sometimes she came and sat with him in the garage to pet the dogs.

'*I don't know if this letter will ever reach you. I came to Senegal two years ago to look for you and Ellena but I found no trace. I am so sorry that I failed to keep in touch. I hope that the loss was only mine and that you and Ellena and all your family have prospered.*' He takes his glasses from his nose, presses his thumb and forefinger into the ridge of his nose, rubs his eyes. He gazes out the window towards the horizon where the blur of dotted trees plume bluey-grey like puffs of smoke. Prospered, he thinks. He pushes his glasses up his nose again and scans the letter, looking for the phrase that made him thrust it away the last time. '*I was hopeful I would find you after I spoke to a young man called Boubacar Dieng, who claimed to remember me and my family, you and yours.*' George doesn't recall anyone by the name of Boubacar Dieng but he has forgotten so much. '*He told me that Ellena had married a Senegalese man and become a teacher like me (I teach French at a secondary school).*' A teacher, George thinks. If only. '*He told me she had sadly passed away,*' he reads. Once again, despite himself, George removes his glasses and lets his eyes glaze. They are like a runaway truck, this Englishwoman's conjectures, sometimes veering so far off the course of his life that she might be talking about another George entirely and then, like this, crashing back on track. The collisions cause him anguish, reminding him of all that he has lost, but the gaps between her words and his reality fill him with a different feeling, a kind of rage that he can't easily contain. He is too old for such strong emotion.

He reads on. '*Later, when I couldn't find you, I decided to help this young man set up his own business as a tailor in Dakar and he admitted then that he hadn't known you and had made it all up. So I am hoping that this letter finds you both safe and well after all. He had lost his sister, and was in a bad way when I first met him, but thankfully she has now returned home.*' George sighs. This is not the part he is searching for. He runs his finger down the page. '*The photo is the one my father sent me in England to show me Ellena at her new school. I've kept it all this time but now I've scanned it into my computer so I'm sending you the original.*' George looks at the unknown girls in the photograph once more to make sure and then drops it into the bin. He reads on. '*I know my father kept in touch with you and paid for Ellena's education and I am so glad of that.*' George spreads out his fingers on the thin paper, fighting his impulse to crumple it again. Here the gap is widest. Doctor Dom, he used to call that man. He stands up from his table, goes out on to the veranda and spits into the dust.

Out in the field the oxen pass by, throwing up mud with their hooves. The boy at the plough raises his arm in greeting. George nods vaguely but he isn't paying attention. He is transported back in time to when he stood at the kitchen door of the doctor's house early one morning. The sprinkler was on in the garden and a fine spray misted the air. The plants glistened. The doctor looked down at him from the kitchen step, shaking his head. George had asked for an advance on his salary to pay for treatment for Miata, his wife.

'I don't lend money. It's a principle of mine,' the doctor said and he smiled at George as if to say that George would understand the importance of principles and how upholding them must take precedence over sick wives. A flap of loose mottled skin hanging under the doctor's chin on his scrawny neck put George in mind of a plucked chicken. George pleaded. He told the doctor about his little girl Ellena, the same age as Adele, the doctor's own daughter, appealing to him as a father. He reminded the doctor how reliable a worker he was. He didn't mention that he'd already spent his rent on hospital fees, that he'd lost his home and that at night he secreted Ellena into the garage where he sat keeping watch and she slept at his feet.

He can still remember the look on the doctor's face, the little smile that played over his thin lips, his cold eyes and twitching head. 'I took you on without a reference, Chief,' the doctor said, and with that veiled threat George grasped that when the doctor called him Chief, it wasn't as a mark of respect to someone older, with more life experience. He understood there could be no conversation man to man with the doctor. The false mateyness of 'Chief' was designed to mask the chasm between them. It was a way of saying 'Stay on your side of the gulf. Know your place.' Now, standing blankly on his veranda, George recalls the urge to put his hands around that scrawny gizzard and wring it, but, instead, he nodded respectfully and withdrew to the garage. 'We all have our problems,' the doctor threw after him as a parting shot.

It was then that George came up with the idea of selling the tools. There were stacks of them in the garage, hanging from the shelves, piled up in the corners. They were not even, strictly speaking, the doctor's tools, because they were old and rusted, obviously there before the family took up residence. The doctor wouldn't have known a hacksaw from a jigsaw, a chisel from a plane. At night, when everyone was sleeping, George worked on the tools, fixing and sharpening, whetting their edges and bringing them to a shine with oil and a rag. There was pleasure in the work, in making good and useful what had been discarded. A man down the road, another nightwatchman, sold the tools on to someone else who had a business. George rearranged the remaining implements so that there were no empty spaces. He poured all the money into Miata's care, but she couldn't be saved. Each time he visited her, she was more insubstantial, as if she were melting into the mattress. He could see through the skin on her hands. Before she died, she made him promise that he would look after Ellena and return to Liberia one day and find the sons they'd left behind. It took him twenty-five years but he kept one of those promises at least, he thinks, rocking on the veranda of the house that he has helped his older son rebuild.

He sits again at the table. '*You know that my parents separated for a while after we came back from Senegal and later my father went*

266

to Ethiopia on his own to work in a refugee camp. Something happened to him there, we think, and when he returned he was ill with a mental sickness. He was in and out of hospital for years. My mother took him back and looked after him. He did recover but he never worked as a doctor again. You'll be sorry to hear that he passed away last month from lung cancer,' he reads. He feels again the unholy surge of emotion he experienced when he read this first time round. 'Sorry' isn't the word for this feeling. He has outlived the doctor. Doctor Dom is cold in his grave and he, George, is still alive. The feeling gives him a pain in the chest. It is like a sticky residue around his own lungs.

George stands again and walks out of the house. He steps down from the veranda and walks around the side to the vegetable patch. He wanders between the rows of beans, cassava and maize. He presses his nose against the skin of a ripening tomato. There were no more tools that wouldn't be missed, he remembers. To pay for Miata's medicine he sold the doctor's radio. He was going to buy a replacement with his next pay packet but couldn't cover up the loss long enough. 'I have to let you go,' the doctor said when he dismissed him, as if he had no choice in the matter.

George had found work at the tool business, lodgings for himself and Ellena with the proprietor. And when the doctor came begging, he refused. The doctor's wife had left him, his life was falling apart, he said. He needed to make it OK for George and Ellena or his daughter, Adele, would never forgive him. His eyes were red-rimmed, his face blotchy, his clothes crumpled and smelling of sweat. 'No,' George said. 'You don't get a second chance.'

George kneels on the ground between the rows of vegetables. He has done many things in his life of which he's ashamed but most of them weren't coated with such thick layers of self-righteousness. Painfully, he takes the feeling out and unwraps it like he unwrapped the crumpled ball of the letter. He'd thought he was a better man than the doctor but he sees now they're the same. He knows he could have given Ellena a better life if pride and rage hadn't prevented him from taking the doctor's help. He didn't even tell her the man had come. He never gave her the doll the doctor brought with him. The damp soaks into the knees of his trousers.

He is still there when his eldest granddaughter, Mary, comes home. She comes round the side of the house with her lopsided walk that always reminds him of Miata and drops her basket when she sees him. 'What's the matter, Grandpa?' she says. 'What are you doing?'

'I'm picking tomatoes for our dinner,' he says. She helps him to his feet and together they go into the house. He sits back down at the table, tears a sheet of paper from the middle of one of his grandchildren's school exercise books and takes up a pen. Others arrive home while he sits thinking. One child is sent to fetch water, another helps light the stove. The littlest one, John, Mary's son, comes and sits on his knee. 'I'm writing a letter,' he tells him, 'to an Englishwoman who was a friend of your great-aunt Ellena.'

'Are you going to tell her about me?' the child asks.

'Of course,' he says. The pain in his chest starts to ebb. 'And I'll tell her about your mother and how she had to run from this house when the soldiers came but now she's back.'

'And the broken mirror. Tell her about the mirror breaking into a hundred pieces.'

'It was a silly thing to try and take,' George says.

'Silly Mam,' John says.

'What else shall I say?'

'Ask her to come and visit,' John says.

George picks up the pen. '*Dear Adele*,' he writes, '*I am sorry to hear about your father. He was very good to me.*'

Boxes

Exeter, Devon, 2007

Richard stood in the expanse of his clean, empty kitchen in his clean, empty house, listening to the silence. Even Enrica, hunched on the windowsill, had subsided into a state of tense hush after yowling at unexpected moments for days, expressing, in a way denied him, the anguish of leaving their home. Now that the crunch had come, the furniture had been moved to his new place, the last boxes of books, vases, odd plates, teddies and Lego were packed into his car, ready for the charity shop, she was mute.

He should get a move on or the charity shop would be closed, but a yearning had hold of him and kept him rooted. He was remembering when they first moved into the house, eleven years earlier. A student-let before, neglected by the owner, it was a mess. His sons, Josh and Adam, seven and ten at the time, trailed after him as he opened and shut doors on to squalid interiors, trying to conjure a vision in their minds of how it would be, once the transformation had taken place; casting the fragile bubbles of his white, sparkling, shiny words out into the dank atmosphere, and

270

watching them melt into the stained carpets or burst on the lethal spikes of the Artexed ceilings. As they moved from room to room, his words became more staccato. 'Power shower,' he boomed as they crowded into the bathroom and he flipped back the mildewed yellow shower curtain. Out of the corner of his eye, he saw his sons were holding hands. The avocado suite and the peeling polystyrene ceiling tiles pressed in on him. Three curly brown mushrooms sprouted from the wall above the bath.

'There's only two bedrooms,' Josh said. It was the first time either of them had spoken since they'd entered the house.

'One for me and the big one for you two,' Richard pointed out brightly.

Josh mumbled something. He was crying.

Richard dropped to his knees so he was on a level. 'What?' he said.

'He asked where Mum's going to sleep,' Adam said.

Kneeling there on the cracked lino, Richard, a committed atheist, had an urge to put his hands together and beg for divine intervention. The level of grown-upness required seemed way out of his reach. He wanted to shout, 'She left me too, you know.'

Adam put his hand on his dad's head and patted him. 'It'll be all right,' he said. To Josh, he said: 'Mum's getting her own house. We're going to stay with her some weekends. You know she's not going to live here. This is the boys' house.'

'Like the lost boys?' Josh said.

'Yes,' Adam said. '*Peter Pan*,' he explained to Richard.

'So will we have a tree house?' Josh asked.

Richard got to his feet. 'Yes,' he said. 'Yes, yes. Come and look at the garden and we'll choose the tree.'

Adam had been right. It had been fine, after a fashion. Richard had acquired the domestic skills to provide them with a home. He had his work, his friends, his boys. It was only when Josh left for university that he realised that he'd made his sons into his life.

He missed them. Not just them but all their friends in and out of the house, the clatter and clutter of teenagers. He missed having to get up in the night and bang on their doors and tell them to keep the noise down. He missed their smell: the cheap-aftershave, stinky-socks-under-the-bed, mint-on-top-of-tobacco scent of them. He missed being needed, someone relying on him, someone to cook dinner for. He didn't know how to switch to being his own motivation. The relish he'd taken in cooking was gone. His meals now were perfunctory, as if eating, if not exactly optional, was only a tiresome necessity. He missed the way their minds worked, their endlessly exasperating questions and mysterious reasoning. He missed a different angle on things. Now he only had his own and it bored him. They called it 'thinking outside the box' in the meetings at work. He was stuck inside his own box where the walls were drab and uniform.

'I suppose you'll be leaving me too,' he'd said to Josh after Adam had gone to university. It was meant to be humorous.

'Dad, you need a girlfriend,' Josh replied.

So he'd signed up for the modern version of the mating ritual: online dating. Despite his best efforts, he found the whole experience shaming. Most of his friends were in couples and would no doubt have egged him on but he couldn't bring himself to confide in them. When he looked at the photo he'd uploaded of himself, one Josh had taken on a cycling holiday in Cornwall in which he appeared fit and vital, what he saw was his own perfidy, as if he were a salesman trying to con someone into buying damaged goods. The effort of presenting himself as cheery, dynamic and outgoing, something the process seemed to require, involved contortions he couldn't seem to stretch to. He persisted for a few months. Surprisingly, women kept popping him in their favourites and sending him messages. He learned to avoid the ones who said they were just as happy curled up on the sofa with a glass of wine as with going out to a concert. As if curling up on the sofa with someone you didn't know could be anything but distasteful, he thought, watching Enrica hiss and arch at a tomcat who'd dared to venture into the garden. She leapt from the sill and shot out of the catflap to confront the intruder. She would have been good at it. You needed that directness and brash self-assurance to survive in the world of dating. He met a lot of earnest women who'd talked about carbon footprints and vegetarianism. Those were the ones who seemed to pick him out. They needed shaking up and a good laugh, these women, but he wasn't the man to do it.

It wasn't for him. For a while afterwards, a feeling of hope would come over him as if by removing himself from the website, he'd increase rather than lessen his chances of meeting a woman he could cherish who would cherish him in return. He sensed it most keenly as he cycled to the office in the morning, a whisper of delight in the pit of his stomach that would spread through him and make him see the everyday streets and passers-by as new and lovely.

That was all a long time ago now. So he was shifting his life in a different way. Downsizing, clearing out, starting afresh.

He'd bought a pet carrier to transport Enrica and lined it with newspaper. It was a bright pink, almost fluorescent box, the only one left in the pet shop. He'd placed it near her bowl with the doorway, a kind of plastic grille that made it look like a small neon prison cell, propped invitingly open. Enrica had spurned it. He was going to have to catch her and wrestle her into the contraption. It wasn't a dignified scenario for either of them.

Later, after he'd cycled to the estate agent to drop the keys off and checked that he definitely was too late for the charity shop, he stowed Enrica, in her pink box, on the floor next to the passenger seat and strapped his bike to the back of the car. Then he set off for his new home, a cottage on the edge of the city with views over the hills. He could no longer remember why he'd voluntarily opted to leave his nice house, with neighbours who would happily feed his cat when he was away and where there was a pub at the end of the road, to live in semi-rural isolation. 'You'll like it there,' he said to Enrica as he drove, 'fields nearby, rabbits and mice to chase. Just you and me.' On cue, she started to howl. 'Crying won't help,' he said.

He reached the T-junction at the top of Stowey Hill and stopped there, unable to decide whether it was safe to dart out or not. He wanted to turn right, but the boxes were piled so high on the passenger seat that he couldn't see if the way was clear.

Straight ahead of him on the other side of the road was the entrance to a secondary school, Stowey Hill High. A woman in a blue dress was attaching balloons around a sign on the gatepost, advertising a charity sale. The sign depicted a counter showing how much money had already been raised, what the target fund was and what could be purchased for the school in Senegal that this one was twinned with: so much for an extra teacher's salary, so much for school dinners for poorer families, so much to fund a Senegalese teacher coming to Exeter. It reminded him of *Blue Peter*, exchanging silver milk-bottle tops for money. He'd sent some off, but he didn't get a badge.

The woman stepped back to admire her handiwork and moved to one side. The sign was framed with red and yellow balloons bobbing in the breeze. The woman's movements were quick and light. Her dress caught the wind and billowed around her brown legs. The occasional car passed between them as he watched her. Something in the fluidity of her movements and the springiness of her step made him want to come closer. It was like the feeling of home, but transposed to a more exotic location. She spun round and seemed to look directly at him, before turning and tripping through the gates. He felt himself grow hot. He gripped the steering wheel. His stomach churned. 'Shh,' he said to Enrica, 'calm down.'

He drove straight across the road and into the school drive. The woman danced before him. As he came alongside, he slowed and wound down his window. She stopped and looked at him as if she didn't quite believe in him either. She spoke.

It was hard to hear her above the cat's din. 'It's you,' he thought she said. 'And there's your bike,' she said, glancing wonderingly at the back of his car. She seemed quite overcome by the sight of it. She turned to look at him again. 'Your arms are bleeding,' she said.

'Just scratches,' he said. 'The cat is a bit unsettled. We had a tussle. We're moving house.'

'I've got a cat,' she said and she smiled at him, a glorious and warm smile.

The blue of her dress was the colour of the sky before a thunderstorm, the same colour as her eyes. With the cat keeping up her eerie banshee cry, the setting sun playing around the curly tips of the woman's dark hair, turning them to gold, Richard felt himself start, tentatively, to smile back.

'Don't I know you?' she said.

'No,' he said, 'but I'd like you to.'

Her cheeks reddened. She took a step back and looked past him to the boxes in his car. 'Um, right. You've brought stuff to donate,' she said in a more neutral tone. 'You're just in time. I'm finishing setting it all up in the hall. Come round to the side entrance. Follow me.' She ran down the drive in front of him, her dress swaying.

If it hadn't seemed churlish, Richard would have turned the car round and gone. He'd have driven as quickly as he could along the uncomfortable road of embarrassment at his corny remark to arrive eventually at that safe, familiar place of regret, of chances let slip.

There was no sign of the woman when he parked the car by the open door. He carried the boxes one by one and placed them on a table just inside. She must have mistaken him for someone else and now was keeping out of his way. He should take his embittered semi-feral cat and leave. He jangled his car keys. He thought of the cottage and all the unpacked boxes there. He marched through the door and into a hall that smelt of boiled cabbage and children's feet. The woman was sitting on the floor surrounded by piles of books. 'Um, sorry about earlier. Can I help?' he said.

'I'm never going to get it done in time,' she said.

They worked together, he steady and methodical in the middle, carrying loads and organising, she in a swirl of speedy movement around him, shifting things from one place to another according to colour or state of batteredness and then, as often as not, putting them back. Her guiding principle seemed to be aesthetic, his practical. She told him about the school in Senegal. There were a million evils in the world, she said, Aids and war and famine and death and she couldn't do much to change them, but she'd set up this project. It was her contribution. The beauty of the twinning, she said, was that it worked both ways. It not only benefited the children in Dakar, it made the kids here more aware too. 'They see how lucky they are,' she said. 'It holds up a mirror to them.' She'd paused in her sorting and was looking at him in that way again.

'Am I being too preachy?' she said.

'No, it sounds fantastic.'

She was planning another trip to West Africa, this time with her son, Joe, and they were going to visit people in Liberia too.

They stood side by side when they'd finished. It still looked a jumble to him but she was pleased. He thought you could say anything to this woman and she would consider it and offer it back to you in a different light. 'Who did you think I was?' he asked.

She turned to him and looked up into his face. 'I thought you were you,' she said. 'But I forgot you didn't know it was me.'

He had no idea what she was talking about. 'Let me cook you dinner,' he said.